blue duets

a novel by Kathleen Wall

Library and Archives Canada Cataloguing in Publication
Wall, Kathleen, 1950–
Blue duets / Kathleen Wall.

Print format: ISBN 978-1-897142-44-8
Electronic monograph in PDF format: ISBN 978-1-897142-91-2
Electronic monograph in HTML format: ISBN 978-1-897142-90-5

I. Title.

PS8595.A5645B58 2010 C813'.54 C2010-903108-3

Editor: Lynne Van Luven
Cover image and author photo: Veronica Geminder
Proofreader: Heather Sangster, Strong Finish
Interior design: Pete Kohut

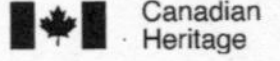

Canada Council for the Arts Conseil des Arts du Canada

Brindle & Glass is pleased to acknowledge the financial support for its publishing program from the Government of Canada through the Canada Book Fund, Canada Council for the Arts, and the Province of British Columbia through the British Columbia Arts Council and the Book Publishing Tax Credit.

The interior pages of this book have been printed on 100% post-consumer recycled paper, processed chlorine free, and printed with vegetable-based inks.

Brindle & Glass Publishing
www.brindleandglass.com

1 2 3 4 5 14 13 12 11 10

PRINTED AND BOUND IN CANADA

For Bill, who taught me the adventures of middle age.

Wednesday, May 29, 2002

One

My morning began with envy and yearning. I've been in my downstairs studio, trying to play Bach, trying to get close to the energy and melancholy, the joy and longing that infuse his music. I'd much rather be upstairs washing my mother's back, pumicing her feet, cutting her toenails, changing her sheets. She's dying of cancer, while I'm trying to play music Bach wrote for the crisp harpsichord on the sluggish modern piano. She has much to teach me about the lightness my fingers need.

Yesterday, we made our most recent visit to her oncologist, Dr. Patel, to get the results of the latest CT scan. She was quite still as he told her that her cancer had reached stage IV.

"So it can't get any worse?"

He didn't know how to answer her because he couldn't tell whether her question was despairing or hopeful. He is an honest man and wanted to answer the question she was asking.

"The pain will get somewhat worse. But you're in the final—"

"I've made the milestone."

"—Months." They were tripping over each other's words, trying to find the language to mediate between their perspectives.

"But it's not final at all," she said after they sorted out the chaos.

"I'm glad you have a belief—"

"Oh, it's not a belief. It doesn't depend on something unseen or unprovable. It depends on me. *I've* decided." She didn't explain what she had decided, but he nodded his head and patted her shoulder as if he knew exactly what she was talking about. They belonged to a fellowship that excluded me. Everything excluded me.

"You can choose to have some palliative treatments. They won't really slow the cancer, but they might make you more comfortable."

"I can choose?"

"Yes. It's your choice."

"I choose not to."

"You can change your mind."

"Probably not. But thank you."

As he finished his notes and stood up, I asked about changes in medication. He wrote out a new prescription, looked me straight in the eye, and directed me: "Keep her comfortable. That's the best way to get quality of life at this point."

My silence, punctuated by pats on her arm and murmured instructions for getting her into the car, wasn't too noticeable, I hoped. But when I turned left instead of right out of the parking lot—because I couldn't possibly face her over an intimate little coffee table—she pounced.

"Aren't we going for coffee? I feel like a big slice of cheesecake. After all, I haven't been a size eight in years." So I drove to our favourite Van Houtte, one that doesn't have mud and trash clogging up the wheelchair ramp, where I ordered a small coffee and a big cheesecake for her and a small coffee for myself. She called across the shop to change the coffee to a large.

Once I got seated, I began apologizing. "I don't know what to say—whether to pick up the tragic note or to be matter of fact."

"Your face says neither of those reflects how you feel."

"Sad but mostly numb."

"Look, it's okay. I've always hated that Thomas fellow who wanted his father to fight 'the dying of the light.' I'm done fighting, and I won't do it. Even for you. I like Leonard Cohen's take on light much better." My mother began to sing the chorus to "Anthem" with her breathy voice, but loudly enough that anyone who wanted to could hear. She raised her voice slightly for the last two lines: "There is a crack in everything. That's how the light gets in." It was a quintessential Mother moment: she loved the slang when I was a teenager and listened to my records when I was at school. Some of them, like Cohen, she kept up with.

"I don't know how to do this," I said with tears in my eyes.

"Make it up as you go along."

"That's not the way I usually do it. I practise for a living."

"Well, you can make it up now. You don't have to figure it out all at once. He didn't say I was going to die tomorrow." She broke off an enormous piece of cheesecake and offered it to me, maybe to shut me up.

My mother accepted the diagnosis of untreatable cancer (they couldn't find the primary site) with the same kind of serenity and detachment she brought to every other unpleasantness in her life: my father, first and foremost; his own illnesses and death; the death of my older brother, Jack, from a heart attack three years ago. She quarantines her feelings, goes away. It's not that she deserts *you*. But she seems to desert herself. I want to find a way to touch her—to rub her back or stroke her hair or massage her feet or simply say the right words—that allows her to know, finally, that I am not deserting her. But she's insisted on a nurse for her morning routine, so I long for the physical fact of her. Ironically, Bach knew exactly this kind of longing, but I couldn't get my hands to express it.

So I'm practising his sonatas for violin and harpsichord. I've been working on them for a couple of weeks now, but only as a kind of abstract music—fingerings, keys, rhythms, melodies. I always start a new work like a day-dreamer who stares at clouds or rocks long enough for an image to emerge. I play the notes and rhythms of my part until I understand it, although I'm still puzzled by what it is I understand. How does music rise out of a life: the cold leavings of a breakfast brought up by the landlady and now brushed aside for the manuscript paper and the bottle of ink, a morning walk in sun or drizzle, an argument with a patron, or a night's coupling that adds another mouth around the table? Does some transcendent vision make its way into the music? I don't think I can ever get to these—the drizzle, the sexual shudder under coarse sheets, the transcendence—and they're beside the point. The stuff of music, the language of music, is ethereal: a mathematics of the head and heart, temporal and temporary; an emblem for the fragile threads connecting the body with its desires to the soul with its wise, splendid indifference. How many paintings or novels raise the hair on your arms?

It's unusual for two musicians who play modern instruments to perform these sonatas since they were originally written for the harpsichord and the baroque violin. But when Kevin agreed to the sabbatical necessary because of my mother's illness, he suggested it would be a good time for us to "cruise the repertoire," as he put it, and build some interesting programs. This is so like Kevin—for him to read my mind. He plays anything happily. I'm the one who couldn't open one more concert with a pretty Mozart sonata.

My hands take pleasure in playing Mozart, the pleasure of being so tidily, rationally in sync. All the notes—and both parts—click elegantly into place, like a well-made wooden box. But perhaps because Mozart needed money and wrote them for the gifted amateur who would buy the music, he didn't think about how he could question or probe the miraculous language he'd found so easy to master. So his violin sonatas, with a couple of exceptions, are polite, decorative pieces. They begin dramatically, as if they had just that moment been forged out of plaster and gilding that speeds across an enormous rococo ceiling in curves and arpeggios. Maybe that's why I'm drawn to Bach's sonatas, to the four-movement pieces with their contemplative beginnings.

A good marriage works in some ways like a sonata, one voice deferring to the other only to come to the fore while the other recedes. One partner has louder needs or a moment of triumph, though the two know this, like everything in a relationship, is temporary. Occasionally—raising children, building a fence, making love—both voices are equal and entwine so intimately they're not sure which is which. But if one of those voices is silent, can one still create counterpoint?

My parents had great sex. That was apparent even to me as an embarrassed, puritanical adolescent who would prefer not to hear the words *parents* and *sex* in the same sentence. I could tell this by the way they touched each other, their hands enjoying the other's skin, hair, shape, and giving pleasure in return. Often there was a special lilt over breakfast, the kind we all feel when hot, muggy weather has broken and fresh wind is coming in from the north—a renewed energy that danced around both of them. I knew in some way that my mother needed the energy from such mornings to get through the times when my father beat her.

Yet sights, sounds, smells can to this day revive memories of my parents' happier moments. My father frequently brought my mother orchids, and the sight of an orchid conjures up, like a hologram, the clear plastic box; the sweet, waxy lack of smell; my mother's always recurring delight in this astonishing gift from a large, practical, freckled man. Were they code, I wondered in my twenties, after I married, these virginal, vulvate flowers? Then I decided not. Now, I'm not so sure.

The sight and smell of a husband barbecuing while his wife sips a drink in a nearby lawn chair also pulses with memory. Old Spice or English Leather mixed with the smell of charcoal, grilling meat, gin and lime. My father couldn't boil tea for water, yet there was a primal cockiness about him at the barbecue. He'd argue with the butcher over the steaks and could land a slab of meat on your plate done exactly as you liked it.

A bottle of Bayer's Aspirin or the smell of cough syrup brings back my father in his most sympathetic role: my mother's nurse when she was ill. He called in sick, pulled a comfortable chair to the side of their bed, and spent the day reading to himself or to her, coming to the kitchen to give orders for another bowl of chicken soup or a pot of peppermint tea.

It wasn't only grief and envy that began my day. Two hours earlier, Rob raced past my mother's door while I was settling her breakfast tray on her lap, barking over his shoulder that he was running late.

"I'll see you off . . ."

"Don't bother. I'll be gone before you're down."

But I went downstairs anyway, to find his briefcase spread open on the dining room table while he dashed to gather his book, his reading glasses, and the paper, with its news about the sabre rattling over Iraq and its hidden weapons of mass destruction.

"Can I help?"

"No. I've got everything. I think. Goddamned meetings." He snapped his briefcase shut.

As he pulled his briefcase off the table, it caught the place mat with his breakfast dishes still on it. The plate shattered, the glass rolled. The cat crept toward the jumble with that particularly feline combination of curiosity and distrust.

"Cripes, Rob. Chill." He glared at me as if I couldn't possibly understand, but I ignored him. "It's all right. I'll see to that," I told him. "Before Brahms cuts his paws or tries to lap up the milk."

"I'm off."

I stretched out my hand to touch the side of his face but felt only the brush of his silk tie (one I'd never seen before) and the nub of his wool jacket. The door slammed. The brush of silk and wool have remained on my fingers while I practised.

During the last month, I've come to realize that moods are like the motifs in music—like the "dum-dum-dum DUM" of Beethoven's *Fifth Symphony* that's become such a cliché. These little snippets of a tune or fragments of rhythm are building blocks or toe holds, places for the composer to play and the listener to grab. Moods, too, are little constellations of sound and thought and feeling that are constantly changing yet always there, colouring, permeating everything you experience. Unlike feelings, which you attach to the event that caused them, moods are pervasive and often inexplicable. When you're listening to Beethoven and hear that rhythm in the final movement, you wonder why it's familiar and where it's come from. You can't quite place it. The same is true of my moods these days.

On Wednesdays, I try to get my mother out of the house. Sometimes we've got a doctor's appointment, but I also arrange trips to the botanical gardens or the mall, visits to her friends, or a card game on the one day of the week when Rob comes home at noon to help me get her downstairs and load her wheelchair into the trunk of the car. At first, he simply supported her as she walked down the stairs herself. Now she's weaker, and has lost weight, so he simply scoops her up and carries her down. I wish he wouldn't be so silent while he does this: I can't tell what he's thinking.

Today she wanted some sunshine, so we went to King George Park and wheeled through the paths for a while before sitting in front of the pool. The sound of the water is restful, she said, before leaning toward me conspiratorially to add that the people-watching is also better here. We cover our innocent spying with desultory talk.

"What were you playing this morning?"

"Bach."

"Sonatas still?" She's disappointed I haven't made a solo career for myself, but she won't say so.

"Yes. He wrote them for harpsichord and baroque violin, but we're going to try them on modern instruments."

"Did you notice Mrs. Henry's fingernails today?" Mrs. Henry is her nurse, the one I envied this morning.

I'm waiting for her to tell me they're filthy: I'll have to find a new nurse. I shake my head.

"She's had them polished a deep dark red. Like that girl's lipstick." Mother nods toward a young woman whose mouth is made violently old by lipstick that's too dark.

"They look nice?"

"I thought so. We used a colour like that when I was a teenager. The polish wasn't so nice, though. It must have been thinner. It never looked as good on your fingers as it did in the bottle."

"Would you like to have yours done?" My mother always had beautiful fingernails, but her illness has made them brittle and ridged. "I'm sure I could find a manicurist who would come to the house."

"Oh, no." She lifts one of her spotted, ropy-veined hands and seems to hold it against the new plantings of salvia and petunias. "My hands are so ugly now. Is there a point, do you think, to getting old?"

"Oh, Mother, I don't know."

"What would your Bach say?"

In my head I listen to the notes I played this morning. "That there's a point to everything. He was orphaned in his early teens. His two wives had twenty-some kids between them, but several died before they grew up. He'd have despaired if he hadn't believed there was a point. There wouldn't have been any music if he'd despaired—not like the music he wrote, anyway."

"I think I'm getting ready to do without my body. It's going to be such a relief—leaving it behind."

I take her hand in mine and look off between the trees, concentrating on not weeping.

"When's Kevin coming to rehearse?"

"Thursday, I think."

"Good. I love *real* music underneath my bed." There's nothing to say. I squeeze her hand but continue holding it.

"Imagine!" she says as a skateboarder twists in the air, the skateboard looking like it's glued to his feet. "Shall I ask for a skateboard when I get to heaven? Do angels skin their knees?"

What do musicians think about when we gather a group of pieces together on a program? Usually, we try for contrast or similarity: we'll program nothing but Beethoven sonatas; or one classical, one romantic, one modern work. I suppose we do this to mimic the way music itself is made, the way it attempts to balance dramatic contrast with formal coherence. But I want you to feel that you've looked at your world, or yourself, or your life, through lenses that reveal something you've never quite seen before, as if the notes I've played have changed the colour and weather of your world. Or maybe the music has drawn some things in close while it pushes others far away, giving you a new perspective. I want to disorient you with beauty. When you leave the concert hall, I want you to feel that the thick impasto of your everyday world has begun to peel away.

"I've been thinking of Mother's courage today," I tried to say casually as I put the curry and rice on the table. The roses Rob brought home two days ago were beginning to droop without ever having opened. I made a mental note to cut their stems under warm water and soak them for a while after I finished cleaning up the dishes.

"She's being too courageous about all this for my taste."

"I'm not sure your taste has anything to do with it." I meant to be playful, but there was an edge in my voice.

"Probably it doesn't." When called on something, Rob can shift gears pretty quickly. "But it's hard on you. You have to play along, which means stifling your own feelings."

"I think I owe her a little restraint. She took one of her worst beatings about my piano lessons, after all."

"Christ, Lila. Why don't you give up on those god-awful memories? They're of no earthly use. Your father was a bastard. End of story." He was sliding some of the rings of onion in the curry off to the side of his plate. "Your korma is wonderful. As it always is."

"What an odd expression—'of no use.' Is that what memories are for—'use'? Useful or not, they're who we are. Lopping off memories is like lopping off limbs."

"My, aren't we colourful tonight? Bad day?"

"Not as bad as yours, I suspect."

Did he blanch, or did I simply imagine it? There's that little snippet of tune again, that motif that gets stuck in my head long after the music is over, trivial and grating, out of context. Ear worms, I think they're called.

"How did your meeting go?" I continued gamely, ignoring whatever it was I thought I heard.

"Boring, boring. What a bloody useless waste of time it was. Between the name and date guys and the anything-goes postmodernists, they're never going to pound out a new curriculum. Early retirement is tempting. Leave them to their folly."

After dinner, Rob and I sat down to watch *Adam's Rib*. We argued playfully over whether the jilted wife had a right to track her husband down and fire a gun at him. Rob thought just confronting him might have been more effective. I thought she felt so helpless that she couldn't imagine doing anything else—hence all her talk about being hungry.

In the middle of the movie, our daughter, Lindsay, called for our tense midweek chat, and I succeeded in keeping my mouth shut about her boredom with her job. I hope I sounded supportive but not too excited (not excited enough to seem critical) when she talked about going back to school. Law school, she thinks, which means her return is over a year away. She thinks her experience in government will give her application a leg up, and she plans to start studying now for her LSATs. But she has new problems with Paul, who doesn't want to come to a family dinner next Sunday. My brother's widow, Margaret, and their kids are coming to Montreal for a week, and we thought that a Sunday dinner with Mother was in order.

"Paul *hates* family things. His family is awful. They're either enthusiastic as puppies about hockey and car racing or cranky when you change the subject. I tried to tell him we're not like that. But then he does his parody of Dad's opinion about something, and you can see his point. He's asked what my cousins *are* interested in. I don't honestly know."

"I don't know about Jackie. Margaret has her job in fundraising for the kidney foundation. Devon plays jazz and classical guitar."

"God, no. Music's right out . . . Sorry."

"It's okay. Look, you can either come without Paul or skip it altogether."

"Skip what?" Rob growled, growing suspicious.

"Sunday's dinner," I mouthed.

"Like hell she can," Rob said as he got up and turned off the TV.

"You really wouldn't mind?" The tone of her voice pulled my attention back to the phone.

"I'd rather have you here, but no, I wouldn't mind." I don't mind, exactly, but I'm heartbroken. Paul knows her grandmother's dying and that the two of them are close. He could cut her some slack about this. Instead, I'll have to do it. The conversation skips a beat.

"You know, Mom, you *could* be angry . . ."

"No, it . . ."

"He's being a prick. I know." There's another beat of uncomfortable silence. "You know one of my—well, not quite one of my happiest memories, but one that's oddly comforting? I was in grade five or six. My friends were punishing this girl—I can't remember her name—for being too smart. We wouldn't invite her to birthday parties or speak to her outside school. You and I were walking back from something—it was spring and I think we'd gone for an afternoon walk to get ice cream. We met her and she said hello. I said nothing back. You were furious. Right then and there on the street. I can still see your arms and hands flying, beating the air. I didn't think you did anything with your hands but braid my hair and play the piano. But it was comforting. Because you were angry, I knew where I should stand."

"Oh, honey. I can't tell you what to do any more. Those days are gone." Everything comfortable is disappearing around me. As though the light is falling out of the air into ashes at my feet.

"I'll see what I can work out and call you Friday."

"Talk to you then."

"Bye now."

Rob was in the kitchen cutting slivers of brie. Two glasses of red wine stood on the wooden tray.

"Want some cheese?"

"I don't think so."

"I'll slice a bit extra in case you change your mind." He was putting the cheese and biscuits on a plate. "Let's sit on the back deck. We can hear your mother from there. Her bedroom window's open."

I opened the door between the kitchen and the deck, and he kissed my shoulder as he walked past with the tray. So we're to make love tonight. I can almost always tell: it's as if he's suddenly rediscovers me. While he lit the lanterns and settled himself in his wicker chair, balancing a glass of wine and a small tower of crackers and cheese, I did a mental inventory. Where have I put the lubricant we need now that I'm menopausal? Once I tried a drop of it on my tongue to see whether I should be careful when I use it. Apparently it comes in flavours, but I haven't been able to pop the question: "Rob, do you want me to taste like strawberry or kiwi?" Would he be turned on by all the buttons on my silk pyjamas or the negligee I bought last week?

"So what's Lindsay's problem?"

"Paul doesn't want to come for dinner."

"I'll talk to her when she calls on Friday. She can come without Paul."

"I don't think it's that simple."

"Why not? It's one Sunday evening. It won't ruin his entire life or give him the clap."

"I think this is more subtle. They're trying to work out who they are as a couple. Are they going to be the dutiful, family-oriented type, or should they spend the afternoon necking on a park bench somewhere?"

"Lila, you are so romantic. I'd lay money that they've had a fight in the last week or so, and this is a kind of ultimatum. Or one of a series of ultimatums. They'll go on until she gives up or walks out. That's the kind of man Paul is." For Rob, everything is about power. History. Intimacy. It makes no difference.

"Well, people do what they can. She'll come if she thinks it's possible."

"Lila. People do what they're made to do."

A quick decision: if I'm frank, all bets are off that we'll make love, and I'm horny. I need him to hold me for a *little* while before he retreats downstairs. "You are so cynical. What's the point to being that cynical?"

"I'm not disappointed when the world doesn't measure up."

"Rob, you're disappointed *all the time.* You eat cynicism for breakfast and again for your bedtime snack."

The stillness this morning (I've just glanced at the clock: it's 3:00 AM) is so complete that I feel muffled in it, except that occasionally a breeze freshens the air and quivers above the sheets. Rob got cold, so he's gone to sleep on the day bed in his study. I've felt oddly disconnected, except when I heard one motorcycle whose path I followed the way one traces a maze and wondered who I was momentarily linked to. And a train blew its whistle at a couple of crossings, the tunnel of sound speaking of long distances, and then soughed as it gathered speed. The birds will begin to sing in forty minutes or so, but now the silence is creating a vacuum that seems to pull thoughts out of my head. I may not even be awake, except that I can feel Brahms, my grey cat, against my thigh. Yet he's so still his weight seems like another kind of silence.

Brahms's body has a stillness like Rob's Shaker furniture. He began to make it years ago when he came back from his first sabbatical in France. I'd stayed home with Lindsay; she was two, and we'd decided she was too young to travel. When he came back, he needed something besides reading and teaching to do with the rough, frustrated energy he seemed to find—maybe it was France, maybe it was being alone—so he began to buy himself tools and to practise mortise and tenon joints before making bookshelves, cabinets, tables, dressers. Working without nails or glue appealed to him, I think. Yet their quiet simplicity is paradoxical, since his anger at the world is often pulled into the work, into the banging and carving of each interlocking flange. There's nothing quiet about making them, but in a room, they're very quiet.

Lindsay lives in a whirlwind of sound and activity, her iPod's earphones over her ears, obscuring the racket she makes as she bangs into things or hums to herself or talks (more loudly than necessary) to others. In her early twenties, she feels her job right now is not to be me, and she's doing it with a vengeance. So there's a lot of silence between us—things I don't say. When she complains on the phone about not being able to find something—her sports bra or her bank statement—I don't natter on about the virtues of order. But there are things I occasionally can't keep my mouth shut about. Her boyfriend criticizes her constantly, and she's settled for an uninspiring job writing letters for the government about health-care issues, in spite of graduating with a respectable honours degree in history. So when she admits she's hurt or bored, sometimes I suggest that she has rights and gifts she's given up on. While I know our different perspectives turn my hopes into judgments, I cannot silence my vision of my gifted daughter. And if I did hold my peace, who would keep that alive for her?

And then there are all the things that my mother, unbelievably, has no need to say. Sometimes I sit quietly by her bed while she falls asleep, thinking that in the unguarded moment just before sleep when we entertain our desires in their purest state, without the limitations of probability or safety or fairness, she will tell me something she needs me to hear.

In my favourite documentary about Glenn Gould, he says that the tape recorder erases time because you can combine dozens of takes to create a single performance. But I don't think he was that good with human relationships, or he'd have known that erasing time has its limits. I want one good long take up to my mother's death, like the prison scene in *Adam's Rib* where Katharine Hepburn quizzes the wife. One long take that says I know from my soul to my fingers what this final music means.

In my dozing, I feel a hand on my cheek, a thought like the ghost of a leaf or spider's web that startles you when you're walking in thick woods. A branch whipping back in your face when the person walking ahead of you forgets you're there and lets it go. I can't quite tell whether it's a caress or a blow. I can smell the rain that fell a couple of hours ago and see the moon out my window. The stillness would almost be pleasant if a sound broke the silence occasionally. I suppose I could begin to sing to myself or to recite the Shakespeare soliloquies I memorized as a girl. But what I really need to hear is something outside myself.

Thursday, May 30, 2002

Two

Tonight on my walk, I thought about the slow changes that measure summertime in an old neighbourhood: the shift from the scent of peonies to roses, the lengthening and waning of daylight as we approach and then, inevitably, descend from the solstice. Usually, I sense a brick-clad, tree-lined stability that's unchallenged until autumn arrives to bring back social time and seasonal change. Tonight, the mood that permeates my days made me aware that, really, nothing *but* change occurs here: a baby walks, a toddler says, "No!" an eight-year-old rides without her training wheels, a teenager dyes his hair violent red, a woman cheats on a husband who spends all his spare time playing golf, an old man dies.

Late this morning, we had quite a storm, just as I was working on Brahms's first sonata, nicknamed the "Rain Sonata" because he used his "Rain Song" as the subject of the finale. Do you believe life can sometimes reflect art? George Woodcock told a story several years ago on CBC about visiting India with Toni Onley. While Woodcock was talking about CanLit, Onley was off painting the parched Indian landscape where it hadn't rained for years. Could this be hyperbole? How would the people who lived there survive without any rain? Anyway, Onley couldn't resist putting one of his signature clouds above the cracked earth. It rained the next day.

The Brahms isn't actually very stormy. It sometimes sounds like an early spring rain, gentle and welcome, that washes the winter's grime off the windows; or like a melancholy day of pleasant but relentless rain; or the irregular beat of rain on a cottage roof. Our storm, in contrast, seemed to be only black clouds and thunder, a "dry storm" as my mother used to call them: all bleakness and threat, a kind of oppressiveness that won't release itself, like someone extremely angry who, on principle, isn't giving voice to his feelings. But clouds, fortunately, aren't like people, and we had a brief but violent shower before sunnier weather invaded from the west just behind the uncanny midday dark.

Mother was alarmed by the thunder and called me upstairs to sit out the storm with her. She took my hand, as she often does these days, and then, in a purposeful attempt to distract herself, dragged out the storm stories of my childhood. How in the days before hair conditioner we would gather rainwater in a real downpour to rinse our hair and make it soft. How we stood on the front porch and watched the rain come toward us in sheets. How Lucy—the terrier mongrel my father was oddly fond of, despite all the time it took to bathe and comb her—managed to escape from the kitchen and join my parents in bed during a thunderstorm. I remember hearing my father talking to her, mocking her gently, and felt safe enough to join the three of them in bed. Not stories exactly, but tiny moments of family solidarity. This moment—Brahms padding in thoughtfully, knowing that people need protection against storms, settling in a round, purring ball by my mother's hip—will doubtless be added to my repertoire when I can make my mother's dying into some kind of a story.

Rob and I did make love last night. He was turned on, it seems, by my rebellion. What next? I guess "what next" is the fast, curiously intense sex he's gone in for. I might once have enjoyed it, but it isn't particularly comfortable now, in spite of the lubricant. I'm puzzled by why I haven't told him this but can't find the right moment to bring it up. Before we make love? He'll say he can't get an erection because I'm critical of him. When? Afterward? It would be a stain on his sexual honour. While we're washing dishes seems neutral, but how do you start such a conversation?

About seven months before Rob and I met, I'd broken off with a long-term boyfriend. I'd startled Steven in his practice room trying to get his hand out of the blouse of a cellist he was working with. (Music students, you should know, are an incestuous and passionate crew; music buildings full of practice rooms occupied by gifted and fanatic young adults encourage such qualities. I can still hear—but even more I can *smell*—their sexuality when I practise in the music school.) Steven was a much better pianist than I, a kind of cross between Liszt and the average seventies hippie—long hair, wild shirts, bell bottoms. He's disappeared, though I expect to find him on an indie label somewhere. He was the sort of boyfriend Father would have hated, which gave me a certain satisfaction without any risk because they never met. Mother, of course, would have barely blinked an eye at Steven's obscenities or his long, wavy hair.

With Steven, I felt free, even forced, to invent myself. Who are you, anyway, at twenty-four? A collection of habits and histories, perhaps. Some luminous moments of childhood comfort and a few brightly coloured adolescent traumas against the out-of-focus black and white backdrop of your family. But you can't give it a name or sum it up in a word, so it doesn't feel like an identity. Anyway, what I suppose my relationship with Steven changed was simply habits. Rather than getting up early and getting into my practice room before the rest of campus was even conscious, Steven and I partied late and got up late. I skipped dinner to practise and got rather thin, which Steven approved of. I flirted at parties. Steven was proud that I was his, and should any guy follow. up my flirtation by even touching me, Steven made clear, in a way I find funny now—a little too much testosterone, shaken, not stirred—there'd be consequences.

After Steven and I broke up, I felt an acidic mixture of righteous fury and abandonment. For at least six weeks, everything seemed to dissolve—habits, practising, social ties. It was the seventies, after all; what was so bad about Steven flirting with a mop-headed cellist who wasn't a very good musician anyway? Our friends felt I'd overreacted. Steven, they kept telling me—when they would speak to me—was desolate. I found a practice room on another floor, cut myself off as much as possible, and threw myself into my classes with a kind of head-down, demonic concentration.

Everyone has a story like this one: an early lover who seems to have given you your body and the measure of your worth; one to whom you've whispered your mediocrities and imperfections, and who has stopped your mouth with kisses. It's just what happens when you're young. I'm left with a perverse addiction to Bruce Lee movies, which Steven was crazy about. I didn't indulge it much for years: I really can't see Rob sitting down to watch *Fist of Fury*. There's little analysis of the relationship between China and Japan, and even less plot besides the unending quest for vengeance. I suspect the history is all wrong. Occasionally, when Rob was travelling, Lindsay and I would watch the videos, laugh at Lee's sounds—kind of a cross between a macaw and a little boy sounding like a big truck—and cheer. When they came out on DVD, I got myself a couple of the later ones. Sometimes when Rob thinks I'm sending emails, I'm really watching my favourite scenes, like the mirror room scene in *Enter the Dragon*. Lee's knack for telling reality from its reflection is hopeful and cathartic.

Steven also left me with a love of the great jazz pianists of the time, particularly Bill Evans. The tunes are remarkable in themselves, but it's the improvisation I envy, the ability to fly loose from the score, to believe you are tethered by your own inventiveness. Evans's training was initially classical, which comes through in the way he gets the piano to express such complex feelings—sometimes by simply emphasizing the right note in the middle of a thick chord. He's not a hard driver the way some pianists are, using the piano like drums with pitches. Sometimes he's almost impressionistic—you can imagine him playing Ravel or Debussy. His performances—particularly with Miles Davis on *Kind of Blue*—let you see how each voice is integral, making jazz not unlike a fugue. Rob doesn't really like jazz, though he appreciates how it makes him seem with it when company comes. But when I told Rob about Evans's death from using too much coke, his stock went up, and Rob lets me put on the odd album for dinner music.

The end of my relationship with Steven marks the first time I felt the fault line between—how do I describe this? It would be easiest to say "between my persona and the real me," but that's not quite accurate. My "persona" continued to go to classes, managed to concentrate when she practised, joked with the caretaker of her apartment building, and paid her bills on time. But the inner self had no substance except for its bruised nerve endings and wondered how on earth all this got done. There seemed no *self* to write cheques and to memorize music. Sometimes these two seem to me like a pair of nearly identical twins. If I can convince both of them to part their hair on the left side and wear the tortoise-shell glasses with the bifocals, they see the same world, though naturally from different perspectives, and look identical. But in times of trauma, they remain recalcitrant and undisciplined, completely determined not to admit their sistership. I've sensed both of them huddling around for the last month or so, humming, in different keys, that little motif that's been making me so edgy.

"What are you doing, little girl?"

"Criminy! You scared the living daylights out of me"

"And you're starting to sound more like your mother every day."

"Every woman's nightmare. Except mine. I like Mother's quaintness." Brahms and I had both our heads under the bookshelves trying to retrieve one of my folk-art tops. I have a basket of them in my studio, and sometimes I get down on the floor to spin them. I spin; he stares, and then chases. He doesn't laugh, old Brahms, but I do.

"But you haven't answered my question." Rob sat down on the single comfortable chair in my study, looking like he'd settled in. I noticed he had a drink in his hand. I must have been concentrating so hard I didn't hear him.

"I'm playing. How was your day?"

"It was fine. I cut it a bit short. Boredom. Sleepiness. I don't know. But I stopped by the patisserie in the ghetto and brought home *chaussons aux pommes* for you and Mother. I thought it might taste good to her, and you need a treat."

"You're sweet, Rob." I put the tops back in their basket and Brahms immediately looked put out. "It's okay, guy." I reached down and scratched the back of his head, working my fingers down his back. "Bored? You were bored today? That's not like you."

"Less bored and more distracted." He smiled significantly at me.

"Listen, honey . . ." Rob circled my hips with his arm and pulled me toward him. I scratched him behind the ears, something he's always strangely liked. This was better than beginning a casual and clearly planned conversation over dishes. "About the raw sex."

"Medium rare. Not entirely raw."

"No, you're right. Not entirely raw. But still a little underdone for me. 'The change.'" I rolled my eyes before he could. Having begun, I might as well keep going. "Could we keep the seasoning light for a while? No red hot chili peppers?"

He patted my bum and let me go.

"While you were playing with the cat, I was bored, and wandered around the ghetto. I ended up in Roche Bobois."

"Roche Bobois? That's a bit of a detour from the ghetto."

"Well," he gestured toward the living room on the other side of the French doors that mark my studio. "The living room looks a bit tatty. What do you say we do some furniture shopping in the next little while? We can start at Roche Bobois. I feel like a new living room."

The last thing I want right now is change, though Rob clearly doesn't understand that. He's helpful about all the practical things, and does stuff like bringing Mother's favourite pastry home. But.

"Come on. If you can find time to play with the cat, you can liberate a few hours here and there to shop for furniture."

"Of course I can." I can't say no. Not after our frank conversation. I can learn from him and appear to go along, all the while being sweetly obstructive. "The art of fighting without fighting," Bruce Lee would say. After Mother's gone, I'll just give in. He can do whatever he wants. He's got impeccable taste. "Sure. I'll look at my schedule after dinner. We'll make it a date."

"It'd be a good distraction."

"I'm sure it would." I should do something. Give him a kiss or offer to refresh his drink. I can't think of a thing that's natural; I feel stiff and self-conscious. I'm standing here holding a basket of children's toys. I pick out a favourite, soft teal and milky brown. "How would that be for a new palette in the living room?"

"Too understated, don't you think?" He tips his head back to finish his drink, the ice falling against his lips. When he kisses me, his mouth is cold.

I let Rob get away with too much when we were first married. Now he doesn't understand what Lindsay and Paul are going through because we never did any negotiating.

When Rob and I met, he had just gotten tenure and owned a house. He had a beard and wore Oxford-cloth shirts and tweed jackets with his jeans. He took his identity as a history professor seriously; part of that identity brought him to the university's series of chamber concerts. I'd noticed him—and he me—at the pathetically mannered receptions afterward. My performance of a Beethoven piano sonata gave him an excuse to speak to me. "I don't know much about music," he began, then his gaze shifted from me into the empty distance as he searched for something beyond the clichés that seemed to crowd the air. He needed help. So we both said, at the same moment, "But I know what I like," and then laughed at our complicity.

"Your performance moved me."

What could I say? There seemed to me a charming simplicity to his response, one so at odds with people's efforts to say something truly clever, which led them into a tangled thicket of mannerisms and verbiage. "Your performance moved me." It seemed the one genuine sentence I'd heard in months, and I instantly admired and liked him for it.

For the last seven months, I'd drawn my will for music around me like a protective cape. As I stood on the mountain in the swirling snow, aloof from my musical colleagues, I could suddenly see they were a group of skeletons tricked out in bizarre clothing that didn't fit properly, trying out roles and words as if they were costumes and scripts. Rob's beard, tweed jacket, and jeans were as a costume as much as Steven's bell bottoms and Max Apple shirts, but I didn't see that because he had such an immediate gift for seeing me. That's impossible, of course; there are too many of you for anyone to see accurately. But his words meant the same thing to both sides of me.

After a couple of more date-like dates—dinners or movies—he invited me to his house for the evening. He hadn't escaped the seventies any more than Steven had; his was simply the grown-up version. He had poised a sleek, sculptured sofa on the obviously antique Oriental rug in front of the stone fireplace, and displayed some Finnish art glass under his Napoleon posters and historic cartoons depicting Louis at the guillotine. He had knocked out the wall between the kitchen and the living room, creating the open space popular at the time. He had Italian cooking pots and the red, white, and black utensils that were standard for anyone who followed Milanese design. With the sleeves of his Oxford cloth shirt rolled up neatly, his hands in red-and-black-checked oven mitts, he looked like an authority in the kitchen. Dinner was a French Provençal cassoulette and a green salad *not* made with iceberg lettuce; dessert was a crème caramel. We retired to his stiff, modern sofa where he touched my hand, nuzzled his beard into my neck, stroked my bare shoulder. Before I got up to leave for the night, he leaned over and kissed me chastely on the cheek.

The courtship was relatively brief. I was seduced by the completeness and civility of his world, and by his ease in it, so different from the unpredictable, sharp romances of the music school, and from graduate classes with their sometimes enigmatic expectations. I was not seduced, however, by him. He quickly figured out I wasn't a virgin, but we wouldn't make love until we were married. So there was an odd divergence between our civilized and even chic dinners and conversation and our grappling and huffing and contortions as we played with each other's passions but refused to completely acknowledge their existence. Four months later, we were married.

I brought little from my own apartment. Since he had all the dishes and pans and utensils we'd need, I left the few I'd bought to my grateful apartment mates. I found myself, a month before my wedding, going through my closet and throwing out clothing—a comfortable caftan I'd made of Indian print bedspreads, a fuchsia peasant tunic and skirt, my pantsuits and bell bottoms. Then I called my mother and cried. After the culling, there were about four outfits left. My father had been dead two weeks, and I felt selfish crying over the phone.

"But I'm *glad* you've called. You've given me an excuse to come to Montreal and go shopping. I still need a dress for your wedding.

Everyone here expects me to see you married in mourning, but I'm not wearing black to your wedding. No one in Montreal will give a holy hoot about what I wear. Nor should they. It's nobody's business but mine. I'll pack tonight and be on the road in the morning. You can expect me tomorrow afternoon some time. I may have to call you once I get into Montreal for directions."

"Are you sure you want to drive? It's a whole day."

"I'm sure. It'll be a beautiful drive, with the trees just coming into leaf. And we'll certainly need a car once I'm there. It'll be an adventure. I have no idea where I'll be eating lunch tomorrow afternoon."

So Mother came, and taught me to shop like a grown-up. How mysterious woman-skills seemed to me then: I had no idea how to find clothes that would suit my new role as a professor's wife and an up-and-coming musician, but she did. Unlike other mothers I knew, she never pressed me to buy something that would have been appropriate for her. She was giddy and extravagant. My clothes took up exactly half the closet when I moved in with Rob after the honeymoon.

These days, Rob occasionally moves a piece of clothing down to his study. In our closet, there are only half a dozen ties, a couple of shirts, and an extra pair of shoes. Yet somehow there's less room for me than ever.

I keep seeing people in coffee shops and on the street who look content with being alone. They write in their journals with fountain pens or sketch the edge of a building and a group of trees. They gaze off toward the mountain thoughtfully, contemplatively; or they people-watch with a detached, humourous curiosity, taking one more sip of a latte, a thoughtful bite of croissant. They have time and space. I envy them. They make me hungry.

Sunday, June 2, 2002

Rob

Three

Julia Child taught me to cook. I'd come back from Paris, where I'd been studying the effect of the French Revolution and the 1832 cholera epidemic on the redesign of the city. I had learned what food truly was when I saw the two Gallic volumes with their fleur-des-lys-sprinkled covers in the bookstore: one white jacket dotted with red, the other with blue. They were unmistakably French, even from a distance. I opened the covers, smelled the new paper, then fell in love with the layout of the page. The Gallic clarity. The useful headings. The varieties of type that distinguished ingredients and equipment from the clear instructions. The wide margins, the crisp lines between the recipes. The illustrations that assumed I knew nothing of cooking, as, indeed, I didn't. Few men did in the seventies. Women found my ability to cook seductive, but it wasn't an accomplishment I bragged about to my male colleagues as part of the gossipy and womanish prelude to department meetings.

I began that evening to read it like a novel, studying Julia's advice for kitchen equipment; her discussion of ingredients; her explanations of how to measure, how to chop, slice, dice, and mince; her advice on wines. Then, barely into her chapter on soup, I flipped to the end—though reading the index of a cookbook is not a sin of the same magnitude as reading the end of a mystery. The index is written in French and in English, and I came to prefer the French names. Soufflé Démoulé, Mousseline sounded magical, though my first attempt at unmolding a soufflé I'd baked for over an hour left a tough mess on my plate. After that, I turned to more basic things. I learned how to properly roast a chicken, how to cook fresh green beans, how to mash potatoes with cloves of garlic that I'd braised for twenty minutes in butter. Cooking green beans for fifteen minutes may sound heretical to us now, but the description of a properly cooked bean, "which should be tender, but still retain the slightest suggestion of crunchiness" was certainly radical. My mother thought vegetables should be well and truly dead, reduced, if possible, to a homogenous greeny-brown that made haricots verts indistinguishable from choux de Bruxelles.

I am tempted to say that Julia Child changed my life, but my search for the proper batterie de cuisine or heads of garlic or fresh vegetables or a proper baguette was really confined only to weekends. Fortunately, living in Montreal made this a bit easier, but in the seventies it was still a challenge. This was before the days when huge cargo planes began bringing us fresh produce from another hemisphere, or before you could buy good tinned chicken stock, which makes Julia's instructions for draining the stock off Campbell's chicken vegetable soup seem almost antiquated. Never mind: it made perfectly respectable sauce béchamel.

Her recipes seem old-fashioned to me now. Sometimes, though, I am tempted to cook something that takes me back to that early time, especially to the things I made for Lila when I was courting her. I made Child's Bavarois á L'orange a month or two ago, and though the flavour you get from rubbing the thick orange skins with sugar cubes to extract their oil is superb, the texture is almost rubbery. Too much gelatin, I suspect. I might be inclined to play with the recipe, except that now I've turned to other cookbooks, first to Craig Claiborne, then those from the Silver Palate, then on to bad-boy Anthony Bourdain and sexy Nigella Lawson. I sometimes wonder if, like my mother, I'll get antediluvian about my cooking in my late sixties, making the same recipes over and over until I am sick of eating. I think not. A new recipe is like a flirtation. You have to imagine how these flavours and textures and colours are going to work together. If you're a creative or responsible cook, you have to imagine where the recipe has gone wrong—at least for your palate. Sometimes—and perversely, I enjoy this—you have to search for ingredients like fresh lemongrass or artichokes out of season. It's part of the chase.

Cooking is one of the few important and meaningful rituals of my life. I'll admit I'm not a patient man. But I'm willing to go to several shops in order to find exactly what I want. My favourite butcher's for free-range chickens. A fruiterer's for the freshest produce. The gourmet deli for the lime splash I like on asparagus. Fresh rosemary and basil. The perfect cheese to go with the new apples. I'd walk miles for good Wensleydale. Or white Stilton with mango if I'm in the mood for something tarted up. I love the orderliness of cooking. The precision of measurement. The Zen of julienne. The order of the kitchen, of a day's cooking, takes my mind off the disorder of the rest of my life.

No two weeks in an academic's life are quite the same. While our teaching schedules don't change, some classes require more preparation than others, particularly if we're teaching something new. Some weeks we're burdened with endless marking of idiotic, dull, credulous papers. Believe me: it takes a great deal of control (and energy) not to say what one thinks of such efforts on the part of undergraduate cretins. Then there are fruitless, often acrimonious hiring meetings dotted among our other responsibilities. The department's pretty well divided between the cutting edge and the old farts, and everyone is scrambling to get *their* candidate to tip the balance. I don't want the balance tipped, so I've been arguing about process endlessly. We have a hiring protocol, Byzantine as it is, for a reason. To protect our integrity as a department. But no one has wanted to back me up on this, so I've locked horns with the department head and the dean. Wednesday, charges of harassment were laid. But there's nothing they can do to me. I'm not going to think about it. This is the weekend, and Lila needs me here cooking. So I'm going to put up a wall right now between the calm of home and the irritation of the office. And besides, there's Elise. But I'm keeping Elise out of this for now. Maybe about 3:00 AM, I'll let her back in.

I loved cooking the dinner for Margaret's visit to Mother. I wanted to do something nice for Lila. Her mother's illness is depressing, an unexpected challenge. I see her trying every day to bring joy or humour or pleasure into her mother's life. When she's desperate, she reads her mother the "Social Studies" section of the *Globe*, or even shows her the comics, as if trying to say, "Isn't life funny?" even while she knows life isn't funny at all right now. She knows how important her practising is to her mother, thank god, so she can take care of both of them at the same time while the morning nurse does the dirty work. She's trying to detach herself from the whole medical process, to live without hope or expectation. So she comes back from their visits to the doctor maddeningly ill-informed. She'll tell me about a change in medication or dosage, but she has no idea—that she tells me about, anyway—what the next stage looks like. She seems to live always in the present. *Now* mother is comfortable. *Now* she seems weaker than yesterday. She's got to have some plan for the next few months—she's got to protect herself somehow, but when I bring this up, she's almost evasive.

Yesterday, when I began to lay out and butter the sheets of phyllo dough that we'd fold into triangles, Lila wordlessly put down yet another biography of Brahms she was reading at the kitchen table and joined me to help. While she and I worked, I told her, "Look, Lila. I can understand you don't want to think about the future. But you need to do some planning. What are you going to do when the morning nurse and a few visits to the doctor aren't enough? Do you have a sense of when you're going to decide that the hospital is the place for her?"

"She's not going into the hospital. Ever. The hospital's no place to die. All they do there is keep you alive no matter what and not give you enough painkillers because you might become addicted. That's senseless." There was no anger in this judgment, and she kept on rolling up her triangles, not even looking at me. Her tone of voice was neutral, almost matter-of-factly flat.

"So you want her to die here? At home?"

"I'd prefer at home. But this is your home too, and if you don't want death here, I understand. I'll move her into a hospice."

"A hospice?" I have only a vague idea what this means. Smarmy nurses and good attitudes toward death. Dumb. "Do you know of any?"

"I've visited a couple in the last month or so. There's one in the neighbourhood. I liked the nurses and the atmosphere of the place."

"*When* have you been checking out *hospices*?"

"Mornings. When mother's been with her nurse."

"I thought you were *practising*?"

"I was doing that too." She isn't looking at me. She's intently folding phyllo appetizers.

"Why didn't you say something?"

"You've been preoccupied. You seemed to have a lot on your mind. I didn't think I needed to have the hospice/dying at home/hospital debate with you since I'd already made up my mind about the hospital. I thought we'd talk about other options when it got closer. I was fairly sure you wouldn't want her to die here, so I checked out hospices."

I've been preoccupied. That's an understatement. That's also why I'm so pleased to be right here, cooking with Lila, thinking about impressing Margaret and delighting Mother.

"Are you upset that I don't want her to die here?"

"Oh, no. I think I'm the one that's inhuman."

I put my right arm around her shoulder, being careful not to drip butter on her bare arms. "Why do you say that?" She deserves this—this lying question. Because there is something inhuman about her calm, though I'm both relieved and insulted by her failure to consult me. We've finished rolling the phyllo triangles, and I pack them tightly into a heavy ziplock bag with wax paper between the layers so I can bake them today when everyone arrives. Lila, knowing that there's rosemary in the chickens I'm cooking, pulls out a couple of stems and begins chopping it finely. The kitchen smells wonderful—butter, rosemary, the astringent after-smell of sautéing fresh spinach, the hint of floury phyllo.

"I don't know why I'm so calm. I'm angry sometimes."

She's clearly fishing for a reaction. "I can understand being angry about your mother's cancer. But that happens to us. *If* we're lucky." Both my parents have been dead for quite some time. There are other losses I don't think about if I can help it.

"No, it isn't that. It's vaguer."

I try a hint of levity: "I don't know anything that can be more vague than anger at life."

It takes, and she laughs at herself—one of her gifts. "You men. That's what I'm angry at," she says, as if with mock seriousness. "My father, who doesn't die, but who is simply there one minute, gone the next. Jack—the same. Leaving me to do this. You're very much here—" she holds up her rosemary-infused hands as if to say she's not going to smear green rosemary blood all over my shirt and leans forward to kiss me. "But you're not, somehow." She cocks her head almost playfully. Her brown eyes are intense, dark and shining. "Work," she pronounces, with a curt nod of her head, and then turns back to chopping up rosemary. "How much do you need?"

"A couple of tablespoons."

"Done," she pronounces, turning to wash her hands. "I'd better go check on Mother."

What was that all about? Goddamn it, she can be so ambiguous. I rub the toasted hazelnuts in a towel to flake off their brown skins, and of course I make a mess of the kitchen floor. Margaret doesn't trust me. Which is why I was so anxious to prepare a stellar dinner to celebrate the family's being together. For perhaps one of the last times. Actually, it was Jack who didn't trust me, and I'm sure he shared his suspicions with Margaret.

A couple of days before the wedding, Jack called to ask if there was to be the ritual stag party. I said definitely not. He suggested that we have a "modified stag," a relatively quiet night of snacking and drinking—though he emphasized a pub was obligatory. I later learned why. When he showed up, he was dressed with almost aggressive casualness, given that he'd never seen me in anything less formal than jeans (with a well-pressed crease) and a button-down, Oxford cloth shirt: he wore tatty jeans and a sweatshirt that advertised beer. Foreign beer, but beer.

"You know, I can't decide," he opened, once we got our drinks: beer for him, a gin and tonic for me. "You have no idea how many scripts I went through before I picked you up. There was the 'nice guy makes subtle suggestion,' the 'educated-man-to-man with subtle threats,' the 'boorish brother-in-law tells the groom he knows his dirty little secrets.'"

"I can see you've decided on the latter."

He raised an eyebrow. I looked him up and down.

"Right," he said. "You get your choice. After Dad died, it was my responsibility to make sure that Lila was making the right decision. It's what Dad would have done." Gregory had died suddenly of a heart attack about six weeks before we were married. We thought about putting off the wedding out of respect, but Clarice, Lila's mother, wouldn't hear of it. The invitations were all sent. Besides, she thought he'd like to see his daughter married to such a wonderful man as soon as possible. Someone who had a future and cared about hers. Then he'd know she was safe. It was as if she imagined Gregory pacing back and forth in front of heaven's windows, nervously checking on the safety of his family.

"So . . . I did a little checking. Some of it fairly formal. Sometimes, all I had to do was make a discreet suggestion and the words fairly fell out of people's mouths. Interesting. How willing people were to talk about you."

"You know how people love gossip . . ."

"Stuff it. Let's start with the easy part. You do indeed own your home, and the mortgage is nearly paid off. Well done, chappy." He popped his fist into my shoulder in a parody of camaraderie—but a little harder than necessary. "You've got tenure, and there's nothing the university can do about that. Lucky for you." He raised his beer to the bartender to signal for another one. "You flirt. With female students. It's even been noticed by your department head, though no one has any dirt for sure, and they're pretty proud to have attracted sonny boy, who's quite the scholar. They're willing to turn their heads the other way until something really happens. Then there'll be *schadenfreude*." He paused to see if I was suitably impressed with his vocabulary. Frankly, I was, and let him know. It didn't matter. "*Schadenfreude,*" he repeated, his pronunciation exact. "Big time."

"Look, university departments are full of gossip and half of it is motivated by other people's jealousy and fearful little fantasy lives. But let's just say this. The gossip doesn't matter. I'm in love with Lila. I won't hurt her. I have every intention of taking care of her. And by that, I don't mean simply supporting her for the rest of our lives. I'm a modern man. She's a gifted musician. She'll have a career. I'll see to it that she has whatever she needs to get that career going, whether it's lessons, practice space and time, or just moral support." I hadn't yet let anyone know that I'd bought her a lovely Heintzman upright as a wedding present. He certainly wasn't going to be the first to know.

He mugged an almost approving nod. "She'll need the independent income. Why is it I don't trust you any farther than I can throw you?"

"Maybe you don't like men. I have a feeling that a lot more went on in your household than Lila's told me about—which is the occasional fist in your mother's face."

"Sounds like a good theory. As far as it goes. But I don't really like *you*. There's something a little self-satisfied about you that sets my teeth on edge."

"You aren't exactly sweetness and light." His third beer had just arrived. I was still nursing my G&T. I'd decided that either he'd give me the car keys or I'd be taking a cab home.

Jack had finished university with degrees in education and phys. ed. An all-round athlete, he'd immediately gotten a good job coaching one of the better high school football teams, with a few phys. ed. classes on the side. He got more aggressive daily, as if he ate testosterone for breakfast. His marriage to Margaret looked solid—well, not so much solid as conventional. Unreflective. Knee-jerk. Their lives revolved around the kids first and work second. It was hard to imagine intimacy—of any kind—between Margaret and Jack. A good vigorous fuck now and then—fairly often, actually—but not intimacy. Hard to imagine a quiet conversation about the challenges the day had brought. Jack didn't seem puzzled by anything. I didn't think I'd met anyone less challenged by life. "Just do something" seemed his motto. "If you do something, everything will turn out fine." Well, he'd done something about me all right.

"I don't have to be sweetness and light. I have to protect my sister. You take care of her, and you don't need to worry whether I'm sweet or not."

"Then I guess I don't have anything to worry about."

"Guess you don't. Just me watching you."

I shrugged.

With Jack dead, I wanted Margaret on my side. I'm not sure what I mean: "On my side." What sides are there here? Do I think that Lila is on one side and I'm on another? No. It's more that I'm on one side, and Lila and I are on another, and maybe Lila is on a third, where she's nursing her mother. I don't want Margaret weighing in. Somewhere out there stands the ghost of Jack. This is beginning to look like an odd version of *Magister Ludi's Glass Bead Game*, the only Hesse novel I ever liked. Or like a surreal chess match from the old *Avengers*. Somewhere, way out there, is my department head and one of my students, Elise. Except today as I've cooked, I've tried to think of Lila and Mother, I've tried to think of Margaret and not of Jack. I've tried to keep my mind on a family dinner. On the order and flavour of each dish. But I kept seeing Elise sidling conspiratorially up to Jack's ghost.

Wednesday, June 5, 2002

Four

The Bach isn't going well. I can't get the lightness or sparkle or speed of the harpsichord. I hope Kevin hasn't put too much time into learning his part. I have, but it doesn't matter. Failure usually teaches me something I'll need to know sooner or later.

So here's another one of those silences that has disturbed me lately. The end of a mangled bar of music, of a baffling conversation. Of a life. My mother's absence in two or three or four months' time is terrifying, but it's abstract and theoretical. The challenge is getting her there with her self intact. Yet her absence now has nothing abstract about it. She hardly spoke Sunday afternoon, but nodded and smiled at the conversation; sometimes she slept lightly for a few minutes at a time, and then awoke, either picking up the thread or not worrying about where the thread had come from. She seems to have escaped from time and continuity. As if nothing mattered. Perhaps everything matters, and she simply can't do anything about it. Perhaps everything matters and she is doing what she needs, although I can't hear it. But her hand, so cool and fragile, so stilled by sleep, seems hardly present.

Margaret must have called me the very minute she got back to the hotel after last night's organ recital to insist we have coffee this morning. "I know someone comes in the morning to take care of Mother, so I know you're free."

I felt bullied. "I need to practise in the mornings."

"You can do that after I leave. We need to talk tomorrow."

I spent the next twelve hours justifying myself. Lindsay was getting out of her boring job and making plans for a life again. If she came to dinner without Paul, it meant she was getting more independent. Mother's decision not to accept any palliative treatment for her cancer was *her* decision. No, I hadn't argued with her about it. But I didn't think I should. Yes, I could dust more often. And yes, Brahms needs brushing. And yes, my mind trotted out all my flaws before it indulged in reasons and excuses. Margaret's importunate call raised an alarm that has been quietly sounding for some months, like that premonitory musical motif that has been hanging around, giving structure to the music but seeming peripheral somehow. Then, in the last movement, when you find that it's been holding everything together, you can't imagine how.

So I was completely surprised when, after we'd ordered our cappuccino and croissants, she asked me if I'd been to the doctor lately.

"You seem listless. You've lost weight. Have you had your thyroid checked? Are you getting enough iron? Calcium?"

"It's only temporary," I told her. "Once things return to normal, I'll be fine."

"What's normal, Lila?" In my memories, this question comes back again and again.

"Oh, I don't know. Not worrying about mother. Having Lindsay in law school. Performing again with a new and challenging repertoire." I needed to protect myself from Margaret's probing.

"Is now really the time for you and Kevin to be trying to learn new music? Why not just hold steady?"

Rob's never been easy with Margaret; she brings out something in him that I can't quite name but don't especially like—a kind of jokey sexism?—a slight professorial arrogance? Ironically, Margaret and I have drawn closer since Jack's death. As a husband, Jack was more like Father than anyone could have predicted from the antipathy—no, let's be honest: hostility is the word—the hostility between the two that developed in Jack's teens and intensified in his early twenties. He loved Margaret and adored the kids, but every once in a while he would erupt with controlled fury, usually at something fairly inconsequential like Jackie smacking her bubble gum at the dinner table or Margaret forgetting to pick up his dry cleaning.

Jack's weapon was his mouth. Better than a fist, but not much. Once, when Devon was young and they still lived in Montreal, his Little League baseball team made some kind of semifinals that Lindsay and I attended as honorary cheerleaders. It was the bottom of the ninth inning, his team was one point ahead, the opposing team's bases were loaded, and Devon managed to drop a fly. His team lost. "Look at them," Jack urged Devon, pointing at his subdued teammates. "Every one of them is going home tonight disappointed because you can't catch a fucking fly ball." His right fist beat a tattoo in his left palm.

Devon knew perfectly well what had happened. He didn't need to be told. What he needed was perspective—the old "this isn't the end of the world" schtick every parent must master and administer with hugs. The reliable "there are always more ballgames . . . proms . . . exams." And there always are, even once you think you've finished with your last heartbreak or fuckup.

Before Jack died, Margaret and I were cautious around each other, as if there were a secret that would be loosed if we spoke of it. That secret wasn't Jack's anger, which was hardly hidden. Perhaps it was Margaret's covert tolerance for it, her inability to challenge it. Dead of a heart attack in his early fifties, Jack now allows us to tell stories of our lives that don't shame us. I remember the year we had an ice storm that crusted the snow thickly and inspired my father to flood the back yard and make a small rink. Jack would condescend to go out to skate after dark with his gawky sister, the kitchen window making a square of light on the ad hoc rink. We skated over our parents' shadows as they stood together, my mother's hand on my father's shoulder, looking out into the night. Much later, there's the one about a goofy family baseball game between Jack, Margaret, and their young kids and Rob, adolescent Lindsay, and me. We barely had enough players for a single team, so Rob pitched until there were no more batters, and then people who had been struck out or who had run the bases took over pitching while he batted and ran his bases. No matter who was on the mound, we made sure that Jackie and Devon and Lindsay "hit" the ball (which means we hit their bat with our pitch). The anarchy made us giddy. (Mind you, Rob was three sheets to the wind, or he'd have never agreed either to anarchy or giddiness.)

Instead of tiptoeing around things we couldn't speak of, Margaret and I have found common, girlish things to talk about. It's safe to moan together about the enigmas of parenting (for some reason, Rob has never found being a parent mystifying). We can share and laugh at the puzzlement we felt when our kids hit adolescence, and hormones and rebellion and generation gaps—not to mention the styles that go with them—made our children suddenly inexplicable and unfamiliar. Yesterday they needed a bandage, a story, a hug to comfort them over an unfaithful friend, a bubble gum ice cream cone. Today, they want to adorn their bodies with as little clothing as possible, they carry talismanic condoms in their wallets or keep an unused package of birth control pills at the bottom of their pile of still thin-hipped panties. For years, I could recognize Lindsay by the smell of her hair, some inexplicable combination of shampoo and the distinctive odour of her skin; then this was slowly replaced by the foreign smell of adolescence, and then masked by the kinds of sweet-sharp perfumes young girls go in for.

So in a kind of jokey relief, Margaret and I whine about shoes and hair styles and the colour of the season's clothing. This year, it's been pink and turquoise, which, since we both wear neutrals and black, is right out. We complain when they change the faces modelling our hair colour—as if a new face on our shade provokes an identity crisis. We complain more when they renumber our favourite lipsticks, whose names we can no longer see without our reading glasses. We know this is trivial; that is exactly the point.

As I hold Mother's hand this evening, Margaret's words rise out of the darkness before me, then sometimes fall at my feet. I remember her soothing, worrying voice, and add to the conversation all the things I should have explained.

"When's the last time you slept through the night?" For some reason, Margaret seems much more worried about my sleeping than about Mother's death.

"Oh, I've never been a very good sleeper. Menopause has only made it worse. You know how it is. The phenobarbital dose that wiped out Heaven's Gate gives me a good four hours. But I haven't started putting chocolate chips in salads." My self-mocking sense of humour isn't cutting any ice. She grimaces and forges onward.

"Mother tells me she often finds you in the chair beside her bed at about four in the morning."

"When did you two get a chance to talk about my sleeping habits?"

"When you were coaching Rob through frying the pommes frites."

"Rob doesn't need coaching."

"No, he needs someone to tell him to calm down and try to be sociable rather than the gourmet of the century."

This snippet arose out of the dark more than once. What did she mean? Simply that Rob needs to calm down? That he tries too hard? That he's not a pleasant person? I'm not sure that being a "pleasant person" has been his goal in life. What has been?

Father approved of Rob, of course. While he didn't live long enough to see us married, the very first time they met, Father gave his approval.

I called Mother to tell her about my engagement. While I was trying to talk to her about it, Father kept interrupting. My explanations intertwined with his growling complaints, like two voices in a fugue, but in different keys.

"What happened to—Steven? Wasn't that the name of the young man you were dating? The pianist with floppy hair, you called him."

"*So what's happened to the floppy-haired young man? Done a bunk? Figures. Nothing reliable about these hippies.*"

"When did this happen, Lila? Are you sure you aren't going too quickly?"

I try to tell her that my timing has been perfect, that I'm sure I know what I'm doing. "What's that horrible expression? On the rebound? You don't need to take someone on the rebound, you know. You're a lovely talented young woman whom some young man is going to love deeply."

"Rebound? Who's rebounding? Is this something about hippies and the stock market? I knew they'd figure out where the power was sooner or later and show their true colours."

"I don't think your father understands."

Rob's older, I try to tell her. A professor. A professional with his own house and fine job.

"Can we meet him? Soon? We could come to Montreal next weekend."

"We'll go to Montreal next weekend over my dead body. I have tickets for the football game next weekend."

"The weekend after?" Mother asks us both. I can hear the different question in her voice—the questioning voice she has for him, not for me. His answer must be a mere nod, for she tells me, "Your father says that would be fine."

I expect things will go smoothly, which alarms me. Have I sold out by marrying a man my father will doubtless approve of? For that matter, what does it mean to sell out to one's parents? We might sell out to the authorities or the military-industrial complex, but to our parents? What does it mean that I can think such a thought—that most of my generation thinks this?

Mother and Father made it to their small hotel by taxi, then Rob and I picked them up to take them to his house for dinner. Rob knew intuitively to shake my father's hand and to lean down and kiss my mother on both cheeks. Then, as Rob pulled on to Sherbrooke, Father took a careful look at his car. It was late afternoon and I had my sun visor down, so I could watch both my parents in its mirror. For Mother, this was a new experience: chauffeured by a professor who wanted to marry her daughter, she was going to enjoy it all—the sights of downtown Montreal, the chic men and women walking along Sherbrooke, the more cosmopolitan European architecture, the glimpse into the McGill campus. She asked innocent, lighthearted questions about the Museé des beaux arts, admiring its neoclassical facade. At the same time, I sensed a giddy relief, an untangling of something tightly knotted.

Father's attention was turned to his more immediate surroundings: he examined the car (a late-model Volvo), he seemed to study the quality of Rob's jacket, asking if it was Harris tweed, which made up for Rob's beard. He asked Rob if he preferred a standard transmission.

He was taking stock, calculating, smiling at me in the visor mirror. The crooked tooth he had always criticized, the habitual bend of my head, my height (I was tall, but Rob was taller)—all these flaws were cancelled out by the value he had put on my future husband. He had no idea of the crisis he caused me in that moment. I had thought I understood Rob's value as a companion, a life partner. Suddenly that value was replaced by a confused desire for simultaneous approval and revenge. It felt as if my love was being played in the wrong key.

"What's normal, Lila?" I have no idea what's normal. Sometimes I don't even think I know what's comfortable or carefree, only what's familiar.

Last night at the organ recital, Mother and I had to use the wheelchair-accesible elevator to enter the cathedral. Margaret came to help me with the wheelchair, and Devon tagged along out of curiosity. Since Jackie was parked with Lindsay—neither of them wanted to hear music last night—Rob was left standing in front of the cathedral, seemingly at loose ends. There's quite a steep incline to the ground floor elevator, and as I struggled to wheel Mother down the walk without tipping her out of her chair, Rob was greeting one of his graduate students, Elise Grant, on the cathedral steps. Rob's protective of his students; he invests a lot in their progress, and sometimes almost goes into mourning when one leaves to do a PHD elsewhere. Elise has been given a scholarship to U of T for next fall, and Rob is understandably proud. So I shouldn't have been surprised when he smiled at her approach and reached out to touch her arm. As he did so, Elise turned her head to look straight at me, a long, cold, appraising look. Then she looked back at him and raised one eyebrow. Margaret was watching too and looked at me quizzically while we loaded Mother into the elevator. A look, a touch. That was all.

"What's normal, Lila?" Margaret was trying to prompt me yesterday morning. She was not going to say, "Your husband's having an affair," because how much evidence did we see? A look. A touch. If she'd said it outright, what she would have said to me is that Rob is the kind of man who has affairs, so it doesn't take much evidence to indict him. I'm surprised at how unsurprised I am. How much it explains. The unfamiliar tie. His sleeping downstairs or penchant for brisk sex. My suspicions are like that bit of melody that's missing: I don't know. I don't know anything.

On Thursday nights when I swim in the university pool, a middle-aged woman spends an hour or so in the sauna, going to and from her locker stark naked, her towel thrown over her shoulder, utterly at her ease. She doesn't have a beautiful body, though her curves and circles are really quite lovely in an unconventional way. She has short, tightly permed hair and an almost simian face. But I envy her for her obvious comfort with herself. A couple of weeks ago, a young blind woman came in from the pool, working her way with her cane around the room until she came to what she thought was her locker. "Oh!"—it was merely a little frustrated, puzzled expulsion of air. My naked companion strode over to ask what was wrong.

"I thought this was my locker, but it isn't." The naked woman asked about the kind of lock, the size of locker they should be looking for, and accompanied the other woman up and down the ranks of lockers until they found the right one.

The blind woman was part of a story she knew nothing about. She hardly knew that the patient voice at her elbow was middle-aged and naked. There was one story for her, the story of a lost locker, probably part of a horde of disoriented stories. There was another story entirely for the onlookers, a humorous story of unselfconscious and generous sympathy.

I am the blind one this morning. The light is just beginning to bloom, making the moist air muzzy. Mother has slept soundly for the last hour or so. I listen and watch as time unfolds: I hear planes take off, a couple of trains blow their whistles as they move west. One of them grabs something just below my breastbone and pulls and it hurts, *it hurts.* I watch the room lighten and awaken; the flowers begin to emerge from the dark. The quilts on the rack at the foot of the bed, the lamps and curtains have become more substantial, as if during the night part of their atoms go wandering, leaving them ghosts, while morning brings them back to themselves.

And I am blind. There's a story going on that's not my story. Except it is. And my companion in the story isn't generous.

Thursday, June 6, 2002

Five

I never sleep this late. Rob must have heard me up in the night and warned Mrs. Henry not to wake me up. Ordinarily the chatter between her and Mother fills the upstairs rooms. Maybe Rob even took Mother downstairs. I was hazily aware of the household going on around me as I almost surfaced from my dream world but was held helplessly just under the comforter of sleep. I think I heard Rob in the shower, Mrs. Henry's arrival, Rob's car starting. His old Volvo needs a tune-up. Its rough rhythms seemed, for the minute he let it run to smooth itself out, to carve out my room the way water carves out a cave.

So as I struggled to wake up, nothing seemed real except the slight breeze and Brahms's occasional kneading of the duvet before he settled himself down in a new curve. I lay in bed and simply smelled the early summer air, sweet with new greenness, and listened to the midmorning rhythms of Montreal: in the foreground were the chickadees and goldfinches and wrens the garden attracts. One confused robin was singing its rain song—I could see that the sky was a sweet blue. Brahms, no longer feeling he needed to purr me back to sleep, left to get some food, perhaps stopping to tell Mrs. Henry I was awake. Shortly after he left, she came in, bringing a cup of coffee.

"Mr. Dowling asked me to bring you breakfast in bed when you woke up. He said you had a bad night."

I smiled and held my hand out for the coffee. "That would be a treat."

I reached over and opened the drapes further, then sat back and sipped my coffee. Soon Mrs. Henry brought a tray with a croissant, a bowl of fruit, and the French press wrapped in its Liberty blanket.

"Mr. Dowling got this ready for you before he went to work. He said you needed some spoiling."

I haven't had breakfast in bed for years. Suddenly there's a still life: the duvet strewn with newspapers; a crossword puzzle half done, abandoned yet again; *Private Eye* mingling with *The New Yorker*; *Playboy* (read for the articles, of course) cheek by jowl with the *Canadian Journal of History*; a breakfast tray in disarray with the leavings of breakfast—croissant crumbs on white china, a sad uneaten strawberry, silverware askew among cloth napkins. All this is Rob's food. He's the one who owned the French press and who introduced me to croissants. He's actually found a small bakery that sells them to you unbaked and frozen, so you can have them fresh from your oven. I search my sub-dream memory and realize that, yes, I remember the smell of baking croissants. Why, of all mornings, has Rob chosen today to spoil me?

Nothing is real this morning. No: that's not quite precise. There's no way to tell what's real. I'm in the hall of mirrors, but Bruce Lee is no help.

When we're learning a piece of music, we depend upon the key, tempo markings, bar lines, and time signature to guide our interpretation. Is it bold, straightforward C major? Or more ethereal and plangent E flat minor? D minor with its antique relationship to the Dorian mode? Is it marchlike four/four? Or does the time signature change constantly, as in Stravinsky's *Rite of Spring*? Adagio or presto? I've taken that guidance, that framework for granted since I was a kid practising on the out-of-tune family spinet. But as I lie here with my second cup of lovely dark roast, croissant crumbs on my pyjamas and in the sheets, that robin still imagining it's going to rain, I realize that I have to learn to read all over again. The alphabet has changed; words have shifted and warped over night, sentences no longer feel like whole ideas. Or like ideas at all. They're something else, something much more primal and instinctive. Ever tried to read the words for *red* or *green* when the letters are in a different colour than the words they make? The word *purple* in orange letters or *green* in blue letters? Your mind doesn't know whether to read the colour of the letters or the letters of the word. I don't know whether to read "love" for this morning's breakfast or "guilt."

An optical illusion of the Escher sort: two railroad tracks, instead of coming closer as they recede into the distance, grow farther and farther apart. Imagine the tension in the train flying down those tracks, suddenly faced with the physics of dissociation. My marriage is just fine. Everything I've noticed has a perfectly reasonable explanation. My husband has been unfaithful for I don't know how long. It's just a matter of gathering evidence and calling him to task. Somewhere between suspicion and a freshly baked croissant, I realized I'll have to put on a perfectly normal facade. It would be a tactical mistake to voice my suspicions without evidence. Why am I thinking of tactics? Tactics against Rob are useless. How do I know that? I just do. I'm finding there's so much about Rob I didn't know I knew.

Or denial. When did I become an expert at denial? Or learn the craftsmanship of suspicion?

Or am I simply hungry to be alone, seduced by those images of people in coffee houses looking through the steam of their coffee and thinking only about themselves and their rich inner lives. How can you tell whether the order for non-fat decaf latte with a double shot of whatever it is that makes this latte as individual as a fingerprint is lonely or self-sufficient? Because we all fake it now and again.

"We'll start with something familiar, shall we?" Kevin asks, getting his violin out of its case. "How about the Brahms 'Rain Sonata'?" He searches through his pile of music, as do I. Our music at the ready, he takes a breath, and I begin the opening chords.

"I love this opening: the repeated chords, the simple melody. Brahms could make melodies out of nothing, couldn't he? . . . Lovely, Lila, the waterfall of notes . . . Go ahead, give it all you've got. It's all yours," he says, flourishing the violin away from his shoulder in the body language of encouragement.

"And then this refreshing little melody . . . heartbreaking simplicity. That waterfall again . . . and again . . . and again."

Kevin often begins a rehearsal wired and chatty. But eventually the music takes over—not just his idea of the music, but the physical part of it: his need to be careful about his bowing, to coax a certain kind of sound out of his instrument and concentrate on dynamics—and then a different conversation starts. We always begin a rehearsal with something we've played often: it's the best way we've found to renew the rhythm and the texture of the partnership.

We take a breath, emotional and physical, after we finish the first movement.

"Such sweet sadness. I never know how much is Brahms's temperamental sadness and how much is longing for Clara Schumann."

"He sent the sonata to her right after he composed it, and she told him it made her cry. They'd never play it together because they were both pianists." Fleetingly, my cynical mind thinks about partnerships. It does this little panicked inventory—about the twentieth for the day. Smells. It keeps coming back to smells, the evidence of the primal nose. I sigh: I'm tired already, even after sleeping late. But Kevin's here to rehearse, and my mother is out on the back deck listening.

I open the second movement with one of Brahms's minimalist melodies, and then Kevin finds an even sparer version of it. The movement almost bogs down in the middle, when Brahms seems to take its motifs apart, reducing them to the simplest terms. Whatever he's made of his life, it lies in fragments before him. It's the dissolution of self that comes with loss and grief. By the end, Kevin's melody is starkly simple. We are watching each other intently for every clue to feeling, dynamics, and tempo that we can find in each other's gestures. I can see from his absorption that we're going to go right on to the final movement with the briefest of pauses. But just a few bars into the movement, he looks puzzled and stops us.

"Not so agitato, Lila. Let's try again."

We go back to the opening of the rondo, and he gives the nod that starts us off. I try to put more silk into the notes, trying to get them to drop like rain. He smiles at me.

For the sake of the music, we are required to be completely frank and open with each other. We struggle honestly with the other's vision of the music. *Vision* is the wrong word, isn't it? Why do we use the word *vision* when it's what we hear with our whole bodies that we attempt to convey? A pleasurable, physical mathematics. Because we have different parts, we have a different perspective on the whole. This is a good thing, most of the time; it enriches our performance, making it complex and many-sided. We disagree over interpretation sometimes, but just keep playing the section over and over—sometimes talking, refining our viewpoint, sometimes not until variety coheres into an intricate whole.

The sonata comes to its quiet, undramatic, liquid end. We smile at each other.

"You okay? Almost lost you there."

I shake my head dismissively. "One of those middle-aged existential crises. It pops up every week or two. To make sure I'm still paying attention."

Kevin nods. "Coffee crisis," he intones desperately.

We go together to the kitchen, where I make him some coffee and myself some peppermint tea. Then I ask if he'd mind sitting with Mother on the deck during our break. Brahms has taken up guard at the end of the chaise; beside him she looks tiny and vulnerable, her white hair a wild aureole.

"That was lovely," she says, predictably, turning her face toward Kevin. "I love hearing you play. You make a dying old woman happy."

"Just doing what I love," he says, tugging an imaginary forelock in salute. "Besides, you still look like you're living to me."

"What have you been playing?"

"Brahms. His first—but heavily rewritten—violin sonata," I tell her.

"Brahms. Of course." She considers a moment. "Was there anything between Brahms and Schumann's wife? I don't believe there could possibly have been. Think of all the clothing. How much time it would have taken to get something going. All those children. And servants. Tell us, dear, what do we know?" she asks, turning to me. She has no earthly idea how startling and painful this is. Decorous walking tours with escorts vs. fucking in his office or in student digs. These days, female students don't have much to take off.

"It's really very gossipy. Most of it's drawn from their correspondence, and from what might have been possible on a couple of trips they took together—with chaperones, of course." My voice feels unreliable, so I take a thoughtful sip of my tea. But I don't think a swallow of tea is going to dilute the sadness that washes over me in this mental space where everything means something else. Where an unfamiliar tie means an affair with the woman who bought it. But Rob often goes shopping on his own; he could have bought it for himself. I resort to the gossipy, avoiding loss and loneliness. "In any event, the first version I read suggested Clara kept Brahms at a distance but was jealous every time he got close to someone. More recently, it's been suggested Brahms almost seems to have abandoned Clara after Schumann's death. He realized he had to choose between art and life." I pour myself another cup of tea, look at Kevin to see if he wants more coffee. He does. My double agent suggests a bit of comedy. A false scent, a bit of a detour when I return.

Back with a cup of coffee, I change the subject to age. "You know, all the pictures of an old Brahms make you think that he was somehow born old and accomplished." My mother is indulging in her usual strategy: get a conversation going and then go to sleep. Or pretend to.

"Like your cat," Kevin says to keep things moving.

"Exactly. He came into the household already middle-aged and filled with longing. What other name could I have given him? But poor old Brahms—the composer, not the cat—had a long musical apprenticeship. The curse of Schumann . . ."

"The curse of Schumann." Kevin says in his Count Dracula voice. He knows all about this, but he's playing along with me for Mother's sake. She's surfaced and smiled.

"Yup. Schumann promised the whole musical world that Brahms was Beethoven's heir. Two things rescued him from safe mediocrity."

"Do tell."

"His mother's death. After which he wrote his *German Requiem*. It was his first big work to get widespread critical and popular approval. The other was turning forty. He couldn't avoid writing symphonies much longer."

"You see, the deaths of mothers have their use." I'm not touching that. But Mother goes gamely on: "How much older was Clara?" she asks, alluding to the fact that's puzzled everyone.

"Fourteen years, I think. You raise your eyebrows, but she was apparently a very charismatic woman and an extraordinary pianist. Someone—Liszt maybe?—called her the 'high priestess of the piano.' I think Brahms knew his longing for her would make him as a composer."

"That's your cat's influence," Mother breaks in again. "You listen to that cat too much."

"Probably. But we should go back to work. Do you need anything?"

"Music. I've already got tea and the cat," she says, nodding toward the end of the chaise. I stop and give her a kiss on her forehead. "Warm enough?" She nods. "I should warn you," I say, turning to Kevin, "the Bach isn't going very well. I can't get it up to speed with the clarity that I'd like."

"You want Gould's ghost to possess you?"

"That's not a bad idea."

"That's a *very* bad idea. Gould isn't my accompanist. How would you look all hunched up over the keyboard?" Kevin twists himself into a parody of Gould gnarled, with his eyes level with his keyboard. "I can't work with gnomes or hypochondriacs. It ruins my concentration."

"Don't be mean. You try being a genius. In my more hopeful moments, I simply think they weren't written for piano."

"Since when has that stopped any interpreter of Bach? *You* know—you're our resident music historian—that Bach arranged his work for anything that made noise. Well, maybe not the penny whistle, but it has been done, and not unconvincingly. Why don't you just relax and see." Kevin puts his arm around my shoulders and leads me back into my studio. It's all I can do not to cry and confess. "Let's just do what we always do," he says. "Play them. We'll figure out how to make them into music."

I don't know anything. How am I going to be less blind, less ignorant?

Tonight Rob was positively uxorious at dinner. He asked about the rehearsal, studying my face intently as if I might suddenly decide to speak a foreign language if he took his eyes off me. You know, the kind of thing a well-trained salesperson will do, along with repeating your name three times in the first five minutes to stamp it firmly in memory. The smarmy over-attentiveness makes you want to hide or give an absurd name.

When someone truly sees you, the mask falls off of its own accord, the way a woman lets her clothing slide suggestively off her shoulders. Every minute Rob pretended to look attentively at me, less and less of me became visible; I was pulling on layer after layer of clothing.

"Brahms came up today—his thwarted romance with Clara."

"Leave it to you and Kevin to talk about the cat." Rob smiled as if he was clever.

"You know perfectly well we didn't talk about the cat. We wondered whether longing had made Brahms a better composer."

"I've always favoured artists who respected their appetites. Tchaikovsky. Norman Mailer. Picasso. Mapplethorpe. Patrick Lane when he was drinking. It gives depth to their work." Rob sipped his glass of red wine, looking at me almost provocatively over the top of his glass. "They know more about the human condition."

"So we're going to jettison Jane Austen, Ravel—who, as far as we know had no intimate life at all—Beethoven. I can't think of anyone who knows more about passion."

"Classical. Neo-classical. Good words for 'cold-blooded.' Nicely covers Austen and Ravel. All that intellectual focus on form. Sublimation, if you ask me."

"I'm not sure I'm asking you. Doesn't seem like your specialty. Art. Sublimation." I am suddenly so tired, and my pulse is throbbing. I pick up the dishes and head toward the kitchen.

Somewhere, there must be a novel that begins "That summer we all wore capri pants." It would be one of those edgy, fragmented postmodern novels attuned to the ephemera of style, hoping to transform style into substance. For all I know, style *is* substance in the twenty-first century. I stand in mine in front of the dishwasher, loading dirty dishes. I can see Rob out of the corner of my eye looking at me appraisingly.

“What happened to the long skirts you used to wear in the summer?”

“They wore out?”

“You look so much better in them. More poetic. Like a musician. Capri pants don’t quite suit your slender calves. Could you replace them? The skirts, I mean.” He’s smiling at me as he offers this friendly bit of fashion advice.

He will sleep in his study again tonight. There will be a plausible excuse: the need to get up early; my bad night last night; not wanting to disturb me; the fact that I keep the bedroom too cold.

Do you remember crossing your eyes as a kid? What made us do that? It wasn’t comfortable. We were warned that it would make us cross-eyed. The trick was to look intently at the end of your nose. Then the world—as long as you didn’t look directly at it—became doubled.

If I don’t look at myself carefully, there are two of me. There’s the person Rob and Kevin and Lindsay and my mother see, the matter-of-fact, professional individual who is marching along obediently, philosophical about the life she’s living, the roles she has to play. Then there’s the hidden person, vulnerable and sly, wounded and anarchic and sad. Such a simple word, *sad.* Not like *despairing* or *bitterly unhappy* or *despondent.* The simplicity of the word is powerful. With its own music. A brief, truncated little tune—just two or three stark notes.

Maybe it’s because I’m so tired. So tired that my soul seems to hurt. I don’t know what else to call that place in the middle of my chest that feels as if a black hole is blooming there. I’m probably exaggerating everything—Rob’s unresponsiveness, Mother’s unnatural cheer. After Kevin left, she spoke with such clarity about the Brahms.

“How could one person be so simple and so complex? As you started each movement, I drank in these lovely melodies—tunes, you used to call them. That word always felt undignified to me. But then they’d get so complicated. Rich. You couldn’t quite tell how they felt—the tunes, I mean. As if tunes feel. Then the simplicity would shine through like sunlight through trees.” She pauses to cock her head to one side and consider that. “Yes, tunes do feel. They almost feel *for* you sometimes. They made me think about my life. About the way I think about my life now." There's a long silence that is either sleep or dreaming. My role is to listen, so I remain still and attentive. She doesn't bother to connect one thought with another as she floats free of logic. "There are times that come back with such simplicity. The weight of you in my arms when you were a baby. Your father's hands, gnarled and spotted with age. Like mine are now." She raises her hands for her inspection in the intense summer light. "Except his were big. He'd envelope your plump little arms or cradle your head." She reaches out to caress the side of my face. "As if he were touching something precious and fragile. As he was. He had—always—a sense of what was valuable."

She closes her eyes with a sigh, overtaken by sleep. I sit quietly, relieved to feel I have no responsibility except to wait and to listen if she speaks. Ten minutes later, she startles me by picking up in almost the same place.

"Sometimes when I drift in and out of sleep, my past sends me postcards. Mostly they say, 'Wish you were here.'" She smiles at her own cleverness. "They're like snapshots, but unlike any we've got in the albums. Can we look at the albums tomorrow?"

"Do you want to look at them now?"

"No." She reaches over to take my hand. "Let's just talk. I can see everything I need to see. My postcards. Jack in his hockey equipment. In his first suit for the junior prom. With that girl you didn't like. I really think you envied her curly hair. You—about nine—sitting at the piano. In a dress I'd made for you—navy with white trim. Your back so straight, your hands just off the keys. Triumphant." She seemed to doze off again, but then said, without opening her eyes, "Some of them are simply places that have been emptied of people. They flash in my mind like slides—with that kind of light behind them. You remember when your father was thinking about retiring, we went to all these travelogues with slides. 'Tired in Tibet.' 'Banged up in Bangkok.' 'Ruined in Rome.' There was always healthy alliteration in the titles. They were silly. Adventures no sane person would go on willingly. But the slides had a wonderful glow. Like my postcards. The back yard with the crabapple tree in bloom. The lake in the Laurentians where your father and I went for our honeymoon. Our church at the blind end of

Griswold. The pictures are so vivid, yet somehow, my imagination has managed to edit out the parked cars."

She suddenly looked cross, frustrated. "Why can't I get a simple view of your father? That's not true. I can sometimes. Naked just out of his bath." She chuckled. "You probably don't want to think of your father just out of his bath, but you should. Vulnerable. Not thinking that he needs to be in charge. He took care of me when I was ill."

"I remember those times."

"Do you?" Her voice brightened, as if my memories made those times more real.

"He was extraordinarily attentive." I'm on uncomfortable ground, as I am each time she brings him up.

"Wasn't he just? Maybe that's why my illness now doesn't seem so frightening. Because it doesn't, you know. You've been spending a lot of time with me at night, so I assume you're worried about me. But really I'm all right. Let's just say it outright. Let's create that clarity I loved in Brahms today. I've had a fine life. I'm tired." She smiled beatifically at me. "Everyone dies, you know."

I can't expect her to pretend that she's playing some childish game, that she sees two of me because she's crossing her eyes. Where am I going to go?

Thursday, June 6, 2002

Kevin

Six

"Hullo!" I don't need to shout quite that loud because Francis has heard me grappling with my bike and come to the door.

"How did it go?" He holds the back door open while I bring in my bike.

"Wonderfully. Terribly."

"Let me take your fiddle and music while you take off your shoes. There's fettuccine primavera for dinner."

"Something smells wonderful."

"It's just the cilantro, darling! Boy, you're no gourmand."

"Cilantro in pasta primavera?" I've never eaten cilantro and pasta.

"I'm trying something different. Oriental veggies. Pea pods. Ginger. A hint of lime."

Francis pats my ass as I take my violin upstairs. When I come back down and into the kitchen, he has his Kiss the Cook apron on, so I do. He hands me a glass of wine.

"Okay. Begin with the terrible part."

"She looks awful, Francis. Dark circles under her eyes. Her hair needs a dye job—lots of silver in the roots. I had no idea she'd gotten so grey. But worst of all, something's sapped her confidence. And her joy in music."

"That appalling husband of hers?"

"Or living with a dying mother." Francis flourishes a gesture that says, "What's to choose?"

"So tell."

"We began with the Brahms G Major, which went well enough. I mean, she did all the things an *accompanist* is supposed to do—follow my changes in tempo and my dynamics. But the music seemed *strange* to her, you know? She could play the notes but didn't know—emotionally—what it was all about."

"Could be she's a bit distracted?" Francis asks as he checks the kitchen timer.

"But there have been other dicey times for her—the time Rob was three days late coming back from some conference—when the turmoil made her *more* in tune with the music."

"Maybe having a dying mother *and* a philandering husband is too much."

"We don't know he's a philanderer. He had a plausible excuse when he came back late from that conference." I defend him against my better judgment. Or am I defending her?

"Which he offered only once he had the whole family worried. Not smooth, that wasn't." He checks the timer again. "I mean, he *could* have been discreet. Why wasn't he?"

"We've never talked about it. I don't know if she thinks he's unfaithful."

"But you do."

"I do. And like you, I think the bastard wanted her to know."

"And do you think she knows?" Francis drains the al dente pasta in his copper colander.

"I think she knows *on some level.* I *hope* she knows. Or do I?" I consider this briefly and vote for painful honesty over powerless fiction.

"You admire her smarts—musical, psychological. Can't blame you for not wanting to see the clay feet."

"*We* know everyone's got clay feet. Another definition of 'gay.'"

"Anyway. You think she knows . . . on some level . . ."

"I think she's aware that it's possible he's been unfaithful. I mean, he hasn't tried to hide the evidence, has he? But she keeps telling herself it's just a possibility, just *one* interpretation." While I'm musing, Francis is sautéing the vegetables in the garlicky olive oil. The bowl of fruit and the cheese is already on the table. "But for some reason, it's impossible for her to admit that she knows." I think of the human capacity for self-deception, of all the straight guys I make uncomfortable. "When was the last time you lied to yourself and knew you were?"

"Oh, about three days ago when I didn't get on the scale because I knew I was losing weight."

"Yeah. And my sight reading's getting better."

We sat down and Francis began pulling strands of vegetable-strewn pasta onto my plate.

"Here you go, puppy."

"She's losing her nerve, Francis. Even before we began the Bach, she started making excuses. She can't sound like the harpsichord. She hasn't got it up to speed yet. Maybe we can do the slow movements as encores. I did my 'Let's just see how it goes' spiel, and go it did."

"So her playing was just fine."

"Not quite fine, but close enough for a first run-through. There's no problem with her playing. It's all in her head. That's what worries me."

"Mmm. I like the taste of that smile." Francis and I are watching *Queer as Folk*, and making out during the ads. "So what are you thinking about to get that kind of a smile on your face?"

"I'm contemplating the prospect of a sexy, middle-aged, single cellist."

"Bad you!" He cuffs me playfully.

"For Lila, my dear. We're doing a single recital in the fall. Here in Montreal, so she won't have to leave her mother. I'm going to suggest we do an all-Brahms concert and include a Brahms trio."

"And your point?"

"Stuart McTaggart. He's a fine cellist. And—completely coincidentally—he likes women. Not in a leering way. That wouldn't work at all—if he were some sort of Lothario. He's . . . nice. Warm."

"So you're setting her up?"

"She can choose to take the bait or not. But she can feel attractive in the meantime. I somehow don't think she feels very alluring right now."

"Feeling sexy is your cure for everything," Francis says to me as he reaches suggestively for my thigh.

"Well, at least it's alive."

I think Francis is projecting a bit when he says I idealize her.

Because Rob thinks all art—except music—is political, he doesn't go to things like gallery openings or readings. Music's abstraction seems safe. But he's paranoid about anything remotely political, and expert at seeing it where it isn't. Since Lila doesn't share his prejudice, she used to go with Francis and me to the odd opening or reading. Used to—before her mother moved in to die.

About a year ago last February, Francis's gallery was having an opening of some stuff from Peru—masks, rugs, pots, some primitive paintings that dripped heat and light and sex and colour. And self-pity. As well they might. Not great art. Perfect for February. I've got to say that for Francis and his boss: they've got the marketing thing down. Francis had to go early to pour wine, arrange canapés symmetrically on platters, and make nice with the dealers who'd come from Peru and the more reliable clients of his gallery.

I picked Lila up later, when we knew the crowd would have thinned out and we could actually see the work. She was waiting for me in her black cashmere coat and a pair of spikey black sandals. I glanced at her shoes meaningfully.

"Rob shovelled the walk," she said, gesturing with her head toward my car. "And you'll be a darling and drive me right to the door of the gallery before you go in quest of a parking place. It's two feet from the street to the gallery, and surely Francis will have shovelled. I can't look at art in *boots*."

I didn't have the heart to tell Francis's boss that playing Piazzolla tangos was culturally clueless. To most Canadians, I suppose, South America is relatively homogeneous, and Argentina isn't really that different from Peru. Anyway, it created a nice ambience. Lila and I had captured glasses of wine and were studiously avoiding the poisonous microwaved nibblies as we moved slowly around the white room to take in the heat of the colours. It was February, as I've said. One needs to remember February. Forget April and T.S. Eliot: February, as Garfield says, is the armpit of the year. Lila and I were enjoying a certain bitchiness that was positively warming.

"Okay. I love that bowl of fruit. But it's so *derivative*. Cezanne. It would be fine in someone's kitchen. But if I see one more mournful peasant . . ."

"And there it is," I say, waving my glass of wine at a peasant almost but not quite hiding his face under his sombrero. “You’ll do what? Throw your glass of wine?”

“No. It’s sold too. I wouldn’t want to ruin somebody else’s kitsch. Elsa Maria Ramos” she read, moving on. “I could get into those if she’d leave out the insistent doves.” The backdrop of the paintings was an interestingly inflected surface of interlocking cubes with doves growing out of every one of them. “Message-y. That’s what Rob would say, and I’d have to agree. Which dictator would these be about?”

“Fujimori. He’s out now. Languishing in Japan.” I turned from the walls to the white plinths in the middle of the floor. “I like the pots better. Francis said it was easier to get good pots than good paintings.”

“Do you suppose we simply don’t recognize the clichés?”

“I don’t think so. That plate—” I was looking at an earthy plate with complex black geometric decorations. “It doesn’t pretend to be anything but an attractive plate. Paintings have to be art. They have to be ideas. But they should converse *quietly*. They’re not supposed to tug on your sleeve like an insistent beggar.”

The gallery had been emptying for quite some time. When Francis had finally finished his duties, he came toward us, wineglass raised in greeting in one hand, his other on his hip in a parody of an Argentinean tango. I’m not sure Francis really knows *how* to tango. Lila, much to my surprise, did, and responded to his gesture. They sashayed like a couple of giddy kids around the emptying gallery floors for about ten minutes, the skirt of her little black suit flaring out and then twisting around her knees. I think I caught a glimpse of red lace from time to time.

“Where on earth did you learn to do that?” I really couldn’t conceive of Lila and Rob doing ballroom dancing on the sly.

“University gym! I had to take gym as an undergraduate, but I’m hopeless at sports. So I did folk dancing and then ballroom dancing. Can you see a whole bevy of girls in salmon gym suits paired up? Waltzing?”

Francis occasionally travels with us. Ostensibly, it’s to look for artists his gallery might represent in Quebec. And he does indeed make contacts and look at a lot of art when we’re away. But I also think it’s for the pyjama parties.

We usually go back to our hotel after whatever reception has been arranged, have a few drinks, and talk over the performance in Lila's room, in our PJs. You try wearing a slinky evening gown (I don't even want to think about what she's wearing underneath to get that profile) or a set of tails with the tight cummerbund and high tie and not wanting to get into your jammies as soon as you can. When Francis travels with us, he joins in. We have respectable silk paisley robes to travel the halls in, but once we're in Lila's room, it's serious jammy time. Emphasis on the serious part. Francis knows how important it is for us to talk about the performance, so he keeps himself in check. But Lila packs food and drink for us, so we talk while we dig into the nuts and the Scotch. Single malt. It's the only thing she'll travel with, so Francis and I have both learned to drink it. She likes a good martini, but ever tried to make one in a hotel room? Too much paraphernalia. She packs nuts because airlines turn crackers into crumbs. Francis hogs the pillows and leans up against the headboard of the bed; I lean against him. Lila sits more demurely—as demure as one can be in silk pyjamas—in the hotel-room chair, which she pulls over to the bed so we can pass the tin of nuts and the bottle of Scotch and the bucket of ice back and forth. I have been known to pad down the hall to get myself a Coke to dilute the Scotch. Lila frowns on this but says nothing. Francis has learned to drink his neat.

We're matter of fact during these sessions. If we're kicking ourselves for something we screwed up, we do that after the lights are out and we've gone to bed. This is not about us. It's about making the music better, about getting the whole of it to the audience. These sessions have gone awry only once.

We were playing the Prokofiev first violin sonata—always a tricky piece for us because it's dark and unearthly, even for Prokofiev. David Oistrakh played the first and third movements at Prokofiev's very hush-hush funeral—a quiet event since he died the same day as his nemesis, Stalin, and the Party didn't want any attention diverted from the Great Man's funeral. There's a section in the first movement, repeated in the fourth, where I play swift muted scales above Lila's soft but sweetly powerful chords, that Prokofiev told his friend Oistrakh should sound like "ghosts in a graveyard." And indeed, there is something uncanny and haunted about the whole, as if a mournful panther were cavorting through its pages, its flanks and desperate highjinks lit by the moon from time to time.

It's a risk to end a concert with this work because it doesn't have much in the way of pyrotechnics. It certainly doesn't give people something to whistle as they leave the concert hall—one of the principles of programming. Give 'em fireworks or a tune to end the concert is my motto. But the Prokofiev ends quietly—another reason it makes audiences uneasy. There's no sense of affirmation. Think about it: when you have six nice, loud, booming, major chords to end a concert, you leave the hall jubilant, as if you actually believe that even while there's AIDS in Africa and terrorists willing to kill themselves provided they can take a few innocents with them, there is also joy and order in the universe. This time, we'd ended the concert with it. Lila's performance was exceptional, but I'd noticed that her voice was a bit tight when she did the program notes. That night, when we arrived at her door, she tried to shoo us away.

"I need a bath or something. I'm cold. That hall was freezing. My muscles are tight. Can you come back in half an hour? Forty-five minutes?"

I'd shrugged my shoulders, willing to defer to her, though I hadn't noticed the cold. It wasn't like I was going to fall asleep any time soon. Not without the Scotch, which was in her room. But Francis picked up on something.

"Lila, let us in. Or we're going to make a fuss out in the hallway. Now you don't want two gay men in silk robes and flannel Garfield pyjamas gambolling outside your hotel room."

She unlocked the door but didn't open it. By the time we'd figured this out and let ourselves in, she was standing with her back to us, pretending to look nonchalantly out the window at the Halifax harbour. Francis handed me the ice bucket.

"Would you be so kind? Take your time. But don't get caught by the pyjama police." In a crisis, Francis gets silly. It has its merits.

When I returned, the lights were low and Lila was sitting in a dusky corner with a large neat Scotch in her hand. She snuffled from time to time but seemed self-contained. We pretended to go through the after-concert ritual, but she was distracted and unfocused.

"What was that all about?" I asked Francis in bed that night.

"Lindsay called tonight, apparently terrified. At least the first time, when she called from the airport. She'd driven to Dorval to pick up Rob. He was supposed to come back from a conference in Vancouver. At UBC. You know, one of his aggressively political/historical things. The first time Lindsay called Lila, she had no idea where he was. She'd called his hotel from the airport and was told that he'd checked out. Only when she got home was there a message saying that a colleague at UBC had asked him to give a lecture on Paris to her class Monday morning . . . So she called Lila again."

"*Her* class?"

"Yup. But it's ski week both at McGill and U of T, which was why Lindsay was home looking after the cat. I told Lila she could check the UBC website and see whether their spring break falls at a different time. She refused."

"Why in Liberace's name wouldn't she check it out?"

"She said something about going down the road of mistrust. Asking questions would change everything."

"Why wouldn't the bastard do a better job of covering his tracks? This was all unnecessary." I thrashed my pillow for emphasis.

"Not if he wanted to scare her. Fear is pretty powerful. She'll be a good girl for several months now. In bed and out."

"That's pretty cynical, Francis."

"Call it experience."

"You got all this out of her in five minutes?"

"Ten. You got lost on your way to the Coke machine."

"How?"

"I turned down the lights, poured her a Scotch, sat her in the chair, got a cold cloth for her so she felt spoiled. Said it reminded her of her father."

"Another bastard. From what I recall. Snippets of stories. Nothing concrete."

"What bastard worth his salt isn't also a sweetie? When it suits him."

Now you know why I love Francis.

Friday, June 7, 2002

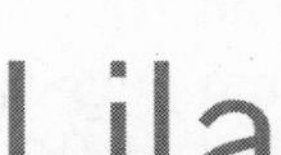

Lila

Seven

How grateful I was this morning when Mrs. Henry reminded me she had to leave for a dental appointment after she bathed Mother. Since it was her day for a shampoo, I'd be left to do her hair. Perhaps one of Mother's motives for avoiding chemotherapy is her silvery white curls. Depending on how she sleeps, it's a wild corona or a sedate cap. When I was a teenager and bouffant styles were in, she had it cut in youthful layers and would patiently, lightheartedly, allow me to play with it for hours, setting it in curlers, combing it out, spraying and recombing it until she looked, somehow, like an adult teenager. Or a stylish adult.

Under the physical pleasure of combing out her hair and drying it, my mind wandered and argued in panic and fury. How it shocks me: though my whole life aches, there is still physical pleasure, the slow contentment of gentleness, the comforting, familiar roughness of my mother's hair. Then, in every silence, there were suspicions and memories. Rob's tone of voice the last time we made love, the unfamiliar raw sound of his satisfaction. His silence as we cleaned up the kitchen after Lindsay, Margaret, and the kids came for dinner. Absence. How do you measure absence, the amount of feeling in the response to a mundane query? "How was your day?" There's no affect-meter for "Fine." The smallest gestures or tones become filled with threatening significance: a shrug or a wave that belongs to someone else, someone he's been observing carefully and often. A turn of phrase—greeting Lindsay with "Dude!" The humming of an unfamiliar tune. Yet here is my mother's hair; she is telling me of Brahms's cuddling last night while a nihilistic iceberg blocks my view of—everything. I feel nothing for anyone; they are all making claims I cannot bear.

My hands worked slowly and calmly while I thought illogically of revenge. Something that would make him choose. Elise and I on top of a building, one of us about to fall. She is young, but I am armed with Bruce Lee's teaching. I can send her over the edge with a well-placed kick, maybe even fool her into jumping with the mere threat. The art of fighting without fighting. My black hair and Faye Wray dress waft romantically in the twenty-storey Hollywood breeze; her cheeks, T-shirt, and jeans are smudged from our struggle, from her lack of balance. The dirt on her T-shirt shows that her boobs are too big for the rest of her body; she looks half urchin, half whore.

Cold-blooded fears and fantasies aside, I made light conversation about the weather, last night's thunderstorm, Mrs. Henry's health, her manicures, Kevin and Brahms, Lindsay's work on her LSATs, and the goofy things she was learning. Mother and I even speculated playfully how doing logic problems would help Lindsay as a lawyer.

"They don't care what kind of lawyer she'll be," I explained. "They're trying to see how well she'll learn the intricacies of law."

"Too many intricacies. Surely, good and right are simpler than they make them out to be?"

"You've watched too much *Law and Order.*"

"Probably. Your father had a good sense of right and wrong."

"My father knew what he wanted. What he *wanted* was right." I suspect there's not enough time to erase the bruising from her body, untie the knots in her psyche. So I need to start soon. But how presumptuous of me to think I can, that anyone can. Or needs to, for that matter.

Mother took one of her worst beatings when she fought for my piano lessons. When I'd gotten to about Grade Four in the Royal Conservatory Exams, Father decided I didn't need lessons any more. His excuse was that my lessons were just the cultivation of a social skill. He'd envisioned me being able to play at parties, entertaining boyfriends with the latest pop songs. I could play well enough to do that now. Probably the real reason was that his insurance sales were flatlining, and the fees for Jack's hockey were going up. "It's my salary. I'll say how it's spent," he told her.

To prove that it wasn't *just* his salary, she didn't prepare dinner the next night. "If it's only your salary, then you're saying I don't do any work for the family," Mother replied when he asked why dinner wasn't ready. "So I thought if it was just your salary, there's no point in my doing any work." He flung his arm out and hit her in the jaw. She staggered back and tripped over a kitchen chair. I was watching from the doorway and raced forward.

"Your mother doesn't need your help. You've done enough," he growled at me. "Get up," he told her. "Get your apron on and make some dinner."

She staggered up. "But there's no food to cook. I didn't do any shopping today. Since it's not *our* salary, I can't spend it. Or spend the time to shop, since I don't do any work." I grabbed at the air as his arm rammed her again.

"I don't need . . ." By this time, I'd gotten past my father's guard and was helping Mother off the floor. She looked hard at me and shook her head as if to say, 'Don't. Don't cave in.'

"You *do* need lessons! I'll take it out of the grocery money. Tonight, you and Jack and I are going out for hamburgers and shakes. I don't know what your father is doing."

"Get out of here," he said to me.

"No." He moved forward. "Don't hit me or I'll tell."

"Stop." Jack was in the doorway, his eyes riveted on Father. You could have threaded beads—large, heavy beads—on that gaze, so intense and focused was it. "If you move a muscle, I'll never play hockey again."

My memory can't sort through the confusion that followed. While Jack and Father argued, I put cold cloths on Mother's cheek. So I don't know what Jack said to persuade Father to give up the fight. What I do remember is surreal: all of us piling into the car to go to a drive-in for hamburgers and root beer floats. We ate in the car, pretending it was more fun that way.

Since we never went out for meals, this part of the memory comes back to me often—whenever I smell fried onion rings; Jack's had filled the back seat with their delicious, heavy aroma. But I'd managed, somehow, to disconnect it from its prelude until just now. It's as if my mood is in the right key to hear that motif in my memories.

There is so much I don't know, yet knowledge seems inadequate to love, anger, desire. I separate my mother's hair into sections and begin wrapping them round the curling iron. I can order the hairs on her head, but not the affairs of her heart. Knowledge solves puzzles, crimes, mathematical equations. But try to connect love to facts, one act and another, one utterance and another, one need and another, and you do not get a straight line.

"I think what steamed me most was how he could make you feel *wrong*. It wasn't something you did. It was something you *were*. He was no more right than you were." This is not the time; there is no better time. "And the beatings . . ."

"But he never beat you. You shouldn't be so angry. I had no idea you were so angry."

"You had no idea? How could I not be angry? He hurt you. He shamed you. He made me . . . familiar with cruelty. He taught me—you both taught me—to see it as part of love."

"Lila! What's happened?"

"Nothing."

She looked at me intently to see if I was being honest. I suspect she couldn't decide. "You're taking this all too personally. When he lashed out at me, it wasn't personal. It wasn't me. He was angry with life, but I was an easier target."

"You can't believe that. That's not how abuse works."

"Do you really think it's that simple? That psychologists can say, 'This is how abuse works. This is how anger works its way into the family. Into *every* family'? I've read those articles too, and they don't describe my marriage."

"It may not have been simple, but it was wrong."

"Yes, it was wrong. Perhaps losing control—being unable to hear the voice that speaks for the best part of oneself—is always wrong. But he loved me."

"How do you like your hair?" I handed her the mirror.

"Not to change the subject."

"Let's do change it."

"It's beautiful. You've done a beautiful job. Much nicer than Mrs.

Henry." My mother's smile, it now seems to me, has always had a plaintive note. Like the small yellow butterfly that bloomed one winter in the house, its beauty magical because unexpected, inexplicable, out of place. It was doomed from the start by Brahms's hunting instincts. I couldn't save it from Brahms by putting it outside: it would freeze instantly.

"She hasn't the practice."

Then she dozed in her comfortable chair while I changed her sheets, changed the water in the vase of stocks I'd bought to scent her room and mask the smell of illness, ran the dust mop, and sorted through the accumulated books and magazines. While I did all this, trying to make her room and her life more comfortable, anger roiled and bubbled. What kind of fictions had she created that permitted her to ignore my father's brutality? Yet there she was, beautiful, transparent, dying, denying.

At its beginning, Rob's and my marriage was almost idyllic. He wanted me to practise at home. It was a romantic notion, I could see: his wife would make music in his house while he was away talking about history and power. During our engagement, I'd noticed him talking with my colleagues, particularly those a little more established. After we were married, he promised to support me, in every way, until I had the career I wanted. The generosity and adulation implied when he said, "Your performance moved me" lingered about our relationship. So I freelanced for a couple of years until more regular accompanying jobs came my way—work with Wayne Riddell and the Tudor Singers, regular jobs accompanying the singers and instrumental soloists who came for the Ladies' Morning Musical Club recitals at Pollock Hall.

In that frank conversation, he also made it clear that he thought I could "have it all," in the phrase of the day. There was no reason for me not to. He was well established in his career, having been promoted for his scholarship quite soon after he arrived. He could support me. He could also support a family. Why didn't I take my time getting established and start our family?

Calm. It seemed such a period of extraordinary calm. Honeymoon, they call it. Blindness. Or fiction. Or, as we say about children, just a phase. It was generosity on his part, that gift of a time in which to grow. Or was it a shell game? A sting? Setting me up for the fall? Now fury and panic ignite over a look, a touch. Over suspicions. But surely these feelings are to raw to be false?

When Lindsay was two, Rob had his first sabbatical. Since he was studying the effect of the French Revolution on the built environment of Paris, he needed to spend three or four months doing research there. But he thought it was impractical to take Lindsay and me with him. How could he find us accommodations with a piano and room for a baby? He came back changed. During the next two months, when Lindsay was teething and he had a deadline for a book manuscript, her nightly crying enraged him. He'd stalk the house, storming. There he was in that refined living room he'd created for himself with its antique maps and modern glass, prowling across Persian rugs and around the Mies chairs like an enraged mountain lion.

"Why can't you do something simple like get a baby to stop crying?" he'd thunder. Why didn't he just leave and work in his office? I'd offer rationally. After a week of this—tense, exhausted, pulled—for here was a crying child who needed one kind of compassion and a frantic husband needing another—all I could do was laugh. Here was the modern intellectual he-man, defeated by a baby being a baby. It seemed, it still seems, the human thing to do, to laugh. There was perspective in that laugh; it came from a place outside all the tension and frustration caused by a baby teething. But I was too close to laugh. I'd forgotten my own safety. As he surged by, he flung his arm out and struck the side of my head. I remember—it's one of those stupid memories that sticks—thinking that this was like musicians arguing about a tempo.

The women's magazine articles both my mother and I had read tell you that you feel shamed and betrayed. I shouldn't have laughed, he shouldn't have lost control. What the experts don't know is that layers of your life, your world, your world view, are falling away. The atoms of your self have gone wandering, the mathematical order of the world has been breached, and you are frightened, above all, about what you are going to see underneath.

That was the only time. Lindsay's teeth came in; Rob's book was published to much acclaim. He got his final promotion and began to make the Shaker furniture that now fills our house. Is he still the man who hit me? If there is a thread that ties a man's beginnings to his end, rather like one of those unending cantabile sections of a slow movement, a seemingly unending and unendable song, then because he hit me once, he could do it again. But he never loses his temper now. Sometimes he growls and grumbles; sometimes he is cold and aloof. What man isn't? Yet can someone be so changed, and only temporarily, by a child's crying and a deadline, or by the success of a book?

This afternoon, Kevin arrived to work on the Bach sonatas. Soon we'll need to decide whether we're going to be able to perform them or cut our losses and try something else. I asked him if we couldn't start with Mozart: it was all I could do to keep the pleading out of my voice.

"It'll help me get my fingers warmed up."

"But I heard you playing as I came up the walk. You sound just fine."

"Please." Of course he looked at me closely to see what I was really asking. "Just a bit of Mozart's rationality and order. Something familiar. The one we played last spring." At this point, I didn't care whether I was crying, though I wasn't, of course. This morning I might have cried, but it was impossible. Discipline is good for something, if only for keeping your dying mother from seeing that you're falling apart. Now I'm too numb to cry. The iceberg is back, blocking the view. There's no point to crying, I tell myself. Occasionally, I've tried to tell myself there may be no need to cry. But I don't believe it. Her appraising look, his single touch. It was like a wrong note in a performance that suddenly makes you question what key you're in. Something about Rob's voice, a lack of believable feeling in it, even when he says the simplest things. Flatness. The shrinks would call it "lack of affect." His preoccupied response to attempts at conversation. Those suddenly shocked looks that say, "What have we been talking about?" His sleeping in the study so I don't have to worry about my night sweats: pretended compassion. I don't believe him. I believe nothing.

Such nihilism seeks the prettiness and order of Mozart. Mozart doesn't stretch one's credulity. Not the way Bach's sonatas do, serene and melancholy and passionate and poignant as they manage to be all at the same time.

"Something's wrong." Kevin put down his violin and pushed me to one side of the piano bench to put an arm around my shoulders.

"No. Nothing."

"It's Rob."

"No. It's nothing. I'm not sleeping well. That's all. Mother. Menopause."

"Lila, I'm tired of your stories. We can't go on working together if you're going to do this. You know I love you. So you know I can see something's very wrong. If you don't tell me, who are you going to tell? So what's up with Rob?"

"Don't you dare."

"Don't I dare what?"

"Accuse him."

"I'm not accusing him of anything. I'm reading the truth that's been on your face a hundred times. That he's cold, self-absorbed. Exploitative." He almost spit that last word out.

"Why don't you set the tempo? For the K. 526?"

"Why don't you stop what you've been doing for over twenty years? Changing the subject. Turning a blind eye."

We sat for five minutes or so while I mulled that one over. Kevin whistled the middle movement of the Mozart under his breath.

"Because I can't do anything else. I don't know how."

The howls that came sounded too animal to belong to me. Kevin put his arms around me while I hid my head on his shoulder and wailed and sobbed. If I could howl it out into the silence between the stars, I could banish that part of me, rid myself of it forever. Then nothing would hurt.

"I've got to pull myself together. I can't do this." I tried to detach myself from him, but he held me firmly.

"Wait. You'll be through soon. Get it out of your system. This time. You'll need to do this again, no doubt."

We must have stayed together on the piano bench for ten minutes, until I tired my grief out.

"Now what's happened? Give me the short version. Detail will only hurt."

"I think he's having an affair."

"You *think*?"

"The evidence is so sketchy. He can't touch me. He can't look at me. Or he touches me like I'm someone else, not a wife of twenty-odd years." Kevin waited through another long silence. "God! Why now? Did he think I'd be so busy with my mother's death that I wouldn't notice? Doesn't he realize that when someone's dying you notice *everything*?" I took a breath; Kevin continued to look confused, so I tried to be clearer. "I saw him approach one of his graduate students at the organ concert the other night. Everything seemed to fall into place—the subtle distance that seems almost like distraction, the absent-mindedness, his sleeping in the study because I've got night sweats. So I can be more comfortable, he says." I can see that Kevin is very carefully controlling the expression on his face. We've known each other for too long. There's rage at the edges of his eyes. "Okay. There's also the fact that he talks of her going to U of T with such pride and loss. She clearly doesn't want to work with him any more, and he's so sad. I was sympathetic. How stupid is that?"

"When it comes to emotions, most of us are a bit stupid. I've never been able to figure out whether desire was subversive or it just sabotaged my life. Any plans?"

"I'm going to talk to him tomorrow night. I'll just tell him how I feel and see what he says. I can't make accusations. I've got nothing concrete."

"Tomorrow?"

"I can't tonight. Cripes. I don't want another day like this. But I'm too exhausted. Too angry. Too vulnerable. I need another twenty-four hours to find some armour. A bullet-proof vest. Some way of protecting myself."

"Mozart?"

"Mozart sounds like a good bullet-proof vest."

"Do you remember when you fell in love with music?" my mother asked this morning. I shook my head at this query, unable to imagine not being in love with music. "There was a series of concerts at the Coronet—before it was refurbished. I can't imagine what it must have been like. I also can't remember the occasion. About four concerts in two or three weeks. Must have been an anniversary of some sort, to make the Canada Council decide to send music out to the hinterlands. Your father had just given me one of the bad beatings, so I couldn't go. But he didn't want to miss them, so he took you. You were about six. Instead of wearing a suit, as he usually did, he went to each of them in a plaid flannel shirt because it was soft enough for you to fall asleep against if you needed to. You didn't. You came back each time electrified. It was almost impossible to get you to sleep. You came back in your dress and stiff petticoat, short white socks and Mary Jane shoes, and pirouetted through the living room. You sat on the floor at the coffee table and mimicked a pianist, pounding dramatically on the table and singing at the top of your voice. Not a week later, he bought you a piano and you began lessons. You had walked into another world. Like the children in Narnia. I believed, stupidly I guess, that music protected you."

As my mother told me this story, I refused to believe her until she came to the plaid shirt. I suddenly saw him again, out of context among the white shirts and grey suits and navy ties, the women in fitted fifties dresses, and I could feel the texture of the flannel against my cheek, where I pressed it up against my father's smell and the sound of his breathing to take in the music better. To make it part of my life, not so otherworldly I could never reach it again. I don't know what to do with this story, except maybe to put it on the shelf next to the stories of nursing my mother. Maybe life at work was better when he was young and could still connect with people who were the age to get their first insurance. What a fiction knowledge is when our memories are so flawed, so determined to construct a straightforward view of the world, of the people around us. Or when all they do is map clouds that shift and make now a rabbit, now an alligator.

Nothing. I believe in nothing. Except Mozart's prettiness.

Saturday, June 8, 2002

Rob

Eight

Goddamn traffic lights. I sit. Then I drive. Then I sit again. I sit and think I'm in deep shit. I wouldn't have to think about the shit so much if I could just drive. Christ almighty. How has this happened? How have I managed to get myself in this fix: fights with two women in a single week? Two women wanting my skin? Then my department head threatening me with discipline over my "unreasonable objections" to our last hiring. Since when was refusing to co-operate with folly called "harassment"? But Lila doesn't want my skin. Lila wants justice. Naive but nice. That could sum up our marriage: naive but nice. Should I tell her that? No, what I've got to do now is take care of Elise. Bloody hell. I tried to explain that I have to look like a Boy Scout around the university, so we should cool it a bit. Then Wednesday night she sized Lila up. Wondering. "What's she got that I don't have?" And Elise has got it all—brilliance, beautiful young body, god how I loved her hollows: her instep, the dip at the base of her throat, the dimple in the small of her back, another beneath her shoulder blade. (It's summer—early summer, but summer—and she'll use any excuse to dress provocatively.) But she doesn't have me. So she wasn't pleased when I cancelled a couple of lunches. Elise, when she is not pleased, is not particularly attractive either.

So I'm not heartbroken about the hiatus, though there's a little crack, as if she took her well-manicured hand and a tiny saw and cut out a slice. Of my heart, then my balls. *Move it, you bastard. It's the pedal on the right that goes up and down. How hard can that be?* How hard it's been to say no, to refuse to take my own clothes off faced with her beautiful *déshabillé*—the skimpiest of dresses, the tightest, shortest shorts. Yet how delicious to be tempted, and to decide when I'd finally give in to temptation. I resisted. I always do. I always have. My thirty minutes of faithfulness to my lovely faithful wife. I'd kept my professorial cool for several months, but thought sometime in the next little while it would be all right for me to give in to all that temptation. I'd deserve it by then. Until Davis comes up with this stupid charge of harassment and Elise . . . bitch . . . stares right at my wife and gives the game away. My lovely wife. She really is my lovely wife, but her timing is a little off right now. I can't deal with her accusations and figure out what I'm going to do about this harassment charge at the same time. Okay, so what's the worst that can happen here? *Don't you know grandpa drivers are supposed to stick to the right lane! Jesus!* Okay. My union will see to it that I get nothing more than a slap on the wrist for being uncooperative. That doesn't sound bad. It'll be very hush-hush. But there's always some gossip. "Harassment" will make them think of sex. Hmm. Might not be too bad. White-haired, scholarly. And a tiger in bed. That's okay.

In the meantime, I can make it a good excuse to end things with Elise. She's off to Toronto in a matter of months, so it doesn't make sense to take any more chances, no matter how much fun it was. That way, I can give all my attention to Lila. Make it up to her. I know every man says he never wants to hurt his wife, but I didn't, I didn't. You mean it when you say to yourself that you don't want to hurt your wife. But you don't mean you won't be unfaithful. You mean you'll be careful. At first you say, "I may get my appetite elsewhere, but I only eat at home," as someone rather crassly confessed to me once. Then you mean this is only sex, a need for excitement and spice occasionally, and your relationship with your wife is something else altogether. Calm. The calm you need to work. (But of course you need excitement to work too. A little electricity, a little danger doesn't hurt the grey cells.) *Get it on, will ya? The speed limit here is ninety.*

Your wife is habit. Watching favourite movies together. Going to her concerts. Wine and brie on the back deck. Helping with her mother. There's something so touching about Lila and her care for her mother. God, the look on her face tonight. The tentative accusation. No, it wasn't even an accusation.

"I feel that something's not quite right between us. You seem so absent and preoccupied. It's gotten so bad that I've even imagined you're having an affair."

Grief. Her face wore this still mask of grief. No hysterics. It would have been easier to react to hysterics, to roll out the righteous indignation. Hysterics would have spiked the old adrenalin and made it easier to act the part of the unfairly accused. But no. Not my calm sweet wife. So when I made my excuses—the challenges of my latest project, which I expect my colleagues to attack—they seemed hollow even to me. If I didn't convince myself, how on earth could I convince her? Damn her! Why can't she be like other women and shriek and wail? Then I could have been angry. I am angry. Goddamn it. Why doesn't she trust me not to do anything that will really hurt her? Because if she never knew about this, it wouldn't harm her at all. If she hadn't been suspicious that night at the cathedral, none of this would have happened, and she wouldn't be in pain now. I don't even think she knew she was weeping. Lila's calm. Which I loved the first time I heard her perform. That tall slender young woman with the long, straight black hair, dressed simply in a silk wine-coloured shift; those reedy arms and bowed head—so still, yet able to draw from the piano such passion.

"Your performance moved me."

My infamous, and entirely sincere, come-on line. She still has the capacity to move me, to make me want her, to make me want to pour myself into that serenity, that tranquility.

Sometimes she seems quite elsewhere. She lives in a world of two harmonious voices that twine beautifully. Yet sometimes she's been quite randy lately, in a way that takes me by surprise. I thought a woman's passions were supposed to subside with menopause, so I'm a bit edgy. I don't know who I'll meet in bed. I get nervous. About whether or not I can get it up. Okay, so Lila has mastered the two voices, but I like to know what I can expect. I like my calm calm and my fevered fevered. My wife calm and my mistress fevered . . .

Mistress. That's what Elise would have been. I'm a middle-aged man who was getting ready to take a mistress. Worse, a middle-aged professor doing a student. Christ, what a cliché. And I've hurt Lila. That frozen face, weeping undemonstrably, unaware of the tears, not even accusing me. Her face utterly still. In grief. What's she grieving? She's intelligent enough to know that sex can be just sex. Isn't she? Or is that one of those guy things that women never get? Or is it one of those guy excuses that women never buy? I can't remember which.

Grief, then. Like patience sitting on a monument, smiling at grief.

Jesus, I can't sit in this park while I contemplate my marriage. I need some music. Aargh. Who the fuck put Leonard Cohen on? Right. Lila borrowed my car a couple of days ago. What time is it? Only nine. I need to talk to somebody. I need advice. From someone who knows Lila well. Kevin? We're not close—far from it. But he knows her. He cares about her enough to put up with me. He makes me nervous because he's gay. Or I make him nervous because I'm straight. One or the other. Or both. He doesn't trust me. Never has. He's been willing to have the occasional beer with me because he loves Lila. I've been willing to have the occasional beer with him because he knows my wife better than I do. In some ways.

Kevin was no use at all.

"What are you doing here, you bastard? Go home to your wife who's sitting there terrified that you're never coming home," he said, blocking the doorway.

"So she's called you?"

"Of course she called me, you oaf. Who do you think she's going to call?"

Shit. I was hoping to tell my side of the story. "Can't I stay a minute?" I pleaded. "Just to get some advice?"

"Look," he said, "I'll be blunt. She's one of the most generous women in the world. She deserves . . ."

"But I haven't done anything."

"Bullshit. You might be able to convince her of that, but you aren't fooling me. Sorry, but I know a prick when I meet one. Having had more than enough experience. Lila's more . . . charitable."

"I want to reassure her somehow," I said, easing my way into the living room and sitting down. "Get her to calm down. If she'd just have some faith in our relationship, we could get back to where we were yesterday. When she didn't think . . ."

"There was no yesterday. There was no day before she found out. Why do you think she was suspicious in the first place? You don't shout at things you love. You don't growl at them either. Your marriage is so fucking compromised. You can't just paper over the cracks. The building's in ruins. The fire department's come and gone. There ain't much to save. A few family photos is about all."

"But how can I get you to believe me? Nothing happened. Why don't you believe that? Why doesn't she?"

"You don't want to be here. I don't have any advice for you. If I had my druthers, she'd kill you when you got in the door and put you down the garbage disposal in little bits."

God, I never realized I aroused such hostility. I began to think he was right about my not being there.

"Okay, okay," I said. "You've made yourself perfectly clear. You're not going to give her the help she needs . . ."

"Giving her the help she needs means convincing her to leave you. And no, I won't do that. I respect her too much. She'll make her decisions. I'll support them. That's what love is," he said, as if I didn't know.

She's fallen asleep with her head on my shoulder. Which is wet. Her cheek is slightly rumpled where it hits the hollow of my shoulder. Touching. Vulnerable. She makes me think of my sister, Claire. Lovely, gifted Claire. Whose death I've never told Lila about. As far as Lila's concerned, I have a younger brother (who's a dork) and that's all. Claire was tall and willowy, like Lila, but had this incredible halo of curly golden-red hair that she wore just below her shoulders. She was a nurse. She had that compassionate bossiness that makes a perfect nurse. Once I stepped on a garden hoe that I'd carelessly left blade upward. My parents were at work, and I was supposed to weed the vegetable garden.

Fifteen, I think I was. Terribly lazy about chores. A bit of a malingerer. My carelessness about the hoe was probably my own fault, a bit of adolescent rebellious laziness.

But when I came into the house wailing as only a fifteen-year-old male can wail, a huge slice in my foot, trailing blood down the back walkway and into the kitchen, Claire simply grabbed a dishtowel, wrapped it tightly, fetched a roll of paper towel, bundled me into her rusty Ford, and took me into emergency for stitches. Crisp and efficient, she was. But care hovered around the edges of that efficiency. She even made up some story for my parents so they wouldn't think this was my usual way of avoiding chores. It would have been a stretch for them to think so—stitches are hardly a good alternative to weeding—but she wanted to protect me. Which I failed to do for her.

When she was twenty-five and I was twenty-two, I was a student in Montreal, and she was working in Trois-Rivières. She called one evening, weeping. The way Lila did tonight. She was pregnant. The father buggered off upon hearing the news, shacking up with one of her best friends. Apparently, while he'd been impregnating Claire he'd also been boinking Susan. Claire wasn't calling about the pregnancy, but about the fact that Susan had called fifteen minutes before and was coming by that evening to pick up a few things that belonged to the jerk.

"I can't do this," she told me. I could barely hear her weeping, the way Lila wept tonight. At the edges of her words. As if the tears were accidental, incidental. "I thought I could have this baby. We'd get married right away, and after a few years people would forget."

It was the early sixties, that time when a person's sexual behaviour was the only measure of their moral worth.

"But I can't have this baby on my own. What would people think of a pregnant, unwed nurse? If I keep the baby, I'll lose my job. But I know what back-room abortions are like. I can't do that either. I can't do that to my body. Or my baby. I work nights. How am I going to find someone to take care of the baby while I work?"

"You could go home," I offered.

"I cannot possibly go home. Our parents would . . . I can't let them see me like this. I loved him unspeakably. I gave him everything, all of myself. And then to throw it all in my face by sending Susan to pick up some underwear and tacky jewellery. Stuff he could have replaced. Or he could have come himself. I wouldn't have killed him or seduced him. I can't stand a world where I've trusted such heartlessness. It's been a month since he left, and it feels like yesterday that I came home and found the note, his things torn out of the closets and drawers."

I could see where this language, this lack of options was going. *I can't stand a world where I've trusted such heartlessness.*

"Just wait. I'll be right there. Don't let Susan in until I get there. It's about an hour and a half—two hours, depending on the roads. You're beautiful. The world needs you. Just wait. I'll be there as soon as I can."

I should have known: it was summer and the roads were under construction. There were detours through small Quebec towns and patches of single lane highway. By the time I arrived, Susan had come and gone with the bastard's prized possessions, and Claire had taken a huge bottle of sleeping pills that she'd used to help her get to sleep after her night shift. I called an ambulance, but she died shortly after they reached the hospital. I stopped trusting time and space, men and women. Re-envisioning that trip, I imagine myself abandoning the fucking roads and detours and simply hitting a straight course for Trois-Rivières. Pulling out the stem of my watch and stopping time.

Lila asked once what happened in Paris. Shortly before I left France there was a commotion at my pension when I returned home after a day's research at the police archives. For some reason, I remember the stone facades of the buildings, the mansard roofs, the cobblestones, but not the face of the young woman, hugely pregnant, who had killed herself.

While I waited for the ambulance, I held Claire the way I'm holding Lila now. Knowing we're all bastards. Time and space make us unfaithful in the end.

Monday, June 10, 2002

Nine

The doctor's waiting room was chaos this afternoon. Clearly Dr. Patel was handling some kind of emergency, so a number of people had their appointments rescheduled. Looking harassed, he materialized in the nurses' glassed-in booth, gazed at the topography of need and illness before him, and decided who could be rescheduled and who should remain. We weren't sent home, perhaps because the nurses know how hard it is to get Mother down the stairs, into the car, and then into the doctor's office. We waited about an hour and a half, Mother dozing in her wheelchair. Our favourite nurse found a blanket to keep her warm and wedged a pillow against the wall to support her head. I pretended to read magazines, though the only words that floated before my eyes—in an involuntary ironic haze—were those from the *Family Circle* magazines my mother used to read: "Can this marriage be saved?" Why was it never "Do I want to save this marriage?"

Rob and I made love this morning. I was wary and cynical when he began to kiss me and caress my nipples; thinking this was a smoke screen that any competent male could manage. A little sex, and presto-chango, she believes he's been faithful. I expected the kind of rapid-fire sex he's gone in for lately. But he was slow and attentive. I don't regard it as proof of anything. It simply was itself. I'm not even sure I'll put it on the scales.

When I'd finished showering and drying my hair, I found Rob in the kitchen baking more croissants, peeling a sexy ripe mango, and adding slices of it to a plate of pineapple and kiwi. The coffee was already made. He'd made synesthesia for me: the tang of sunshine in the breakfast nook he'd built, the warm fragrant colours of the fruit, the brown and golden aroma of coffee and croissants. Was this my husband the lover of good food, the careful cook, the man with whom I've built a life of lovely rituals? Or was this the guilty husband who thought he could buy my consent or my blindness by reminding me of this life, one that will only be destroyed if I choose? Any coherent interpretation is dangerous. Maybe even inhuman, since none of us is coherent. His lovemaking, his cooking, make sense in one context and mean something entirely different in another. I am beleaguered by what I don't know, in a thicket of brambles so tangled no compass will get me out. I don't know how to mourn. My father's death taught me nothing about my mother's. I don't know how to negotiate the anger and humiliation and vengeance that roil and argue and chatter. I can't choose between the desire to lash out or the wish to creep away and hide.

Then he started this earnest conversation about the new repertoire that Kevin and I are working on. How was it going? Was I finding the new music satisfying? Did we have any thoughts about what we'd program together? He looked right into my eyes in a way I don't think he's done for quite some time, except for that odd night about a week ago. Perhaps he cares. Perhaps he was trying to compensate for infidelity he'd committed that very day.

I've tried to think of it from his point of view. What options does he have, besides playing the good husband if he wants to stay married? But why would he want that?

Saturday night, I thought of live electrical wires writhing on wet pavement, exploding transformers, the endless views of pyrotechnic precision bombing televised during Desert Storm while Rob responded to my concerns, remaining cool and seemingly unfazed.

"I don't know what to make of these accusations of yours."

"They're not accusations. They're just feelings. I'm trying to be a modern adult and take responsibility for my feelings."

"Well, I can't take all this in. I feel like a lion in a cage. I'm going out for a drive."

I was sure he was going to her; I could imagine the two of them rationally, intimately, talking, drinking a conspiratorial glass of wine in crystal goblets, considering the best way to deal with me. I called Kevin, of course, who said that straight men like to drive while they think. (Many gay men, I've noticed, don't drive.) I didn't know whether I wanted him to come home, or whether I'd hoped he'd never return so that I could get on with the business of writing him out of my life. I didn't want to make decisions. I want to get everything that reeks of him out of the house, but planting his pots, his clothes, his antique maps on the front lawn is a cliché. I forced myself to focus on creative vengeance. I'll sign him up for eHarmony and photoshop his head onto Arnold's body. Or better yet, I'll find a site that promises casual sex.

We talked this morning longer than we've talked in months. I was almost seduced by his interest in me. Then his motive was clear.

"What are you going to do, Lila?"

"About?"

"Don't be coy. It doesn't suit you. About your suspicions, my dear."

"I don't know."

"You said last night you didn't have any evidence. That's because there isn't any. Couldn't you simply trust me? We'll go on as we have been?"

"Going on as we have been is not going on at all. Because we haven't been 'going on.' We've been going exactly nowhere. I'm invisible to you. You've forgotten how to be tender or simply friendly. I feel like a piece of furniture in your life. Useful, maybe even attractive, but no more than that."

"I don't know what you're talking about. Nothing's suddenly changed. How I feel about you hasn't changed."

Elise was everywhere; I saw her dark, accusing look at me in Rob's face, in the shiny surface of the coffeepot; it was her voice speaking softly on the radio in the background. What was she doing right now? Was she even thinking about what she'd done to us, to me? Or, having done it, having appeased some hot wicked desire, was she nonchalantly putting on her thick black mascara, studying the laugh dimples in her cheeks, making sure they weren't turning to wrinkles? Is she slicking the dark blue eyeliner along her lid with self-satisfaction? She shouldn't. On a blonde, the smouldering eye is overdone.

"It isn't simply my suspicions. It's the way you've acted over the last six months. Your preoccupation, your anger, your emotional if not literal infidelity. And you know it. Or you wouldn't be doing so right this morning what you've been doing so very wrong for months."

He shook his head in this impatient gesture, as if I had said something predictably obtuse. "What have I done that's so wrong? A few mornings back, I left you breakfast so you could sleep in."

"It isn't what you've done. I don't think. I can't prove what you've done. It's what you haven't." This is not the moment to begin a discourse on figure-ground relationships.

"So we're going to go on about omissions." His voice was ugly. He was testing. "I haven't given you a Cadillac or a fur coat."

How do you count omissions? Because he was going to make this about what you could count, see, name. As an historian, he thinks evidence is god. But how do you interpret what's not there?

I'm closer, but this isn't quite right. There's another omission. Somewhere inside me. Like a space that holds an ache. And a desire.

"Mrs. Jameson?" The nurse scanned the room for any response. She's new.

"Right here, dear." Mother started to wheel her chair forward, getting her blanket tangled in the wheels, dropping the pillow behind her. I picked up the pillow, sorted out the wheels, but didn't say anything about the folly of trying to manage on her own.

Once Dr. Patel joined us, Mother began with the disclaimers. She could see he had some kind of emergency. He didn't really need to squeeze her in.

"What did you need to rush off to?" My mother was uncharacteristically direct and nosy.

"I had an old patient who was in some . . . umm . . . distress. I wanted to be with her."

"Will you charge off to be with me when I'm dying?"

If Dr. Patel was shocked at her bluntness, he didn't show it. I pretended to study the trees out the window.

"Of course," he said as he reached out to take her hand.

"Good," she said, looking him straight in the eye.

"Pain?" he queried.

"Not much. What you've given me is fine for now."

He looked at some tests taken a week ago and nodded. "Good. Let me know if you need anything more. There's no reason for pain." His voice is warm, but his face is strained. He knows he's failing us. Failure is inevitable. He's trying to do it with compassion. Will compassion make any difference?

"How soon?"

"A couple of months. Maybe three."

"Is there anything I should be doing?"

"Eat as well as you can, as much as you can stand. Avoid infection. Your immune system has self-destructed. Spend time with those you love."

"Dream," I would have liked to add.

If I were a man, it would be much easier to describe the effect my mother's dying is having on me. In fiction at least, men can get a hard-on over the most surprising things: the speed of trains, horses, biplanes; large animals crashing out of the bush; mountains, icy and phallic, particularly the thought of climbing them or falling from them. The unexpected hard-on is a useful device that has come to stand in for male desire. What I feel is a craving more difficult to describe.

I want to fashion for Lindsay a holograph of herself as she is, without angst, her voice not muted by rebellion or need, without fear of desertion because she knows she always has her remarkable self. When I see people take joy in their work—the librarian eager to share what he knows with you; the baker ecstatic about a surprising combination of flavours and the pleasure they give others; the potter in rapture over the shape of clay that begs to be held and used—I realize how idiosyncratic and generous joy is. I don't yet know what will give Lindsay joy, but I'd like to build into my holograph a mirror that will echo it back to her.

I want to stretch time and energy so that Kevin and I can perform all ten of Beethoven's violin sonatas in a single concert. It's not physically or musically possible. But I want to do something whole and complex—like exploring every corner of this poignant and profound music that occasionally turns giddy out of some high spirits one cannot quite imagine flowing from this depressed, lonely, misanthropic man. Perhaps it's the unimaginable that I want to celebrate. The deaf maker of music. The defiance of silence.

I want to find in myself that naked woman in the locker room. A casual generosity. A gentle fearlessness. I don't expect, or even want, the ease of literal nakedness. Rob's infidelity—I suddenly realize I know he's been unfaithful because I never want to take my clothes off again and imagine myself taking baths in pleated and buttoned white cotton camisoles and petticoats like a Victorian woman. I will be naked only in music, where each performance is a kind of emotional stripping. I think of musicians like Anton Kuerti whose performances balance between beauty and morality and philosophy.

I'd like my mother to see me in that nakedness before she dies, to see a legacy that gives her some peace and satisfaction.

These are as physical as any lust.

After the doctor's appointment, I took Mother back to Van Houtte's for a cup of Lady Grey tea and a scone. I was still struggling to be talkative.

The minute we had ordered our tea, she began enigmatically. "I'm hoping that in heaven we all have separate rooms. I'm not quite finished becoming myself and need a bit more privacy. To finish sculpting. You showed me those statues, once—what were they called?"

I was completely puzzled. My mother's death-bed whimsy continues to surprise me.

"You know. The blocks of stone with things like a hand and a head reaching out of them."

"Ah. Michelangelo's *Captive Figures*. It's been years since I showed you those."

"It was right after your father's death. I remembered them because they were statues of me. I was lucky that your father died when he did." She looks at me to see if I am shocked. I am only curious. But also guilt-ridden. "I need to talk to you about your father."

"I'm sorry for dumping on you the other day."

"You shouldn't be."

"Where did you keep your sense of self all those years. Your integrity?" Today, I was sure that she had a sense of honour; yesterday, I was not.

She waited until the waitress finished dispensing teapots and cups and scones, studying the young woman benignly. "I'm not sure I had a sense of self apart from my role in my family. I don't think women of my generation did. It wasn't something they expected from life." She stopped to butter her scone and pile on strawberry jam and Devonshire cream. "Integrity? That meant protecting my family as well as I could. I had some principles I wouldn't compromise when my children's well-being clashed with my husband's will: your music lessons and Jack's undergraduate degree. Your father wanted him to do business, but Jack wanted to be a teacher. Your father didn't think that teaching was a fit profession for a man. So I fought for Jack. But if integrity was protecting your family as well as you could, then sometimes it meant taking a beating."

She turned her head to look out the window, at the street where people's bustling seemed so far from death and self-judgment. She had run out of breath. I reached over to touch her cheek and turn it toward me.

"What happened?"

"Your father's death, of course. I couldn't prevent that. I couldn't really protect my family. Do you have any idea what that felt like?" She looked at me, suddenly angry, her eyes flaring blue. "To have the good you believed in vanish? I hated myself for a long time. And then hating myself became pointless. Like a child crying itself out. Sometimes, my memories would be of nothing but shame. Things I failed to do; things he did to me. And then suddenly a smell or a snippet of tune or even a bit of colour would remind me of a happy moment, and the shame would go away for a while. Each time it went away longer. But I have to admit that in heaven, I not only want my own room, but I don't want to meet your father for a while. I don't know how I would react if he said to me, 'Do this.' Whether I would say, 'No.' This is all very silly, I know. What I'm really hoping for, looking for, is an ecstatic, joyful absence of self when I die."

Mother has fallen asleep on the way home, so I've been driving around Mount Royal Park. I would much rather be ferrying my mother from place to place, on this earth, than going home. Where does honour lie? In being honest to the vision of my marriage that has materialized like a holograph over the last forty-eight hours and asking Rob to leave? I cannot do that. Who will get my mother down the stairs?

Or in waiting, learning, unfolding, risking, seeing what emerges? Being true to a partnership that's lasted a quarter-century? If I am watching him, how do I make music, reflect my daughter, take off my spiritual clothing? How do we do the simplest thing—hand each other a glass of wine, touch an arm—without measuring the truth or falsehood of every gesture?

Wednesday, June 19, 2002

Kevin

Ten

The pounding at the front door baffles me: there's no fire and salespeople usually aren't that aggressive. I carefully put down my violin, plunge downstairs from my studio where I've been working on the Brahms trio, and whip open the door ready to be surprised or annoyed. There's Lindsay looking like Dracula's wife on a bad hair day.

"Shouldn't you be at work?" I bow her into the house.

"It's my earned day off. Which is why I was doing grocery shopping."

I motion her into a chair, the most comfortable one in the room. She needs comfort.

"I was picking out grapes. You know how impossible they've made it to buy grapes? Those waffle weave bags? You can't buy just a few grapes any more."

I make sympathetic noises hoping to get this story moving. I feel like Jack Webb on a *really* slow day.

"That was when Mrs. Hammond pounced. 'How is your family doing?' She gives a sympathetic smirk. 'Pardon?' 'I've heard your father's been accused of sexual harassment—an unlikely story if you ask me,' she adds quickly. 'We're just fine. Family solidarity and all that.' Except that a family can't have solidarity if no one knows what's going on—which she's reading all over my face. Cow."

Fuck. I knew it. I can't decide whether I hate the bastard more than ever or wish it weren't true for Lila's sake. It's that impulse toward jubilation that tells me what I feel. "Who's brought the charge?"

"I have no idea. I also have no idea what to do. I'm sure Mom doesn't know."

"Could the cow have been making it up?" I'm trying not to get my hopes up too soon.

"Not Mrs. Hammond. She's not above needling you, but she wouldn't lie."

"Well, someone's got to find out what's going on. Your mother needs to know."

"Would you . . . ?" She looks near tears.

Ah. It becomes clear why she's on my doorstep and not her mother's.

"I can hardly ambush your father on the way home and ask what's up."

Lindsay smirks. Good.

"Or do you simply want me to tell your mother about our suspicions and let her take care of things?" She shakes her head emphatically. "Wait a minute. Who are you worried about here?"

"Mom. Of course."

"It's your dad who's been accused of harassment."

"My dad can take care of himself."

I am sorely tempted. I restrain myself, and promise myself a treat for my good behaviour.

"Let me think about this. I'll make coffee. Or tea? Francis baked last night so there are some great cranberry muffins."

"Tea?"

Tea made, muffins warmed in the microwave, we sit side by side at the breakfast counter looking out the window rather than at each other.

"Okay. So you want me to use my sources and find out whether Mrs. Hammond is right and see if I can find out who brought the charges?" Lindsay nods, her eyes still fixed on the back yard. "And then you want me to tell your mother?" She nods again. I turn to her. "Don't you think your father may have reasons for not telling her? Maybe the charges are so ridiculous that he knows they'll be dropped. In the meantime, he doesn't want to worry your mother."

Lindsay snorts. I swear she's got tea up her nose.

"You need a tissue?" She shakes her head. "What was that all about?"

"Even though I went to U of T, it's pretty hard—if you're my age—to ignore my dad's reputation. I mean, nobody's said he's fucking his graduate students, but a number of people have implied that he flirts. Or at least that's the word they use with me."

"Mmm. You sound pissed." This is one of Sam Spade's strategies: float a theory and see what it gets you.

"When I was young, Dad was okay. The last six or seven years, though, he's seemed distant. Earlier, he took me to soccer practices, got up for early morning swims, brought home books from the library when I had papers to do but didn't try to write them for me."

"Do you know what happened?"

She studies the back garden, which doesn't have that much to look at: a lot of grass, a few tubs of flowers. She stirs her tea. She peels the paper off another cranberry muffin. "I'm starving," she explains, sighs. "What happened? I got uppity? I grew breasts and pubic hair?" She chews thoughtfully and then shakes her head. "Mom gives him permission of some kind. Maybe just by being nice, doing her best."

She's figured out the fifth law of thermodynamics: "That's a hard one. Sometimes nice isn't all that ethical. It lets people off the hook."

Her face suddenly clears. "Yeah. Yeah, that's it. So you'll do it?"

"Where your mother's concerned, I'll do just about anything. I know a few people on the inside I can ask without raising alarms. I'll tell her as soon as I've figured it out."

"The sooner the better. While I was driving over here, I realized that Dad's been a little tightly wound."

"Does that worry you?"

She squidges up her face. A grimace, really. "Not exactly." She stares into the bottom of her mug. "Yeah, a little."

Being adjunct faculty has its advantages, though the pay's not great. My source tells me she's heard rumours; she'll check them out and call me back. Human Resources people must love gossip because she's back to me in less than half an hour. In this clandestine, whispery voice. I do love a good spy novel.

"It's harassment, all right. But no one can quite say who he's harassed or who's bringing charges. There's a gossip about a former student of his. Elise Grant. But apparently she's leaving for Toronto at the end of the summer to do a PHD. She's already been accepted. So no one can figure out why she'd bother to bring charges. She's got what she wants. She's leaving. It'll just be a pain in the ass."

"Could it be serious? Whatever the cause?"

"At this stage in his career? No. There'll be a letter in his file, but he's senior enough to ride it out if he's smart."

"What's smart?"

"Not fighting. Apologizing."

"*Mea culpa*? Fat chance."

So I call Lila to see what her afternoon is like. I need a little musical advice, I tell her. I bike right over to find her looking a little better than she has lately. She's dyed her hair again. Made an effort with her make-up. She's wearing a beautifully cut, slim little black dress with creamy orchids splashed all over it.

"You've put your foot down."

"How can you tell?" Is she feigning surprise?

"Because you look so much better. Your self-respect has returned," I tell her bluntly. When she looks puzzled, I lean toward her conspiratorially and say, "You've done your roots."

"I'm not sure dyeing my hair—I'm not sure it means anything at all. It doesn't mean I'm hopeful. It doesn't mean I'm trying to win him back. It's just time I dyed my hair."

This is exactly the right answer. She should dye her hair because it's time to dye her hair. Past time, actually.

"You don't have your violin. I thought you were having problems with . . ." She can't finish her sentence because I left things too vague to begin with.

"Actually, it's Rob who's having problems. I come bearing gifts. Or not." I've been fairly jolly up to this point because this whole thing has been a vindication of my powers of observation. But suddenly I realize I have no idea how she'll take this. "If the Trojans wondered whether the horse at the gates could possibly be a present, I don't know what you'll think of this. Aren't you going to offer me some coffee?"

"You're stalling."

"Lindsay came by today, rather put out by a conversation she had among the grapes in the supermarket. Some busybody . . ."

"Which busybody?"

"A Mrs. Hammond?"

Lila rolls her eyes. "She's the most unreliable person on this earth."

"This is true."

"How do you know?"

"I have my sources," I mutter darkly. I might as well keep to the espionage theme. "Mrs. Hammond suggested that Rob has been charged with sexual harassment by one of his students." I put up my hand to stop her. "I called a friend who works in Human Resources. He's being charged with harassment; at this point, there's no 'sexual' in front of it. She put her ear to the ground—my friend—but didn't pick up anything. Which is funny in itself. Though gossip associates him with a student."

Lila is disastrously still. "And her name?"

"Elise Grant."

"The one who stared at me brazenly last Wednesday. Bitch."

"Excuse me? Your husband's an adult. This isn't entrapment."

Lila brightens suddenly. Takes me completely by surprise. "Yes, it is. She's trapped him for me. I finally know something." Lila buries her face in her hands. I can't tell whether she's laughing or crying, but some pretty extraordinary sounds are being muffled by her hands.

"Your mother?" I tactfully remind her.

She stops immediately, as though she'd bitten off her feelings, torn them with her teeth.

"My mother. A week ago, my mother talked about protecting her family through my father's beatings. About the passivity, the silence, the hopeful *ethics* of doing that. I now see the temptation. If I don't say anything, we can all *pretend* this has gone away when the hearing or whatever is over. And pretty soon pretending will become our reality. I wouldn't have to find the energy to be angry. But there'll be this great big silence in the middle of our lives. How would I play Bach or Prokofiev with any honesty?"

"Why don't you worry about yourself instead of Lindsay or your mother or Prokofiev's ghost? Lindsay's at the age where parents find—through no blame of their own, of course—clay feet. So this is just part of normal for her. But you're trying to cope with your mother dying, and your husband is out poking students?" Lila gives me a withering look. Why is it my job today to annoy people into paying attention? To make up for all those times when I annoy them without meaning to. Penance. "Why not worry about yourself?"

"Because I don't deserve it."

"What you deserve is a slap upside the head."

"Exactly." Her voice is cold, ice-bound.

I put my arms around her as if she is about to fling herself off a tall building. Is this the abused child thinking? Too simple. I have this tricky relationship with monogamy, so I can't imagine how a woman feels when a partner has been unfaithful to her. Does her sexuality evaporate, and along with it her self-worth? Then it suddenly dawns on me: if it's her fault, she can fix it.

I'm holding her and rocking us back and forth and theorizing, then I suddenly realize how still she is. It's possible that if I let go, she would simply collapse. There's an image for this in a bad pulp movie somewhere, I'm certain: her soul has left her body and been replaced by . . . what?

"Are you there?" I ask.

"Sort of. Will be. Mother'll be awake soon. I'd better have my disguise back on by then. Because, as you so perceptively point out, she's busy dying. The timing on this is shitty. Well, I'll just have to make it of no consequence. As far as she's concerned."

"You can't fix this, Lila. This isn't like practising. You can't simply discipline your way to some perfection that Rob is going to find so compelling he'll stop being unfaithful. Because it's not your fault."

She wasn't crying: she seemed to have given up on emotion in some odd way. Her soul *had* left her body, and she didn't trust feeling. She trusted conduct. I shook my head slowly in puzzlement and disbelief. Can one really live that way?

"Don't you see? Mother's dying. I have absolutely no control over that. It's going to happen. At its own pace, in a time frame that has nothing to do with me. And I have to get her there. I have to attend to that. Carefully. Lovingly. How do I find the energy to do that if the rest of my life is falling apart and I believe there is nothing I can do? For that matter, how do we know there's nothing I can do? It's that 'how do I know' that keeps me going."

"The 'how do I know' that makes you dye your hair?"

"Nope. That was for me."

"You may be okay, then. You may *just* be okay."

Monday, June 12, 2002

Lila

Eleven

I've lived for years within bar lines, within metronome markings. When did I learn that music was paradoxical—that it depended on control and hyperbole, discipline and excess—and that real expressiveness was the struggle, the conversation, between these? About the third year of my music lessons, when I'd moved on from simple tunes for kiddies to simplified versions of Bach, Beethoven, Handel, I hated the discipline of the metronome: my fingers wouldn't obey the orders of this little wooden pyramid that had to be propped up to give me an even beat. When I worked on a new scale or arpeggio, I knew the metronome was lying—that my fingers moved evenly and the metronome was erratic. But with skill came the discovery of what it means to give yourself over to the beauty of order. The egotism and the self-abnegation: you need proud, iron-clad technique and the willingness to give that technique over to someone else's voice. Narcissism and the possibility of community: it takes a kind of self-absorption, the making of a world of order that wraps around you like a protective cloak to develop that technique. But its very purpose is the possibility of community, whether with your audience or with other musicians. The first thing musicians do—or that the conductor does for them—is to decide on the tempo. Music, like life, can only move in time. We can only work together when we agree on the tempo. Only once we've agreed on the flow of time can we create something.

My mother had bought the metronome—a little mahogany pyramid with its tiny swivelling hook at the top of the secret door, a door that allowed it to look more like a decorative piece of furniture rather than an instrument of torture—by economizing on the groceries.

I wasn't very old before I discovered that I could distract my mother from pain or fear—whether she'd been recently beaten or had done something that might earn her a beating—by staging a late-afternoon concert. It was the fifties, when little girls still wore short, full-skirted dresses to school. So I'd come home from school and practise—the backs of my thighs and knees prickling from the wool needlepoint bench cover my mother had made depicting lords and ladies dancing. While I was diligently working through my scales and exercises, I would plan a concert for Mother. I'd find her in the kitchen staring out the window. The day's housework was finished, but it was too early to begin dinner, so she gazed into a world I couldn't see. I would pull her into the living room, into a slipper chair on wheels I could move near the piano, pull out the sides of my dress in a Mary Jane curtsey, and begin. She liked it even better when I played with the metronome.

Twenty years later, I learned to live with the time signature of motherhood. First, breastfeeding and nap times; except that I was the insecure conductor, unsure of how quickly or how slowly to go, how much to dictate, how much to give in to Lindsay's rhythm. Dr. Spock said to set the schedule, so I did—disastrously. It made no sense to Lindsay's need for sleep or her hunger. So I gave in to the cadence of Lindsay's needs for the next four years. Rob made the sun porch into a music studio since we'd given her the front bedroom, so I could practise while she napped. But nothing could be counted on. She might sleep twenty minutes or two hours. I took only the easiest gigs until we shifted to the jubilant timetable of nursery school—two reliable hours every afternoon—enough time to learn repertoire but not enough to grow as a musician. Then I followed colours and moods: sullen music lessons, adrenalin-rushed swim meets, anxious school dances; then the rotation of the university year—times when Lindsay was away and the house seemed to float from its moorings, and times when she came home and weighted the house with her noise and frustration.

So Rob's defiance of constraints seemed fresh and daring. An antidote to my obsessive order. A balance, a fulcrum for the antitheses of my life. Part of his attraction. I've kept my life and my tempos and our child measured within bar lines while his scope was the universe, its history, and the quest for power. In the meantime, he's defied its rules and strained against its norms. So have I in some way conspired?

Whether he's been unfaithful or not, I've seen him from a different perspective, through the lens of my anger and my discontent, and it's not a vision of him I can take back. I've seen habitual coldness, scorn for the world, impatience with views and feelings he doesn't share. Maybe it's his midlife crisis, a dissociation from a world in which he feels he's made no difference; perhaps the fractures in our relationship are simply collateral damage, something he cannot help. But should you say "he can't help himself" about any adult?

On the other side of the scales are twenty-seven years of marriage; thirty years in the same bed, the weight of one another's bodies, a daughter we've shaped together, meals prepared together, bottles of wine shared, fires and candles lit. Every sense there is, everything that makes us a body in the world—the taste of food, the texture of a baby's skin, the images of movies and photographs and paintings, the scent of one another's sweat or of the huge lilies in the garden or the early morning smell of his perfect lawn, the sounds of lovemaking and sexual satisfaction and anger and music—we have shared.

Anger and love. Two of the most powerful forces on this earth. Sometimes I feel almost like an onlooker in that battle, as if it has nothing to do with me. My days now are often like those dreams where you flee from a horn-plated monster and can't move fast enough, except when I'm practising or taking care of Mother. Nothing I can do will change the outcome. There's no reason to run toward either anger or love. Neither will rescue me. At other times I feel suffocated by a fracas being acted out on my chest while I try to sleep quietly next to my husband.

I'll have to support him through this. I don't believe in his innocence, but I'll have to pretend that I do. I don't know whether a serene smiling wife will help get him off, but I don't care. The young woman will have to marshal her own metaphysical forces, as well as her evidence. This will be like one of those battles by single combat, where the will of the supporters and the will of the universe play themselves out.

In the meantime, I'll dream of revenge. A blowtorch. I'll singe her blonde eyebrows and melt the thick mascara off her lashes. Melt the bronzer she uses to disguise herself as a golden goddess. I'll fool her super into letting me into her apartment. I'll sew baby shrimp in the curtains of her living room. I'll spray skunk scent all over her skimpy garments or use puce spray paint to coat her entire closet and its contents.

After Kevin left, I sat quietly and composed myself. Kevin's many comments about my dress or my hair or my height imply his vision of me: calm, musical, unfailingly elegant. So I tried to get his presence to pull that woman out of me while I waited for Rob to come, waited to decide how I would tell him I knew. For once, I thought about power. I thought about style and power.

How some people, like my mother-in-law, gain it by interrupting whatever you're saying to make clear that her life is terrible. You might be telling her the story of a friend of yours who has been diagnosed with breast cancer, or of a parent trying to cope with a son with ADHD, but she simply covers your voice with her own. Her knees hurt, she misses her husband, the dog is sick and needs to be given pills three times a day, and the woman in the apartment next to her talks loudly on the phone all night. Others gain it by bullying. Young girls are wonderful at the verbal mockery that commands compliance. Some get it through threats—of anger, disapproval, violence if necessary. I've never understood the desire for power. It's a craving that has always seemed demeaning to me, as if one weren't complete in oneself. It's an admission of weakness, not of strength. Now I want it.

I want Rob to feel that, first and foremost, I am supporting him out of principle. I want him to sense a new independence, borne perhaps of having faced his infidelity. And that as anger and love battled, love could win—maybe. Except, of course, I have the anger fully under control. Men admire that.

When he arrived home, I was busy in the kitchen with Mother's early dinner, but he smelled the fragrant coq au vin. When he popped his head around the kitchen door, I told him dinner would be later tonight because the chicken needed to cook longer. I knew a late dinner meant a hasty retreat to his study and would buy me time. I considered cloth napkins and candles on the table but decided that was too much. I wanted dinner to be pleasant and comforting, not romantic. I powdered my nose and put on a quiet lipstick.

The first half of the dinner conversation he was solicitous, wanting to know how Mother was today, how my practising had gone. When he asked whether I'd given anything else a good polishing, I heard the first natural note in the conversation, the first time he was neither deliberate nor guarded. He was referring to the fact that in the afternoon while Mother sleeps, I haven't been doing what I normally do: read history or biographies or study parts. Instead, I've been doing anything to pass the time that doesn't seem entirely pointless or trivial. I've reorganized my music, polished the silver, cleaned the fireplace, pruned the lilacs, rounded up every piece of brass I can find—from parts of light fixtures to knobs on furniture—and had a Brasso party. I rather like the smell of Brasso.

I looked up from my plate and we smiled at each other. It was time.

"Kevin stopped by today on his way home from a lesson at the university. He's concerned you're having some difficulties. Something about a harassment charge?"

"Christ! These committees are supposed to be discreet."

Then suddenly it occurs to him that this is not simply a friendly, sympathetic conversation. It happens at the speed at which you fall flat on your face when you take out the garbage in the flip-flops that are slightly too big and catch on the fieldstone walk. Nothing faster.

He pauses, looks at me appraisingly, as if to read my reaction. I've made my face a pleasant mask—I hope. I want to make it hard for him to react to me. I'm on a fact-finding mission.

"So that's it, eh?"

"Sorry?"

"I'll tell you what it's about, but you won't believe me. The department had two hirings coming up this year." I nod my head; I remember the rants after the "sociable" dinners. "The candidates they chose for both positions were disasters. I tried to stop things first by claiming that they'd gotten the procedure wrong. When that didn't work I said some rather intemperate things to Davis. There were witnesses standing in the hallway. He took it to the dean and presto! A harassment charge. That was a couple of weeks ago, the day you learned Clarice's cancer had gone to stage IV. You can see why I didn't say anything."

"Before Lindsay was born, I had a terrible time, and you helped me through that. I want to help you through this."

It was as though a ghost had drifted into the room, magically lit a fire and the dead candles in the waning dusk. Rob smiled at me warmly, simply. I don't know this man. But I tried to smile warmly back.

"It's terrified me—the thought of your finding out about this. It's one of the reasons I've been so distant. You'd smell the fear if you got too close. I didn't know what to do when you thought my pulling away meant I was actually having an affair. You have no idea how trapped I've felt." He reached across the table and took my hand. Despite the warm summer evening, both our hands were ice cold. "You're cold." He began to chaff my hand, and then got up to bring me the silk shawl I keep in the hall closet, draped it over my shoulders, and bent down to kiss my neck, then turned my face toward him to kiss my mouth. His tongue slyly circled my lips. "Um. Coq au vin. And a rather nice wine." His tongue licked the corner of my mouth. He turned my chair toward him and kissed me again. "Let's leave the dishes for morning."

"I'm sorry, but I'm too tired. I'm wrung out. Mother's in more pain, and I had to talk to Mrs. Henry—Genevieve—. Really, we can't go on calling her Mrs. Henry. We had to talk about a higher dose of morphine. Then I had to call the doctor about it, because obviously he'll need to prescribe more. The two of us have no idea what 'more' should be. I have to take her into the doctor again tomorrow when he has a free moment, and you know what a production that can be." He was learning over me, his hands on the arm of my chair. The expression on his face changed obediently from friendly lust to solicitous concern. "And then, of course, I've been worried about you. I really didn't know whether to bring it up or not. So I argued with myself all day."

He cocked his head sympathetically. "You were right to bring it up. It's always better to talk about these things, don't you think?"

Then why didn't you tell me? I silently wonder. Evidence. He can't keep his emotional stories straight.

"Perhaps you'll help me get Mother downstairs tomorrow before you leave for work, and I'll simply make her comfortable down here. Then it would be easier to take her to the doctor when he has a free moment."

"Of course, dear. Do you want me to stay and help you? There's no reason for me to go into the office tomorrow. I can work in the study until it's time for your appointment. These days, going in to the office isn't that pleasant. Shall I just stay home?"

"No. Thank you. We'll be fine, I'm sure, if you get her down in the morning. She can forego her bath for once. And Genevieve can help me get her into the car."

"If you can't get in until afternoon, call me, and I'll come help." He kissed me again, lightly, on my forehead, and then stroked my hair. "Let's get at these dishes, then." He playfully pulled me out of my chair, toward him in a hug. I loaded the dishwasher while he scrubbed the pots and pans. Then I went to check on Mother. What I really wanted was the privacy of her en suite bathroom: I threw up my entire dinner. The bile burned in my throat and mouth, coating it with bitterness. It was also a relief.

While I was pregnant with Lindsay, I nearly went under. That's a tawdry metaphor, but for some reason all the language about depression is worn, rudimentary, like brick-and-board bookshelves. Mental breakdown. What on earth does that mean? It's a diagnosis, not an experience. Black hole? Grand Canyon? Only art—poetry and music and painting—seems to convey what we experience. Mark Rothko's enormous black stations of the cross in the chapel in Texas. Bach's C Minor piano concerto. Language is social; the Black Hole of Calcutta—which used to be my ironic nickname for it—is not.

Absence. Of self. Of desire. Of joy. That thick absence has penetrated the region just below your lungs, which are filling up with it, so your feelings can't breathe. You sit by an open window with the breeze and sunshine on your skin, unable to feel pleasure. That abyss between knowledge and feeling. You know everything's fine and you feel your life's a disaster. You sit at the edge of a cliff with peace and contentment floating just out of touch in midair.

It had taken me a while to get pregnant, so we were eager parents who painted and furnished the nursery long before the baby was due. It was the seventies: colour-coding for babies was right out, so we painted the room a lovely ambiguous grey-blue-green and furnished it with blues, greens, yellows. Now that I think about it, the only forbidden colour was pink; clearly the rules about colour and babies weren't quite gender-neutral. You could dress a girl in blue but you could not put a boy in pink. We bought mobiles, stuffed toys, Fisher-Price. The room was a shrine to the future. Except, in defiance of the common wisdom that women are serene and balanced during pregnancy, I seemed to feel more and more every day that the future was pointless. It was not something I could explain, so I was silent, simply napping more—which Rob took to be perfectly normal for a pregnant woman.

One day he came home to find me standing in the middle of the room, turning slowly round and round. Beside my feet on the floor was a box of enormous garbage bags.

"Hi. What's up?" In my frame of mind, I couldn't fathom his naiveté, his hopefulness.

"I wanted a last look at it all."

"A last look?" He said this, of course, with panic in his voice. This could have meant anything: that I was leaving him,that I was about to burn the house down, that I knew I was going to die in childbirth. But to his credit, his response was calm and warm. He put his arms around my shoulders—my belly was too big for a proper hug—and said, "Tell me about it. Why last?"

"Because I can't do this. I can't have this baby. Or I can't keep it. I need to pack everything up for someone who will." I glanced down at the box of garbage bags.

Pregnancy made me naked in the most unexpected way. I know that expression sounds wrong, because for the most part pregnant women, who hid their bumps under flowing maternity dresses, were sexless then, even though they're sexual in the most powerful way possible. But my sense of my human inadequacy—how could I possibly be responsible for the life of a child?—was so overwhelming that I knew it was visible to everybody. I couldn't imagine myself able to get a baby to go to sleep because I myself was so tense and frightened. They'd find me rocking in the chair clutching a starving, wet, wailing baby. I wouldn't be able to bear it then. I'd have fallen in love already. So I needed to take care of this now. I was a crystal on a chandelier, turning in the wind, studying my child's nursery. If one of the other crystals should so much as touch me, I would explode, sending bright glass shards everywhere, into the walls, lodging in the carpet, lancing my daughter's transparent ear, her tiny fingers, her unwavering blue eyes.

I was also emotionally naked whenever I practised. I would sit at the piano and weep while I played late Beethoven or Brahms or Chopin. Music moved me with a depth it never did before and rarely has since. Everything I felt as I played turned into script—the kind we'd later find as background on greeting cards and wrapping paper and silk scarves, nostalgic as we've become for the hand-written word. But the words wrote themselves on my body. Then they leapt off my body into the air, tracing filaments so thin and keen, I could not leave the piano. If I otherwise felt nothing, music made me feel too much. It spoke of all the essentials of life: that fragile shade of green that dusts the trees in spring. Winter days when a white sky and white ground make a day into a blank page and there are no words.

How would I ever perform if every time I sat down to play something profound, I wept? And so Rob found me ready to pack up Lindsay's things for a proper mother. "Tell me about it," he instructed again, his arms around my shoulders as he steered me out of the nursery into the living room, pulling me close to him on the hard, modern sofa.

"I can't explain."

"Sure you can. Take your time. I'll go order some Chinese food, and you think about it."

I gave him the short version: I'd be a rotten mother and I couldn't play without weeping. He nuzzled me; he kissed me; he gave me a gentle mock "knock upside the head." He paid for the Chinese food, set the table, opened the containers of food, and steered me into the kitchen.

"For now, just eat. I'll make you some jasmine tea. We'll sort this out after dinner."

I discovered, surprisingly, that I was ravenous. And I could still taste food. He told me about his day. He had, I remember, a very funny story about one of his colleagues at their department meeting that day.

"Jacobs wears these tatty old tweed jackets. The seats of his trousers are always shiny, and they're always creased 'round the crotch. It's the only real 'perma press' I know. His shirts, of course, are un-ironed, and he wears a skinny waiter's tie that's covered with splotches of soup and spaghetti sauce. He never speaks at meetings. He sits in the back corner of the room near the windows and silently glowers—when he doesn't ostentatiously read *History in Canada* while the rest of us debate regulations and course offerings and voting rights for instructors." Rob twirled another bunch of chow mein noodles onto his split wooden chopsticks. I'd noticed my breathing had changed.

"But today he decides to speak. He raises his skinny, liver-spotted hand politely. Nothing." Rob spears a bunch of broccoli and munches it. I can tell that he's spinning this story out as long as he can.

"He raises his hand more aggressively. He's not quite the eight-year-old boy who knows the answer, but close." Again, another pause to serve himself rice and take another helping of almond chicken.

"Bathurst, you know, is virtually blind beyond six feet. You know those Coke-bottle glasses he wears?" I nod. "Finally, Jacobs is practically waving him down, and I clear my throat as loudly as I can to get Bathurst's attention. I sit near the front and off to the side so I can survey the room and read body language. Sometimes it's more reliable than words. 'Dr. Jacobs has something to contribute,' I say with my best formality when I've gotten Bathurst's attention. Jacobs would like to smile at me, except that he's spitting mad. At the very moment when Bathurst invites him to speak, this breeze comes in and blows

Jacob's papers all over the floor. Marilyn, who's sitting next to him, is pawing through her enormous purse, trying to find a tissue to wipe his spit off her face. 'Never mind,' he mutters. He's standing now, trying to gather up his papers, but watching Marilyn's search. 'You wouldn't have liked it anyway.'"

Rob had been acting much of this out as we went along, and by this time we're both laughing more than the story deserves because we need to wring the panic from our bodies.

"Let's go sit in the living room. No. Let's go stand in the nursery. Come on. You can do this." He takes my hand and pulls my cumbersome body along behind his fit one.

So as we stand in the middle of the perfect, beautiful nursery, he holds me and says, "You'll be a fine mother. This is probably all hormones. Plus maybe a shard of reasonable fear. Every parent ought to worry a *little* bit. Too many think parenting is just something natural." He points to all the baby-raising and child-rearing books on the shelf next to *Winnie the Pooh* and *Goodnight Moon*. "And this isn't the end of your performing or your music. We have money for a babysitter if you need. You can keep practising and performing."

There is no place in this house to howl. There's nowhere I can go to give tongue—and body—to what I'm feeling. My bedroom is right next to my mother's. The bathroom will only echo with my howls. So I sit here by my mother's bed, trying to cry as quietly as possible. I'll use her bathroom to wash my face when I'm done. Rob thinks we have made peace and will be hoping that I join him for reruns of *West Wing* tonight, and I must.

Wednesday, June 26, 2002

Lila

Twelve

"I think it's time for me to go." Mother begins our visit to King George Park with this little bombshell. She smiles at me. Clearly she doesn't expect me to notice how artificial her smile is, but I'm hyper-attentive to what people don't say these days.

"Time for you go to where? You want me to find you a washroom?" I'm trying to respond to her almost manic cheerfulness with my own.

"I'm not blind, Lila." Her voice is suddenly harsh. I've been expecting her to be angry about dying, but somehow I didn't think it would be aimed at me. "You've been spending too many nights in my room holding my hand." I must look surprised or puzzled, because she continues, "Oh, yes, I knew you were there. I wasn't sure you wanted to talk in the middle of the night. I thought my hand was enough. So I'd just go back to sleep. Morphine has its advantages." She reaches over with her hand and cups it around my cheek. "You're getting thin, dear." She pats my face. "I think I know why, but let's leave that for now. These have been magical months, really they have. I've felt so cared for. Most of my friends' kids park them in nursing homes and visit once a week."

"I could see you through to the end."

"Of course, dear. And you will when I'm in the nursing home. There won't be this pall over your whole household, that's all. I can tell that you and Rob are . . . Well. A little compartmentalization isn't a bad thing. Life in one box. Death in another. That's how it is, anyway. We never really know death while we're living. We don't even understand our lives any better while we're dying. Though I had my hopes." She smiles as a young man rides by on a unicycle. "You've done enough. Don't argue with me."

"It's called 'palliative care.' Not a nursing home. They keep you comfortable. But I *am* going to argue with you." I'm on the edge of tears. "I *need* you at home." I want to tell my mother what the real problem is, that I thought Rob had been unfaithful, but because there was this harassment suit—for what, I honestly didn't know—I was hunkering down to support him. Death in one room, infidelity in another. An unearthly balance.

Between the trees, a young woman dressed entirely in brown is settling on one of the benches, trying to balance her cup of coffee on the slope of the bench while she extracts pain au chocolat from its sticky bag. She licks her fingers, then wipes them on a serviette and pulls a slim book out of her large bag and settles back. Absently, I wonder how she's going to manage coffee, croissant, and the slender hardback. She pulls a pile of serviettes from the bag, unfolds one on her lap, and nestles in the pastry. She's concentrating on her careful pleasure.

"Why don't we just wait . . . ?" Some things are not said: Worse. Dying. Helpless.

"Because I'm worried about you *now*." It's been a long time since I've heard my mother that angry.

"Okay. There's nothing for me to do but come clean. I'm stressed out. You're right."

"Stressed out? You're regularly throwing up in my bathroom. That's beyond 'stressed out'—which is what *every* North American complains of these days. *You're* sick with worry."

"You're right. There's no point lying about throwing up, given that you're so good at pretending to be asleep." A young man with a lizard-like spiky Mohawk spins by on his skateboard. Were the tips of the spikes blue? "It's Rob."

"What's wrong with Rob?" She's still prickly.

"Well, it isn't 'wrong,' exactly." I want to tell a story. I want to get outside the details I haven't been able to find the right context for. "I woll reherse," King Arthur's knights used to say when they came back from a harrowing adventure. "Rehearse," from "harrow": to wound or lacerate. To draw a harrow back and forth across a field. Both of which I've been doing. Going over the same ground again and again until my mind is frayed with pain and I've lost my way. I want to tell a story; I want my mother's comfort. "Do you remember when Margaret and I took you to the organ concert?" She reflects, then nods brightly. Her moods change on a dime these days. "While we were getting you into the elevator, Rob greeted one of his students. Elise Grant. She's going on to do a PHD at Toronto this fall. Full scholarship."

"Lucky her."

"Indeed. I'm not so sure I'm in the mood to wish her luck."

"Oh, dear." Mother raises her brows.

"That night she gave me a long appraising look that made me suspicious. I must have picked up some change between Rob and me, because I suddenly felt everything was clear. Things I didn't quite know were bothering me." The woman in brown has finished her coffee and croissant and is licking her fingers again. Then she pulls a water bottle from her purse, pours a little on a serviette, and wipes her fingers, drying them before she settles back into her book.

"You're going through the change of life, dear." How does she know this too? "Why is it men never know what to do with a menopausal woman?" Her eyes look into the distance, where memory is playing itself out among the trees where the young woman reads quietly. "It's true your body isn't your own. That it's got its own out-of-this-world thermostat. But your desires are your own, maybe for the first time in your life." She pats my hand tentatively, as if this rite of passage made by every woman lucky enough to live into her fifties might explain what I'm feeling. My brain spins to sub-Saharan Africa and women dying of AIDS; my story is a luxury.

"I waited a couple of days while I thought about why I felt betrayed. Why I was made so suspicious by a look. All I could come up with was a cool tone of voice. Emotional absence. Lack of interest in sex. At first I came to the same conclusion you did, that it was my being menopausal."

"But it isn't." She's said this very softly.

"I can't convince myself any more. I decided to be adult about it all and told Rob how I felt. That he'd been unfaithful. In some way. I didn't claim I had anything more than suspicions."

A tinny version of the *1812 Overture* reaches us. The woman across the park rootles around in her purse, pulls out her cellphone, opens it up, studies its screen, and turns off the ring. She drops it back into her purse.

"What did he say?"

"He was all over the map. He got defensive and went out driving for hours. Then came home and held me while I cried myself to sleep. The next morning, he was positively . . . I don't know. Not flirtatious. Not quite. On his best behaviour. As if he'd been lying awake the whole night thinking about what our marriage was made of. Outward things like food and companionship. Oddly enough, that made me more suspicious. Because love isn't tangible. It irradiates everything. It's light and heat that can't be manufactured with a slice of mango and the smell of excellent coffee. Then he probed ever so gently. What was I going to do? I was honest. I told him I was going to trust my suspicions. Not him. He was going to have to wait for me to decide."

"Good for you!" She punches the sky in enthusiastic approval, the way the crowd does when there's a touchdown. The coffee drinker, who's gotten up to throw her cup and the large supply of used serviettes in the trash can close to us, turns as my mother gestures. She smiles at me broadly.

"Good for me? I've won a prize?"

"Yes. Exactly. Your self."

"That isn't what it feels like. It feels as if I don't know what love is any more. It's like this big absence. If Rob did his professor thing and gave me a pop quiz with a single question, 'What is love?' I'd fail"

"Well, that would be like Rob—the pop quiz. But you'd fail because he had."

"If you think he's failed, you'll love Act Two. Kevin learned that someone is charging him with harassment. We don't know who or why. Rob maintains it's because he was cranky about this spring's hiring." My voice is uncertain.

"Do you feel vindicated?"

"No. I feel awful: trapped. No matter why the charges are being brought, I can't do anything 'til it's resolved."

"Why?"

"I don't know anything. I don't have any evidence. Besides, when I was in trouble before Lindsay was born, he was remarkable."

"But this isn't about what you *know*. This is about what you *feel*."

"This isn't just about what I feel. There has to be some rationale, something just about my decision."

"Since when? When was falling in love about justice? How many nice guys did you turn down for dates because you could see from the beginning it would go nowhere?"

"But that was *before* we got all tangled up together. At its deepest level, love is about justice, about doing justice to who someone is. About seeing them, appreciating them, acknowledging them, reminding them of the best of who they are and the story of how they became themselves."

"My dear, ethical, romantic daughter. Let me be more blunt. *Can* you do justice to the person Rob has become? Do you want to? Life's too short."

She's right, and I smile in a way that tells her so. Something has shifted my perspective—or one of my perspectives—a couple of feet to the left so I suddenly see and want something different. I smooth out the gravel at my feet with my toe. "I know. But staying with him for now is the only thing I can think to do. It's awful. He knows I'm watching him. I know he's . . . what do I imagine him doing? I need a nice, cold word. *Judging* is too personal. *Assessing*. Or *appraising*. The way you'd evaluate an antique, turning the object over in your hands, reading the name of the maker on the back. A date if it's there. What is it worth? What am I worth?"

"Of course you're worth it. You're beautiful. Gifted. Compassionate."

"You're also my mother. And you've just described half my friends, most of whom I wouldn't marry." She's playing with her zipper. "Are you cold?" She shakes her head.

"So? If he doesn't value those things—beauty, compassion—what good is he?"

"I'm not sure what he values. What does a very sexual man nearing sixty want? I feel like I'm supposed to guess. And I can't possibly know. He won't tell me. That would be cheating. *I am supposed to be the one person in the world who knows him*. That's the test. That's how you know a lover. Want. I ache with it. I'm not even sure it's for him. For a state of mind created by—what? Respect and pheromones?"

"But *no one* knows anyone else. We're lucky if we know ourselves half the time."

She's right. At best, we promise to learn, to be curious, to keep track of each other, to learn about each other's shifts and changes.

"Still, I can't help thinking of possibilities. Like a breeze out of the north on a hot, muggy day. We may be forced to begin again, I think to myself. But I can't let myself feel too hopeful, because if I do, I'll stop watching him. Naiveté and hope. I swear, they're the two things he hates most. I don't know what to do. I second-guess myself three times a minute. Should I be hopeful right now? Should I be suspicious? What does he want me to say? What does he see in my facial expression, my body language? Hope for the future? Distrust that will keep him in line? It's like watching the two of us in a three-way mirror. Getting an unfamiliar glimpse of myself where I least expect it." I kick the gravel, sending some of it flying onto the grass, and think of the naked woman in the locker room, of her complete nonchalance, her indifference about whether anyone sees her. She has a vision of herself, and that's all that matters.

"Stop playing with stones and sit down." I sit. "You don't have much control here. You can say all the right things, you can read his moods and his needs and he can still be unfaithful." She reaches out and kicks one of the stones I missed. "I know it's a family joke—Rob and power. But sometimes one partner has the willingness to risk it all; to throw it all away really does give them power. The world's not safe if they're not in control. And there's power in not caring. Or in caring more for power than anything else."

We sit silently for quite a long time. I can only keep hopelessness at bay by thinking about how my mother has learned this truth. For in spite of my moments of hope, I have known that Rob held the balance of power.

The sun has moved and has been shining directly in our eyes for about ten minutes. While both of us have turned slightly so it falls on the side of our faces, it's starting to make my eyes ache, and mother is squinting.

"Should we go? You don't look comfortable." I get up, ready to wheel her back to the car.

"We're not done yet. Why don't you just find us some shade?" I don't know what to do about my mother's relentlessness, but I wheel her into the shadows at the other end of the bench. I glance around; there's no other place nearby with a place for both of us to be out of the sun, except for the bench where the young woman sits, reading, I can now see, poetry in French. We can't intrude.

"Aren't you tired?"

"That's for later. I'll sleep well tonight."

"Promise?"

"I promise. As long as somebody doesn't come in to wake me up. I'm going to get much sicker soon." She must see the grief on my face, for she quickly goes on, "No, don't worry. It's just a way of avoiding Rob. It's going to be difficult to be relaxed and civil—to be natural. The easiest thing is simply to find an excuse to stay in my room. Exhaustion will do nicely." A heroic smile accompanies these words: "Maybe it's time for me to move out."

I cannot fathom such loss, not only of my mother, but of the chance to craft compassion and beauty while she dies. I still want to create the long take, single and whole, that time cannot wrench apart, the single interpretation that holds together across time, the antidote to her understanding of her complex, contradictory marriage. I shake my head no slowly, and she silently assents.

"Screw bar lines," I said to myself a couple of hours ago. Rob is oddly preoccupied by something down in his workroom, so I've put on some Bill Evans CDs. *New Jazz Conceptions*—friendly and accessible. *Big Fun*. The difficult *Conversations with Myself*, where Evans lays down a foundation track, then is recorded responding to the foundation, and then to the two voices together—all on Glenn Gould's beloved New

York Steinway. He knew how to talk to himself, he said (more or less) in his liner notes, better than anyone else. Then *Kind of Blue*, to take me back to the familiar. Unlike some jazz pianists, who hang their improvisation on rhythmic drive, Evans is almost impressionistic in his interpretation of the standards. They've got an organic flow that has nothing to do with bar lines. While we listen, Brahms and I are on the floor, spinning and chasing tops.

I realized even before Mother finished saying, "Maybe it's time for me to move out," that I'd done something wrong. I've tried to word that differently, telling myself, "I've done something regrettable" or "I've done something selfish." But *wrong* is the right word. A wrong note, one that the editor tries to splice out; one that compromises the integrity of the performance. In my need for sympathy and clarity, I told her a story she shouldn't know. It will colour all of her final days, making her a prisoner of her room, making her feel anxious and helpless.

Then came fury: he picked this moment in my life to go tomcatting around. He'd waited until I was most preoccupied and most vulnerable, thinking . . . Well, I don't know what he was thinking. That he could get away with it? That I'd cave or be so needy I'd beg him to stay? That I wouldn't notice?

Bill Evans talking to himself made music.

Saturday, July 6, 2002

Rob

Thirteen

I love shopping for wood. First, the smell. LeggettWood Bois, where I've been buying wood for years, has layers of smell, like layers of memory. The smell of wood-mulched paths at the cottage we rented one year. Of the flower boxes Claire and I built with my father. The smell of turpentine and paint lodge right next to the smell of freshly cut cedar boards.

Then colour. To the untrained eye, wood looks like wood. The inexperienced eye doesn't see the grain. How much do I want? Given my plans, do I need it good one side, or should both sides be flawless? I got out my plans to begin figuring how much. I had to think about the beauty of the wood compared to how much I wanted to pay. Wood's not cheap. What most people buy these days is tarted-up laminated particle board. This is not a project I'm going to try to do on the cheap.

I'm going to make a music cabinet for Lila. Now she keeps her music in utilitarian cardboard boxes that she labels and lines up on the music room bookshelves. So yesterday, while she was out with her mother, I measured how much music she had. I've designed a flexible cabinet. I'll make grooves that allow her to move the partitions between letters or composers. Half of the top will give her space to store her musical reference books; the other half will have a slanted bookstand where she can rest books she's consulting. I was tempted by some cherry, but I've decided on white oak. I've wielded my measuring tape and know how much I need, but I've got to wait for one of the guys to come help me shuffle the wood and see which boards I want. The help in here isn't great. They know they're the only game in town if we want good wood. So I'll hold up this joist, jingle my keys, and try to look as bored as possible. A couple of the staff have seen me and signalled they'll get to me when they can.

The music case is part of the "new beginnings" redecorating. She finally found time last week to go to Roche Bobois. She was cagey, claiming that while some of the pieces were indeed quite spectacular and the leather was luscious, she also thought them expensive and larger than anything we'd need. We don't need, she pointed out, L-shaped seating for sixteen. She was exaggerating, of course. It wouldn't hold sixteen. But I took the hint and simply ordered the sofa and an ottoman—two pieces instead of three.

While I'm waiting, I'll indulge in a little fantasy. It makes time go. An email to Elise. There's something delightfully impersonal about the theoretical, virtual connection between your keyboard and someone else's email box. When the cultural historians try to grasp the essential nature of the early twenty-first century, email will be one of the elements of the *geist* they'll have to study.

But tone in an email is a challenge. Unlike a phone call or something handwritten, emails have hardly any tone at all. Unless you work really hard to create one. What tone would I like to create? The naughty version of "cautious optimism," I guess. I'm not sure I want an affair after this whole thing is over and Lila calms down again. whole thing. What do I mean by "this whole thing?" Clarice's death, of course. I don't want her to die, but I also want Lila to have the death over with. It's taking so much out of her. Also Lila seems more concerned about the harassment suit than seems reasonable. I keep telling her there's nothing to worry about, but maybe she doesn't trust committees. I probably outrank most of the people on the committee and draw more research dollars into the university coffers and add more points to the *Maclean's* ratings with my publication record than the lot of them. I've put paid to her suspicions of an affair by being an attentive lover and cook and saying nothing about her night sweats and the fan she aims directly at the bed. Though I've taken to wearing pyjamas to protect myself from both. But I'd like the idea of an affair. The *possibility*. An antidote to tedium. Some things are better if they're roughed up a little. Suede. Oil paintings.

So an email to Elise. Something to keep her interested, something allusive, elusive. Let's see. I'll begin with a bid for sympathy, patience. It's summer, and committees grind slowly. I'll show some polite interest in her life. That's another feature of our e-culture. People are so busy keeping themselves connected and up to date that they've forgotten the virtues of polite interest in other people. "Sorry," we smirk to the best friend having lunch across from us whom we haven't seen in a month because we're so busy. "I've got to take this phone call." "I *am* so important," we imply. But I'm more than politely curious. She found a summer job in someone's constituency office, and I want to know how that's going, how she likes it, if it's told her whether she belongs in academe or the "real" world. She's also a wonderful collector of gossip, and I'd like to know what she's gleaned. For some reason, she's rather undiscriminating about her accumulations, her jumbles of gossip treasures. Which of course makes chatting with her even more rewarding. There's a startling, little-known but important fact about a budget coming down cheek by jowl with some dirt on an opposition MP.

But along with all this stuff that might be matter-of-fact friendliness and might not be, I need something ambiguous to pique her ego and make her write back. A compliment. An almost underwhelming compliment—a curiously underwhelming compliment—if I'm not amassing too many qualifiers. Double entendre would be good. Brain/head. Skin/surface. Nope. Eyes/insight. Better. Ah. Here comes Ken to help me shuffle wood for Lila's cabinet. I'd better warn him that this is going to take a while. I need perfect pieces. I'm looking for luxurious grain you want to feel with your hand.

My life feels like the "Facts and Arguments" page of the *Globe and Mail*. Or how that page might look if they asked me to reorganize it. Facts in their little hermetic boxes. Yes/No, For/Against columns.

Fact: I love my wife. I love the life we have. Clarice's lingering death is compromising the *ambiance* of pleasure we create with food, wine, the lawn and garden, music. But that death too is a fact. It can't be helped. Oddly enough, it has made Lila more beautiful to me. What is it about a woman's tiredness that's almost erotic? That day about a month ago when I let her sleep in and baked fresh croissants for her. How I've domesticated flirtation! Anticipating her languor, her passivity that night, aroused by the little parenthetical lines in her cheeks that appear when she's tired.

Fact: Sometimes that's not enough. It doesn't have enough edge. Jolt. The quietude feels like cotton batting. Then the cravings start. I don't do chocolate. That's for women. Sometimes I buy a case of exquisite wine or a bottle of remarkable, complex single malt. But that dulls the senses, which I want roused, not deadened. I want something individual. A particular kind of beauty. A beauty the colour of honey or topaz to complement Lila's monochromatic pale skin and black hair. Were I honest, I'd say a mirror. I shouldn't need a mirror, but I do. Maybe we all do. The right mirror. Platinum. All shards and spikes around the edges. Something startling so I see myself afresh. I've found that beauty twice in my life, once with a breathtaking, dangerous brevity. I keep looking for it in the faces of the students I teach, but they're usually too naive to appeal to me.

Here's today's opinion piece. I am so grateful for Lila's support while I wait for all the committee members to come back from their various safe holidays to rule on my fate. I swing back and forth. They can't touch me, really. My research record is stellar. I'm getting SSHRCC grants in a time when all the money is going to dopey interdisciplinary group projects, and the book I'm working on about the democratic side of Hausmann's redesign of Paris is nearly complete. Scholars tend to see the way the broad streets allowed the powerful to watch the lower classes, but the boulevards allow all kinds of surveillance to go on. I've got a publisher who's waiting with bated breath, knowing it'll be controversial enough to sell.

But you never know with committees. They're unpredictable. All it takes is one person out to get you (and my research record has aroused not a little envy), with enough imagination to figure out how to bend the committee's task to his will. Yes, his. The vengeful in academia are largely men. Insecure men. Comparing their intellectual pricks at the urinal.

Yet Lila's faithfulness has been . . . I've been trying to think of the right expression. I've thought of her as a compass or a rudder, but these metaphors all imply navigation, direction. At this moment, I'm not going anywhere and I don't need any guidance. Centre of gravity. She pulls me toward some meaningful centre where thought isn't the only thing that counts. But when I'm there, I can't quite say what *is* important. Ironically, although she's a musician, it's very quiet there. Your senses need to be sharply tuned. No laziness; no over-the-top appetites. Maybe that's why it's both comforting and cloying. Yet I don't want to be any place else.

Sunday, July 14, 2002

Kevin

Fourteen

There's got to be a self-help book somewhere that lists all the ways to avoid dealing with family conflict; aside from taking separate vacations or being a workaholic, giving a party has to be at the top of the list. Because if you throw a party, there's all the practical stuff you've got to do that makes avoiding each other seem natural. You've got to plan menus, do the shopping and cooking, create the atmosphere. Then cooking. I've always admired couples who could cook together. We're not one of them. Neither are Lila and Rob, for different reasons. Rob's a show-off, and doesn't want to share the praise with anyone, even his wife. I am a hazard in the kitchen. I'll helpfully unload the dishwasher while the dishes are still dirty. People who cook together have a kind of dance: when one zigs, the other zags. When Francis zigs, I do too. We bump into each other a lot. He's spilled a number of things all down the front of me, none of which, fortunately, were boiling.

Then there's the party itself, which, if you've invited the right people, may slipslide on the surface of things. If you're careful, you invite some patient soul who figures out there's tension in the air and decides it's his or her job to sparkle, to give off light, to set a certain tone, to start conversational hares. Finally, the cleanup.

As soon as we arrived, I could tell this was an "avoid life" party. And the avoidance wasn't coming from Clarice, who was a little on the manic side for a woman in her late seventies dying of cancer. By the time Francis and I arrived, Lindsay was already there, so we didn't know why she was alone, where lovely, feckless, and snarky Paul was. Paul is *very* attractive, obviously someone who obsesses about his body more than a little. But if it weren't for Lindsay, I couldn't tolerate more than five minutes of conversation with him. If he gave me a chance to speak, I'd have no idea what to say.

The first thing I noticed was that the room was full of marshmallows, and people were sitting on them quite tentatively, as if getting comfortable was hazardous: they'd either melt into the cracks or find the hidden whoopee cushion. Rob, as usual, was looking the professor-cook self in his Craig Claiborne navy striped apron, shirt sleeves rolled back several times to reveal the hair on his arms and keep his cuffs out of whatever lovely sauce he's going to disguise our food with. I swear, that man could cook nothing but soy burgers and tofu and find ways of making it tasty. I don't quite know whether or not that's a compliment. I mean, shouldn't you be able to taste what you're eating and not just the sauce?

Anyway, once we'd been seated at the edge of the marshmallows and made our flattering remarks about the canapés, Clarice leaped on Francis.

"Forgive me, dear, but what do you do? You're an artist? Is that what I remember?"

"Well, I did Fine Arts at university. I got the craft down pretty well. I can throw a pot or do a respectable engraving with the best of 'em. It's the 'pretty well' that gets me in trouble. I like 'pretty.' It's not art. I work in a gallery in Old Montreal."

"Do you like it?"

"Yeah. For now. I design our windows. My boss, Josh, even pays me to scour Old Montreal, St. Catherine, St. Denis, for whatever I need to do a show-stopping window. When we get some great pottery or glass, I like to stand and watch people walk by. Stop. Back up." Francis took a pull on his drink, hoping that someone would jump in to change the subject. He likes to be the centre of attention on his own terms. But people were simply waiting. Francis wouldn't talk about anything controversial. Realizing this, he soldiered on gamely. "There's a catch: Old Montreal takes its minimalism seriously. Onyx jewellery in beds of red lentils or amber in brown rice was about as far as Josh was willing to go. I'm trying to loosen him up. I've been collecting antique linens and can't wait for a shipment of porcelain that'll look gorgeous swathed in damask and old lace."

Francis stops again. There's a wild look in people's eyes that tells me they're desperately trolling through their minds for light conversation and not finding anything. I'm not either, so I prompt Francis. "You've already started to use some textiles."

"Ah, yeah. Banners. Very simple. A bit of damask or a simple brocade. Neutral colours, of course. Taupe, gold, cream. Black. Black is always good. I use a lot of fishing line to get it to defy physics. Variety and balance. Symmetry is out. Doing windows is my biggest treat."

"Do you ever worry about getting trapped in that job?" Rob queried with the best of intentions on his carefully composed face. Bugger. Given our last friendly meeting, he's trying to pretend I'm not here. "It can't pay you much."

"My job suits me just fine. I've also started designing the catalogues. After you've got a certain amount of comfort—which Kevin and I have—money doesn't make up for everyday pleasures. I like my life—the easy hours, the art world, meeting people who care about art. Some of them are a little pretentious, but . . ."

Rob guffawed. "*Some* of them?"

"*Some* of them. Most of them are interested in beauty or craftsmanship. Not a bad thing in the twenty-first century. I've had a surprising number of clients who are worried about artists being paid fairly for their work. The world might be a better place if more people cared about beauty or craftsmanship or whether artists got paid fairly. Instead of shifting their lives along some kind of ladder—success, money, possessions—that doesn't really exist."

"*Doesn't really exist?* Tell that to the statisticians."

Rob took a sip of his wine and, unopposed, droned on. "Some economists have figured out that you can measure a person's happiness by the way his income compares with his peers' and neighbours'. If he makes more, he's happy. If he makes less—it might even be millions—he's not." At this point, the air was getting a little steamy.

"What Francis means is that the ladder doesn't have rungs that you *count*," defended Clarice.

Rob nearly snorted. "What kind of ladder would that be?"

"If you were dying, you'd know." Clarice vibrated with fury.

"Nobody here is dying, Grandma. We're all living. Unless one of us is a vampire, of course."

"I see you have new furniture," I said with false brightness. "It's splendiferous!"

"I thought the room needed brightening up. Leather's a great investment," said Rob, holding forth.

Lila's face was hard to read. Was she pissed? Amused? Time to change the subject again. "Something smells wonderful."

"I was going to cook a lovely rabbit stew, but Clarice vetoed it. So I'm making Bourdain's boeuf en daube," Rob said with evident satisfaction at his self-sacrifice.

"Thank you," I mouthed to Clarice, inwardly blanching.

She gave me a quick, impish grin. "Almost as bad as sitting on the backs of dead cows," she said in an undertone that could nevertheless be heard in the entire room, which had grown quiet.

"Come on now, Clarice. You're willing to eat it. Why not go the whole hog and use everything you can?"

Should we be embarrassed at how quickly food can switch the topic? We got lost in the lusciousness of Rob's cooking. Lila and I worked together to shift the subject into more neutral territory, until a gentle snore from Clarice changed the topic.

"Why don't the two of you and Lindsay go sit on the deck or go for a walk while I get Mother to bed for her afternoon nap and Rob and I clean up the kitchen?" Lila asked, looking from Francis to me.

"A walk?" I queried. "Start dealing with some of that chocolate pâté?"

"Perfect," Lindsay agreed while I was preoccupied with helping Lila ease Clarice out of the wingback chair they put at the head of the table for her. Rob took over from me, and we all gathered at the front door to put our shoes on. We straggled until we got our stride. Then Francis popped the question.

"Where's Paul?"

"Paul's in Hull, where he got a better tech job. He hadn't been very happy with his work, so when the offer came up, he jumped at it."

"Joining him?" I asked. This is not a good time for Lindsay to leave.

"I don't think so. I'm not really wanted. Actually, the point of taking the job was to get away from me."

"Sometimes people who find change hard need to go to extremes. Just to get themselves moving," Francis offered.

"Are you okay?" I asked.

"Yeah. I'm relieved to have him gone." She studied the planters at the edge of the corner lawn attentively while Francis and I traded surprised looks.

"Does your mother know?"

"No. She's got her own problems right now. I didn't think it was a good time to bring it up. I made up some story about a family commitment. That wouldn't send Dad into a rant. God, he can be relentless. Did you hate your dads for a while?"

"Didn't have a chance," Francis responded. "Dad buggered off before I could."

I merely shrugged my shoulders. Mine's been a great dad to my two sisters. Whether he couldn't stand my being male or couldn't stand my not being male is unclear. We're civil to each other. Family meals—like this one—are just the ticket for us. We don't watch football together and get down and dirty about our feelings. I don't watch football. He doesn't feel much. There's silence as the three of us contemplate our fathers.

"I don't think I know *any* men my dad's age who aren't like him: driven by something, blind to anything they can't explain. They're giant egos half full so they need constant reassurance. Except you guys, of course," she says, linking her arms around our elbows so that we look like the Three Musketeers coming down the street.

"We're not his age," Francis said slyly.

We arrived back about half an hour later. The kitchen was spotless. Lila and Rob were sitting on the back deck, Clarice dozing on the chaise longue. We all gathered out there and I pounced. I've been waiting for this.

"Lila. Do you know Stuart MacTaggart?"

"The cellist? Teaches at McGill, doesn't he?"

"Yeah. Composition sometimes. He also plays principal cello with the McGill Chamber Orchestra, but he's not entirely happy. He told me last Friday that he'd like to work with you, but he's terrified of asking. With us, actually. He'd like to do some of the trio repertoire—Beethoven or Brahms."

"Terrified of me! Kevin, you're exaggerating. He hardly knows me."

"Apparently, he was a few years ahead of you when you were doing your graduate work. He says there's some myth about you that won't die. Some guy messed with you and you cut him dead. No excuses or extenuating circumstances for you. You picked up your life and went on with it. So he wonders if you're a bit—chilly. He's come to our last three concerts in Montreal, though, and thinks you're awesome."

"He's a fool to be frightened of Lila." God, Rob's blind. He thinks people only fear power. Sometimes beauty and passion and rigour and perceptiveness frighten us.

"Myths saturate a community, Rob," I explained. "They just stay there—if they don't morph into something even more extreme." I wonder if he got the innuendo. Probably not. No point paying attention to gay little powerless Kevin.

"I don't know, Lila. If this guy has to send an emissary, you might think twice about having to deal with him."

"But the repertoire, Rob. Brahms, Beethoven. Gorgeous trios. It would be something entirely different."

"And a whole new body of works to learn," Rob growled. "Maybe not the best timing?" Rob nodded toward Clarice, who still appeared to be sleeping. Clueless and mean with it. *I've* figured out she sometimes pretends to be asleep, but he just soldiers on.

"Can I hear one of them?" Clarice asked in response.

"You were supposed to be asleep. Do you want to go to your room?" Lila threatened jokingly.

"I did sleep. Now I'm awake. I'm excited. Put one on for me."

I was afraid that Lila would put on the Brahms Opus 8, a youthful work he revised thirty-four years later that reeks of Brahmsian longing. But she found the Beethoven Opus 1. It's cheerfulness itself.

Rob frowned momentarily. "It's pretty. Would it cheer you up?" I'm shocked Rob will admit that cheer is needed.

"Look. Think about it for a day or two. We can talk more if you like. I think it would be great to do an all-Brahms program for the concert we're planning in the fall, if we could pull off new repertoire by then. I should warn you, though. He likes women. Women like him. There's some very hetero kindness lingering about him . . ." I did this thing with my fingers only gay men can do convincingly. Well, maybe not convincingly. Unconvincing may be the point.

Rob snorted. He had been swirling amber fluid in a *very* correct Scotch glass. Scotch up your nose? I was tempted to ask. Interesting way to get the full bouquet.

"Kind. Well then. He'll make a great musical partner." It takes a musician to get the intonation of a response perfect, one key for the husband, the other for the violinist. Her words were supposed to soothe Rob, but I picked up some frisson—maybe anxiety, maybe excitement, maybe both.

We sat quietly for several minutes, listening to Beethoven's improbable cheer. Clarice had closed her eyes again; Rob was looking at Lila, who was staring off into the trees.

"We should all go so you can get Grandma into bed," said Lindsay abruptly, nervous, perhaps, about the silence, realizing that its meaning is different for everyone. "She's had a long afternoon."

"Yes. We should go," Francis said, making our excuses. "Thanks so much for a lovely meal and," turning to Lindsay, "an informative walk. Take care, all," he finished, turning to kiss Lila's cheek.

"Francis." Rob extended his hand in a manly handshake.

Francis smiled, not entirely sincerely, and swept out the door, his eyes telling me to be right behind him.

When we were on the street and could see that Rob and Lila were preoccupied with saying goodbye to Lindsay, Francis asked, aggrieved, "Why did you do that this afternoon? Why not ask her during a rehearsal? You cornered her."

"I wanted to make sure she'd take the bait. I didn't think Clarice would let her fail to take an adventure."

"Well." He winked at me. "You've certainly set the cat among the pigeons."

Thursday, July 18, 2002

Lila

Fifteen

I hadn't remembered him very well. Grey, taller than I am, he was still boyish: the curly, carefully trimmed hair, jeans and a white shirt with the sleeves rolled up, probably a dress shirt he'd performed in hundreds of times—all its pristine stiffness gone—pressed into friendlier service. He'd remained slim. He didn't have the authoritative padding even fit men like Rob put on in their forties as a badge of their success.

I haven't told Kevin we're meeting because I couldn't tell him why. I'd have to make up a story or he would think I didn't trust his judgment, and that's not true. Besides, Kevin knows accompanists learn to work with all kinds of people: the egomaniacs, the insecure ones who need your constant praise, the cold professionals. You do it matter-of-factly, being professional yourself. You put everything of yourself aside: you are brain, musicianship, and fingers only. Kevin and I could have worked with Stuart this way. I didn't think he'd spring any surprises on us. I remembered him as a shy, fervent musician. Kind, as Kevin had said. But with fire in him. Some of us were mystified about his failure to marry; there was gossip about his being gay because he was so comfortable with women. I knew he wasn't.

I've been listening to the Brahms first piano trio since Kevin proposed we work together. Brahms wrote it when he was terribly young, then rewrote it in his forties. It's so layered: you can hear the young Brahms being revisioned and tutored by the old Brahms; you can hear two stories in counterpoint, one of reckless young love, one of old wounds. When I put the recording on last week, the very first notes reminded me how much difference the addition of the cello makes to

Brahms's style. He wrote beautifully for cello: I sometimes think it's his introspective voice

Stuart stood up when I entered the coffee shop late, nearly tipping over his cup of coffee, and pulled out a chair for me. I explained I'd had troubles getting away and then again parking. Without sitting down, he asked what I'd like.

"Herbal tea? Would they have some chamomile? Or something floral? I don't know how exotic their teas are."

"Completely exotic. Can I bring you a surprise?"

I nodded. He returned with a cup and a pot of rose petals that dropped me straight into a garden.

"This is lovely. I've had rose-hip tea but find it too acidic."

"I love floral teas after concerts."

"I've been highly irresponsible. I can't remember when I came to one of the McGill Chamber Orchestra concerts."

"It wasn't that long ago, actually. Last October. Kevin tells me you've been preoccupied." He smiled as if to say he knew that was a polite understatement but couldn't offer meaningless, uninformed comfort or condolence. The clichéd "I'm sorry for your loss" that has become the standard line on cop shows. *Sometimes* the understatement is convincing.

The frayed edges of his white collar tempted me to open a door. "She's holding her own. For now. I'm not fooling myself. We're just stealing some time."

"*Carpe diem.*"

"Exactly. Musicians are good at that, don't you think? We *play* in the moment. Why not live in it?" I constructed a fake segue. "Is that why you want to do the Brahms with us?"

"Oh, I have a dozen reasons for wanting to do the Brahms. The chamber orchestra and my teaching are quite satisfying." He stopped, as if his motives weren't entirely clear to him. "Right now I need to do something more personal, even intimate. I compose too, and I'm working on a small scale. I guess I want to see, from the inside, what a limited number of voices can do. I'd also—this isn't just flattery—I'd like to play with you. You're an extraordinary musician, you know. As is Kevin. The two of you could teach me a lot. Right now, I need—this is probably the onset of middle age—to do something different. Something new." He smiled, but without crinkling up the corners of his eyes. It was a gesture without feeling.

"I know exactly what you mean. Renewing yourself. Rethinking how you see the world, being aware of where you see it from. Before it becomes habit." I stopped briefly to consider the explosion in my household. Is that what this was? "Look, can I get you another coffee? You look like you could use something warm."

He let go of his mug almost defensively. "Thanks. I'd better not. Too much coffee makes me edgy. Great for the vibrato, but not so good for the intonation. Actually, not good for the vibrato either. Makes it too uncontrolled."

I looked at my watch. Genevieve was with mother, but Rob had agreed to call late in the morning to see whether I'd gotten home and whether he should come home for lunch and take over. That was the kind of thing he was doing these days. Being completely thoughtful. I wasn't convinced.

He noticed the gesture. "Do you have a rehearsal this afternoon?"

"If I'm out past noon, my husband will have to come home to stay with my mother. I'd rather he didn't have to." Stuart continued to sit quietly, his hands open around his coffee mug as if he were announcing his defencelessness. "What's wrong?" I reached out and fingered the frayed edge of his cuff, then put my hand on top of his.

"Don't worry about it. It's not existential. Well, not exactly. And it's not romantic. So it won't get in the way. Nothing worse than trying to play chamber music with someone in the throes of . . ." He stopped abruptly. "I shouldn't have said that."

I sighed. "Oh, cripes. Where *do* the rumours come from?"

"I'm sorry. For bringing it up. What a dolt."

"Well, why not bring it up?" I looked at him hopefully. "New repertoire. Isn't that the cure for almost anything? You couldn't be more helpful." The frayed cuff was inexplicably appealing. "We could have a run-through in a couple of weeks, and be honest with one another. If it really isn't going to work, we'll know soon. Before any of us has invested a lot of time."

"Do you have your schedule?" I don't go anywhere without my diary, and pulled it out of my purse. "Could we set a time? You could check with Kevin and get back to me. And it's the Brahms No. 1 we're talking about? What do you think about doing it with the Beethoven No. 1? Too much?"

"Kevin's suggested an all-Brahms concert. We've got a couple of the violin sonatas pretty well under our fingers. I don't think I should take on too much new repertoire right now. I don't know what will happen. If my mother should need to go into palliative care, I'd want to be with her as often as possible. I don't feel like being pulled in two right now." I didn't want to splice together bits of Brahms with quick visits to palliative care and call it a take.

"No," he said, shaking his head gently. "No. Of course you don't. Do you have parts?" Practically without skipping a beat, he reached down for his briefcase. I expected scuffed leather, in keeping with the frayed white shirt. It was space age.

"That's cool." I reached forward to stroke the fabric.

"For carrying my laptop." He had reached in and brought out the piano and violin parts for both trios.

"Ever hopeful?" I reached out to take the piano part.

"Ever prepared."

I checked my watch again. "I've got to get back to my mother. Sorry I was late."

By this time we were standing. He leaned over the empty cups and saucers and kissed me chastely on the cheek.

I had the Brahms trio on the car's CD player, so as I drove home, I thought about what it was going to mean to our sound to add a cello. Sitting in a Montreal traffic jam (why are Montrealers proud of the irrationality of their driving, their willingness to double park on Sherbrooke in the middle of the day?), I listened and smiled. For several days, I've felt trapped between Mother and Rob. Mother wanted me to do it, to seize the adventure. Rob suspected any change. But I was happier than I'd been in weeks. Especially in the first movement, which I was listening to for the second time today, the cello adds a large generous calm, a depth to the sound. As the traffic began to melt away as it sometimes does, the scherzo started. I've heard it called a goblin dance, but I'd prefer to say that it's full of a slightly malevolent joy that echoed my own.

Because of the traffic jam, I was late again and found Rob sitting with Mother looking through a weathered brown photo album. He looked like a babysitter, someone who's not supposed to be comfortable in your home but tries to look dutifully attentive. She'd pulled herself into a corner of her chair as if he had cooties, leaving Rob to perch on the edge of his new leather. It was all I could do not to laugh.

He glanced up as I entered, nodded, but said nothing because Mother was in the middle of a ramble about why we'd taken this particular holiday in 1966—our visit to Mackinac Island and then the Bridge for the Labour Day Bridge Walk. His silence gave me a moment to observe, a moment full of unwilling judgment. As he sat there dutifully feigning interest in the photographs, I thought about the new views Stuart and I both needed. I had no more hard evidence now than I'd had before, but because I was seeing him differently, that mattered less. And as Mother pointed out a couple of weeks ago, when have feelings been based on *hard* evidence? Instead, I think we're going to find it taxing to survive the air of deliberation that has fallen over every sentence, every gesture, every touch, asking everything but ourselves to carry extra meaning. Whether that young woman stands between us literally, or whether she simply stands overhearing and shaping every conversation, she's changed something.

"Do you remember this holiday, Lila?"

I walked over to the other side of her chair to look at the pictures. They were taken with the Brownie camera I'd gotten for my thirteenth birthday and held with photo corners on the black pages of the album. Some of them had curled, snapping a rebellious corner off the page. Somewhere Mother had gotten some white ink and had written captions under each of them. There was a struggle at wit: *Mother's Bed and Breakfast* was written under a photograph of my mother in a dress cooking at a Coleman stove with the Mackinac Bridge for a backdrop. *Daisy warns the Bridge* was written under a snapshot of the shepherd mix whom mother and I had trained; the lack of perspective makes it look like she's barking at the bridge.

Mother turned the page. "Your father was very funny about the trip to Mackinac Island." There's a picture of Father sitting on the steps of the Grand Hotel with *The Lord of the Manor* written in white ink underneath, another of Father holding the bridle of a horse nonchalantly, as if this is something he does every day and is about to mount it. Under this is written *To Hounds!* Mother looked at Rob. "We clearly didn't belong there, you see. The island is a rather swish resort for the wealthy. We'd been camping and all looked a little rough." She pointed to the picture of my dad with the horse. "It has no cars, you know, so you either walked or took a horse-drawn carriage. We walked."

"Gawking enviously, I'm sure," I added.

"Except your father. He walked up to the steps of the Grand Hotel with Lila like he owned the place, sat down on the steps to tie his shoe, and told Lila to take a picture with her new camera."

"But he told stories afterward," I reminded Mother.

"Did he?" Rob put in, ever polite.

"Oh, such stories! I had to keep telling myself and the kids what really happened or his stories would have taken over our memories. In his version, we stayed at the Grand Hotel and rode there in the carriage. He was practically on a first-name basis with the driver."

"Did you let him know you were on to him?" Rob asked.

"Oh, no! What good would it have done? He knew he was making it up. We didn't have to point that out. But we had to keep ourselves from being . . . seduced."

"It was a perfect holiday," I suddenly remember. "He was unfailingly cheerful. I remember it took me off guard."

"He'd wanted to walk that enormous bridge. It seemed a feat of engineering he ought to celebrate. Perhaps he'd found something as big as he was." My husband is probably screwing a graduate student, but my mother's got perspective on her life. Well, that's something.

"Why didn't we take many vacations? I'd always assumed it was because he was—in a way—too big. For us and him to fit in the car." I'd pulled up a chair beside Mother, and she continued to turn the pages. We'd found someone to take a picture of us in the Ford Fairlane, each of us leaning out a window and waving. We looked like a happy family expert at carefree vacations.

"I'd guess it was money." Rob looked inquiringly at Mother.

"Does anyone want lunch?" I asked. They both ignored me.

"You'd be only partly right. Gregory liked the cachet of going back to the office and describing his carefree holiday with his family. But he also liked to think the office couldn't run without him. If there was enough money in the bank account to pay for the kids' back-to-school supplies and new clothes, I'd tell about someplace we should take the kids. If there wasn't, I played to the side of him that thought he was indispensable. Sometimes it worked, and sometimes it didn't."

"When didn't it work?" I need some perspective too.

"Your father wasn't very curious. The little corner he had built seemed to him the best place to be. Sometimes, I simply couldn't goad him into leaving that corner. I wanted to see the world. I wanted you kids to see it. But he was happy right where he was."

"Well, he might have been," Rob muttered.

Stuart hasn't remembered. If he was unguarded enough to say he knew something about the case against Rob, but didn't bring up that scene twenty years ago, it's because he hasn't remembered.

The May after Rob returned from Paris, on a perfect early spring night, we went to an artsy party organized by some musicians I knew. We went because Rob thought we should. It was another example of his sane principles driven by self-interest. Lindsay was nearly three, and the bother of finding and fetching and taking home a babysitter might well have kept us home. But Rob said we needed to get out and have some adult time. The babysitter was quite young, though Lindsay went to sleep easily out of a wise self-interest I'm afraid she's lost as an adult. Sarah was the sitter's name, I think. She wore cut-offs and the most peculiar top that looked like a man's cast-off pyjamas. In that enormous flannel shell, she looked altogether too young to leave Lindsay with, so I decided we had to be home early.

It was a beautiful night. And although this was the pre-deck eighties, the party spilled out into the back yard. Our hosts had even put up some dusty lanterns left over from the year before. It had rained that morning, so my high heels sank into the grass. I solved that by nipping into the downstairs washroom to strip off my pantyhose and spent the rest of the party barefoot. The grass was new and soft.

Lindsay was sleeping through the night, so I was getting my body back. That sounds like a non sequitur, but when you don't get enough sleep, food—particularly sugar—is tempting. I'd bought a new dress; the Princess of Wales had brought dresses back into style. It was royal blue, with a nipped waist (how proud I was of my new waist!) and a full skirt.

Lilacs. I remember the smell of lilacs. And an incredible red wine that someone claimed had chocolate notes—as indeed it did. Much of the party is a blur, as parties often are. They're largely forgettable. After a certain point, the conversation gets silly and trite. Why do we want so badly to be invited to them, to the point where we sometimes balefully think, on a quiet weekend, that people don't like us? Out of the usual blur of this party rises a handful of intense sensory details, all of them in colour. The evening was the colour of lilacs; it was the royal blue of my dress and the quieter, intense blue of a spring sky at dusk and the intense red of the chocolate-y wine. Rob was drinking too much wine. About half an hour before I thought we *really* should go home, I let him know. But I'd rehearsed a funny way to put it so he wouldn't think I was being heavy-handed. The minute you lose your cool with a man, you've lost the battle; they do so admire self-control.

"Hey, look. We should think about going in a while. You don't want Sarah sleeping through a three-alarm fire."

"Relax. We deserve some fun. We've been good parents now for weeks and weeks. And weeks. It's Saturday night. She can sleep in tomorrow."

Rob went back to the conversation with one of the musicians about the Canada Council—all the time thinking that he's being incisive and brilliant—and the musician was giving me funny looks, like "Take this guy home, will ya?" I jumped in at the first break.

"Look, Rob, the babysitter was dressed in pyjamas. It was a sign," I said with self-irony. That was before we all used scare quotes. "She wants to be to bed early."

"*What* are you *talking* about? Oh, that. Look, Lila. Relax. Have another drink. I'm going to. We'll leave in an hour or so." He looked at his watch to see what time it was. "Yeah. We'll be out of here before midnight. That'll be early enough. If she's old enough to babysit, she's old enough to stay up 'til midnight."

Stuart, whom I knew vaguely from a couple of my graduate classes, overheard all this, so when Rob walked away to refill his glass, Stuart raised his eyebrows in query. "Are you worried?"

"Sarah's kind of young. Barely thirteen. I don't think we should keep her out past ten-thirty. I don't know what good she'd be if there was an emergency. Which there won't be. All the same, it's not a good idea to push it. Now that I've got a baby, I have this ridiculous sense that any carelessness might be pushing it."

"I know what you mean. Look, do you want me to take you home? He can follow when he's good and ready."

"I'm not sure I want him driving."

"I can have a word with Dave. He'll make sure he's okay, get him into a taxi or something."

"Look, why don't I call the babysitter and see how she's doing?"

"Yeah. Come on in, and I'll show you where the phone is."

Sarah was clearly groggy. Never mind that *you'd* be groggy if something happened to your baby in the middle of the night. *You'd* know what to do. *You'd* be propelled awake because it was your baby.

The evening's colours had spilled all over the sidewalk, the lilac became a greyed mauve, the "royal" had been bleached from the blue. My daughter or my husband? My daughter. Stuart was standing just far enough away that I wouldn't feel he was lurking or pressing. I turned to him.

"I'll take you up on that ride." I didn't know whether to tell Rob I was going. I weighed the possibilities while Stuart continued to look both nonchalant and attentive. I didn't want a scene. I didn't want to fight about or explain my decision. "Could you ask Dave to tell him I've left? But not 'til after we're gone?"

"Sure. How 'bout I meet you on the front porch?"

The car radio was on. We made sporadic, desultory comments about the weather and the full moon.

"Do you want me to come in?" he asked after I'd guided him through the last turn.

"No." There was nothing else to say, except to be more polite. "No, thanks. I'll be okay."

"What if Rob's a bit . . . What if he's pissed when he gets home?"

I shrugged my shoulders. "What if he is? There's not much I can do about it. I can take care of my daughter—that's about it. That's all that matters."

"No, it isn't."

"He won't be, though. He'll be a little embarrassed. That's all."

"Are you sure?"

I put all my acting ability into the next two words. "I'm sure. Thanks for the ride."

"What about the babysitter? Should I take her home?"

"Oh yeah. Good grief. Good thing you thought of that. I'll pay her and send her out. She doesn't live far."

Thank goodness Sarah was too young and too sleepy to worry about getting in a car with a strange man. I checked on Lindsay, who was sleeping peacefully on her back. I eased her thumb out of her mouth and turned her over on her tummy just to do something. Then I changed out of my dress, found a magazine, and settled down in the living room to read until Rob got home. Sarah hadn't closed the drapes after dark, so I walked to the window to pull them shut and noticed a car strange to the neighbourhood parked one house down the street: Stuart had come back after taking Sarah home and was on watch. I thought of waving to him, of acknowledging this extraordinary act, but I closed the drapes instead. Loyal to my husband in gesture, if not in thought.

It was a gift of an evening. It had been warm enough to leave the windows open, and I could hear spring rustlings of not-quite leaves. I sat under the only light on in the house, turning the pages of *Architectural Digest*, absorbing nothing. My consciousness was just beyond that closed curtain. I heard scraps of conversation from two people out for a late-evening walk in counterpoint to the click of her shoes, the softer thud of his on the pavement. Occasionally, gusts of jazz came from the neighbour's house when the wind changed slightly. Miles Davis: *Blue in Green*. Bill Evans on piano, giving them a foundation of rhythm and motif, and then flying free of it himself. I was lost in sound, in the music of a night beyond that curtain. I felt the night was singing because there was a stranger out there protecting me.

Rob got home about two, cheerfully drunk. He teased me about being overly conscientious, about believing my baby couldn't do without me.

"Don't I remember you standing in the middle of Lindsay's room, ready to pack it all up because you were going to be a lousy mother? You're too good a mother. I need some attention too, you know." He had me by the wrist and was leading me upstairs. I quickly realized he was too drunk to make good on his desires, so I followed him up the stairs willingly. Playfully even. He turned on the bedroom light and then began kissing me and started to slide the straps of my nightgown off my shoulder when he was overcome with a wave of nausea. I rubbed his back while he threw up, then helped him get ready for bed. I turned off the bedside light and lay in the dark, staring at the ceiling, listening to the breathing of my husband, who'd instantly fallen asleep to the accompaniment of a mournful train whistle and the sound of tires. My music. Ten minutes after the light went out, I heard a car start and slowly drive away.

I've told myself this story too many times. It disappears from my life for months to rise up when I've lost my purse, when Lindsay is cranky, when a run won't settle under my fingers. When I need care. I'm sure I've intensified the colours over the years, the smell of earth and grass become layered over with the scent of every intervening spring. I'm sure I've made us more awkward and silent than we actually were: we didn't know then—and he certainly doesn't know now—that this story is a talisman. When I've got anxious insomnia, one of the ways I settle myself down is to replay the story in my head, detail by detail.

Whenever I wonder why the music of the young is dominated by lyrics about love and love lost and love consummated, I get metaphysical.

Because music itself is about desire. Because it floats on the stream of time, you can never *have* a piece of music. You can never *have* any work of art. Even if you pay millions to be able to hang a Monet over your fireplace, it eludes you.

Some people try, of course. They buy every decent recording, hoping to own the definitive performance. As if that isn't an oxymoron. Or they buy all the variant scores. They memorize it so that it becomes part of them, but that's not ownership. It's on loan. It's not even on loan from the composer, to whom it doesn't belong either.

It's the music of the universe—planets spinning and grazed by the light of stars, trees easing into bloom, the silent pain of being human and mortal and the cries of love—that someone has briefly, fleetingly been able to hear. If we're lucky, we hear echoes.

Friday, August 2, 2002

Rob

Sixteen

This is a beautiful lawn. Nicest lawn on the street. Sometimes I love to do what I'm doing now: sit on the front steps and water it by hand. It's inefficient; what a lawn needs is a really good soaking, not a little shower now and then. I haven't let Lila tart it up like the back yard with perennial borders and pots of annuals. Green grass and foundation planting. This calm expanse of velvet green. Sitting on your front steps on a beautiful afternoon and rhythmically swishing the hissing hose from side to side—you have to admit that's soothing.

It matches the sound of the cello coming from inside the house, a sound I'm particularly attentive to today because I wonder what it's going to mean for Lila to be working with Stuart McTaggart. They've just begun a slow movement—must be the second or third. Lila began with these calm chords at opposite ends of the keyboard—quiet extremes. Then the two voices, the violin and cello. It's too intimate, slow, and full of possibilities. Too thoughtful. And they're taking their time, as if they want to be deliberate about everything. There she is with McTaggart only. I think I'll just study my beautiful lawn and consider my victory.

Davis and I both got letters today from Human Resources indicating that the committee had sought legal advice (not wanting, clearly, to be slapped with a counter-suit) and decided that the harassment charge will be dropped. Davis stood in my doorway, trying to be contrite. He said he hoped there'd be no hard feelings. I played the humble victor: of course there wouldn't. I had my life and my freedom. When the rehearsal is over, I'll tell Lila.

I feel pulled in two directions, like the chords that Lila has moving toward one another from the high and low registers that never meet. There they are again. Except now the piano is decorating her part; it's no longer so austere. Pulled in two. I had coffee with Elise today, a public cup of coffee on campus so the spies, if they reported anything, at least couldn't say it looked clandestine. Even out in public, that frisson arrives unbeckoned. How refreshing to feel something you don't have to think about or summon up because it's what you *should* feel. Just this *whoosh*—rather like a sprinkler you've just turned on—of spontaneous feeling, blood singing in your veins, whispering in your ear.

I'm sometimes surprised by how much I love Lila; a little gesture of hers, an expression on her face, something she says will suddenly waken deep affection in me. But all the same, it isn't like that powerful *whoosh* I feel when I see Elise. Lila has calmed down, and we're going about our business of being a contented married couple. Now she'll calm down even more. We had Kevin and Francis over for dinner a couple of weeks ago. Last week a younger colleague of mine, a new chap with his new wife (they say ugly is the new handsome, which is the only way you can explain her marrying him), came by for evening coffee and dessert. I made a caramel almond torte with spiced mango compote and found some common ground with him that will be useful when the fights start in the fall.

And Lila's mother. We've got a partnership there. I've been careful to be aware of Lila's need for support—practical as well as emotional—with respect to her mother's dying. I've also taken over some of the cooking so she could get the Brahms trio up and running. It's a wonderful time of year to be cooking—the fresh vegetables are coming in. Tiny courgettes. Fresh peas. New lettuces. One night we even had fried zucchini blossoms. I've tried to be an observant lover again, to add some of the romantic frills that used to be part of our lovemaking, as if I need to seduce her with my attentiveness. Which perhaps I do. This has not been wonderful for my performance, this self-consciousness, but she doesn't seem to mind. She seems both content and slightly distant. I can understand that. She's got a lot on her mind, what with new repertoire and her mother's health, and both of us have felt the weight of this harassment suit. She hasn't taken up the suggestion I made about full skirts: the image of her slim thighs under a full skirt is a turn-on, but perhaps there aren't any in the stores.

As Elise and I sat down to our coffee, there was the opening politeness, questions about each other's health, comments about the beautiful summer—all the small talk we could muster to cover our delight at seeing one another, delight we could only put into weather-code and breathless enthusiasm.

"You look rather pleased with yourself," she opened when we ran out of meaningless and meaningful inanities.

"Relieved, rather. I got the news today that the harassment suit has been dropped."

"You weren't really worried."

"Well, it could have made things complicated. It made me contemplate early retirement. No more imbecile undergraduate essays to mark. No more inane department meetings. No more supervision of graduate students who undertake useless and arcane research projects that make me read into the night."

"No more graduate students to flirt with." Ouch.

"There's that," I admitted.

"So you saw it coming—the dropped charges? And sent your ambiguous email?"

"I hope it wasn't too ambiguous."

She smiled through all this, her brick red lipstick precise against her pale golden face. She was wearing a very short skirt and crossed her legs provocatively, as if she were wearing so little underwear she knew no one could see it. Which is indeed a possibility. She knows she's beautiful. (I don't think Lila knows how beautiful she is. Hers isn't the sort of beauty that turns heads, except those of the very discriminating. It's a quiet, simple, wise beauty.) Elise is young enough to have a perverse kind of feminism that says if men are going to think with their pricks, she's happy to take advantage of it. Her body is her fortune only because that's the game men play. She should go into politics. She'd end the punishment of political women who don't shelve their sexuality. She'd scratch out the eyes of a reporter or minister who suggested she got where she is by sleeping around or who commented once too often on her appearance. If it didn't mean breaking a fingernail.

"Lila must be relieved. If you retired, she wouldn't have the freedom to do six exquisite concerts a year." Unfortunately, Elise has the politician's typical disdain for culture. It makes her a little crass.

"Six *well-paid* exquisite concerts."

"You loathe *everything*. Except your wife. You never meant to sleep with me. You're like the dog who chases cars. You wouldn't know what to do if you caught one."

"Want to try me?"

"I don't think so. It wouldn't be fair to Jean Claude."

"Jean Claude?"

"My lover. For a little over two years now. Great in bed. Stamina, you know?"

It really is a beautiful lawn.

I'm sick unto death of the loathing I feel. I can hear them behind me, Lila, Kevin, and Stuart, the three thoughtful voices; even though they're entirely new at this, they're making something recognizably beautiful. I can almost hear them thinking as they go, talking to one another with their hands, their musical voices.

Have I always felt such loathing? The academy often gives its imprimatur to cynicism and distrust. On the scale of nasty, inhuman feelings, these fall somewhere between false rigour and misanthropy. Cynicism is intellectually respectable. Who, knowing even the tiniest bit about our world, doesn't find it easy to be cynical? It's one of our critical faculties; our lack of trust in the authorities of the past, our recognition that they were inevitably wrong, compels historians to put the record straight. At the beginning of my career, my scholarship was a conduit for the mild contempt I felt for the world. But my attitude was also a kind of disingenuous masquerade. I wouldn't have married Lila or fathered a child if I felt the contempt, the hopeless cynicism I often pretended I felt. But now it's like a sweater that's too small. I've taken it into the change room where you try on clothes. I can't get my arms out of the sleeves or the neck over my head, and I can't ask a clerk for help.

I can hear that they've finished the final movement—it's obvious by its energy—and I suspect they're packing up, so I turn off the hose and wind it up, preparing to go in. But just as I open the screen door, they're beginning again. Lila, then Stuart, finally Kevin. It is the most beautiful, passionate calm I've ever heard. They're studying one another with engaged concern for the music, studying the way their bodies express the nuances they want the music to articulate. My mother-in-law is sitting on the sofa, her eyes bright with tears, so I sit down next to her and hand her my handkerchief. There's longing that's suddenly fractured, like a windshield you've thrown a rock through, longing broken into little pieces. Then a momentary promise of order and serenity. With barely a break, Stuart begins the second movement, the jaunty scherzo with its calm interlude. Lila has some difficulties with the arpeggios at the end of the scherzo, but shrugs her shoulders and begins the Adagio.

Lila once said that someone called Brahms "the musician of the unsatisfied." What better time than this for thinking about what I love?

Elise was quite right: Lila and her music are one of the few things I don't loathe. I love my daughter. It's a love I almost fear because it's so primal. Do you remember the first time you smelled your child and felt a quick thrill of recognition? I fear that I could hold my little girl in my arms forever, reading a book, rocking her to sleep, protecting her. So I've withdrawn because she's better off without the love so benighted and misanthropic a father can give her. That's clearly worked well. Still, I want her to become independent, self-sufficient, to find her own way in the world. Her own way *with* the world. Yet I didn't know how to teach her integrity, besides forcing her to stand on her own.

I loved my parents, my sister. But they're gone. I loved my work once, the adventure and engagement and discovery it brought me. But that too is gone. At some point it became humdrum. I still love to cook; there are still new tastes to discover, the order and pleasure of the kitchen. But that's hardly a vocation.

All these—Lila, Lindsay, my family, my work—were such simple loves. When did I get hungry for something more? Who would expect our tastes to be satisfied with Gregorian chant or roast chicken? Beautiful in and of themselves, they lack the complexity humans crave—even strive for. Nothing in life is really simple. But as I sit listening to these musicians making something whole and unified out of Brahms's fragmented desperation, as I listen to my wife play with such feeling, with such intuition of the needs and reactions of two other people, I realize how dishonest that is. You take the complex and make it simple in the most important parts of your life. That's where the beauty lies. But it's not what I want, it's not what I want.

I'm so lost in these thoughts that I don't register the end of the fourth movement. I'm brought back from my thoughts by the electricity that has been building in the room as they begin, tentatively, to talk of performance. They've made a decision without making a decision because it's so natural. I turn to Clarice to see how she is. Does she need anything? Would she like a cup of tea? A glass of water? I am hiding, masking myself in the pedestrian. I don't want any of them to talk to me yet. I bring Clarice a glass of cranberry juice just as they are packing up. I can now trust my voice.

"That was remarkable. It would have been a solid performance, but for a first rehearsal as an ensemble, it was . . . Well, I'm lost for words. I was deeply moved."

As Lila cooks dinner, she is understandably preoccupied, humming little snatches to herself and carrying on an inner conversation that's part of being a musician. I make myself useful by getting Clarice upstairs, taking up her light supper, making her comfortable, and then reading the paper out on the back deck. At dinner, though, it's time to talk.

"You're pleased. I can see why."

"These partnerships that simply *happen*. They're impersonal yet . . ." She looked beyond the window to find a word, her pale face glowing with joy. "Passionate. Passionate conversations. They're a miracle."

"I don't want to steal your thunder, but I've also got some good news. The harassment suit has been withdrawn. Clearly they knew I'd sue for inappropriate disciplinary action and decided to let it go."

"I never understood why she did it. After all, she was on her way to U of T and surely the academic world is small enough that it'll get around that she accused her supervisor of sexual harassment. That can't help her career."

I don't interrupt soon enough because at first I don't really understand what Lila is going on about. All this time she hasn't believed me. She believed the harassment suit was proof I've had an affair. "Lila! Stop it! I told you I wasn't . . ."

"It doesn't matter."

"You could call and check my story, if you'll stoop to that."

"It doesn't matter. You're out of the woods. Isn't that what you wanted?"

I think about this a second too long. "What I want is you." I am leaning toward her as I say this. She slaps me sharply. We are both silent. She stands up, takes her plate to the dishwasher, and, without turning around, explains.

"I'm too tired. I'm going to bed. Leave the kitchen. I'll pick up in the morning. But please don't wake me up. Sleep in your study. That's a better idea."

Except it's no explanation at all.

The night twenty-some years ago when Stuart McTaggart took Lila home from that party, when I came home, I'd fully intended to engage in a little conjugal coupling. I didn't think she'd so much as kissed McTaggart gratefully on the cheek, but I guess I wanted to assert my ownership. As I fought the nausea with my head on Lila's shoulder, I found myself smelling her. There was no smell of sex, no hint of a recent shower. What relief I felt. I could simply throw up and go to bed.

Saturday, August 3, 2002

Seventeen

I've never exploded like that. It was unexpected, spontaneous after weeks of control and premeditation. It meant everything and nothing. It meant "I don't believe you and haven't for some time," and it meant "I'm so hurt by your lies." It also meant "I just don't give a fuck any more."

Not wanting him to follow me, not wanting to say another word to him, I grabbed an old Walkman of Lindsay's and retreated to Mother's room. She was asleep, of course, but I was in no mood to talk. I wanted instead to think about the rehearsal, to revel in the music and the magical partnership.

No one ever knows what art's about, what the *Mona Lisa* means or what Tolstoy really wanted to say when he wrote *War and Peace*. It's over thirteen hundred pages long: he obviously wanted to say a lot of things. Music has an added challenge: what the composer wrote down is a guide. Musicians take a key signature, some notes on a staff, some sketchy instructions about tempo—allegro or presto, and suggestions about dynamics—ppp or just pp, and *realize* something the audience hears as music. Yet Glenn Gould's allegro might well be somebody else's presto. The composer's art doesn't fully exist until it's performed, and then it isn't just his vision any more.

So when all this complicated stuff happens as naturally as it did yesterday, and you hear some kind of integral whole emerging, when somehow your collective realization of those minimal instructions creates something for which we only have imprecise words like *vision*, *integrity*, or *unity*, you know that something otherworldly is taking place. Art is always a conversation. Sometimes it's simply between the work and the audience. But musicians must converse with the score and with one another, and there are all kinds of challenges to that conversation.

But when I was listening to a passage in my mind's ear, Rob's voice would break through. Like the postcards my mother's mind sends her, except these were high tech and came with sound. I'd be able to feel the fullness of our sound as a trio, the cello voice coming up through my feet into whatever part of my body—my core, the core that remembers all its pleasures—and I'd hear Rob saying something biting about a colleague who wasn't producing enough scholarship. I'd hear Kevin and Stuart and me talking to one another through the shaping of a phrase we all shared, and then Rob would break in, telling me that his pommes frites were never going to fry up crisply if I didn't julienne the potatoes more finely. One of us would see something new in a motif Brahms brought back to play with again, and the others would begin to try it out for themselves when Rob would begin snarking about an exhibition or a play we'd seen. I could hear the whole we'd almost created and understand what we'd made it of, but that would be interrupted by Rob's raving about the beauty of his latest graduate student.

I'd been using Lindsay's old Walkman as a cover, but I finally gave up and listened to "In Performance," to Eric Friesen talk about Glenn Gould. It was some anniversary, and they'd decided to replay parts of Gould's *Solitude Trilogy*, radio documentaries he put together in the sixties and seventies. They began with "The Idea of North," his first one. Gould's narrator is a surveyor whom Gould chose because he sees space as a language, a philosophy of life. The sound of a train clacking over tracks permeates the whole; we feel trapped in a train car with this fellow who talks about going north as the moral equivalent of war. You have to become truthful with yourself because there's no one to protect you from the lies you tell. In the north, you must—I could see this old geezer in his plaid flannel shirt, his surveyor's tripod thrown over his shoulder—rely on your own built-in sense of direction, develop a gyro-compass of inner direction. You must be ready to travel from the known to the unknown.

Then they gave us a segment from "Quiet in the Land," the last of the trilogy, this one about the Mennonites. Gould had juxtaposed a movement from a Bach cello suite to Janis Joplin singing "Oh, Lord, won't you buy me a Mercedes-Benz" and the personal stories of Mennonites. At first, Gould's montage made me crazy; I couldn't follow the voices. I know his passion for the fugal lines of Bach, but I'm not sure fugues work with words. Following several conversations at once is different from following lines of notes that also make some coherent harmonic sense together. But Friesen had said these documentaries were as close as Gould came to composing, so I kept trying.

And then I began to laugh at myself. Because my brain was sounding like Glenn Gould's documentary tonight. Luckily, they filled up the last twenty minutes with part of Gould's second remarkable recording of *The Goldberg Variations*.

When I heard Rob locking the back door downstairs, I slipped into our bedroom to get my pyjamas, then back to Mother's room, where I washed up. I wasn't going to sleep tonight, not for a long while. Bach or Bruce Lee? I could take *Fist of Fury* and my laptop to bed. Except that I'd spend the entire movie planning my own revenge, which I didn't want to think about right now. So while Rob was in the bathroom, I went downstairs to fetch my copy of *Goldberg* and my copy of Gould's recording. I was going to short-circuit my noisy brain and my wonky gyro-compass by studying.

You find the theme and variations everywhere: in Bach's *Goldberg* of course; everywhere in Brahms, most famously in the "Variations on a Theme by Haydn"; in Elgar's *Enigma Variations*. It's what jazz musicians like Bill Evans do all the time, take the tune as the theme and see how it can be played with, what can be built on it. My mind is composing themes and variations, building stories as cacophonous as Gould's "Quiet in the Land." That would be an ironic title for my thoughts: they weren't quiet at all. The inconsistent variations, in radically different keys, tootled and tweeted.

Variation One: I need some clarity.

"I was deeply moved." What the hell did he think he was doing with that, I wondered at about 2:00 AM. The little echo of our first words together. Part of me says he might well have been deeply moved. Another part says it was blackmail. Sentimental mumbo jumbo. It doesn't matter. What deeply moves him no longer matters to me. He was lying when he said the charges have been dropped. The substance probably isn't a lie. But there's a lie somewhere. Is there some way to check? You want to be sure before you abandon a man who stuck by you through your own bad times and cooked while you practised and attended all your performances and fathered your daughter and made sure your piano was well tuned and maintained. Being so suspicious made me feel guilty. When I feel guilty I want to cut him some slack. Clarity. God, how I'd love some clarity.

Variation Two: I've gained something. I think.

My anger is turning into self-preservation and self-respect. I won't let his voice take over one of my inner twins, forcing me to look through bifocals that distort and darken. I refuse to see the world his way. Perhaps the only clarity I will get, then, is that of my own perspective. Perhaps that's the only clarity any of us ever gets. If so, it's a pretty isolated, self-absorbed, selfish sort of clarity. You can't build a world, a community, a trio, particularly a family on that.

I'll make sure he takes the best of the pots and pans and his favourite cookbooks. There's the extra set of china that he likes more than I do. I'll pack it up for him. He can pack up his own goddamned tools.

This morning, we avoided one another by mutual, wordless agreement. His lies and the slap that rippled out from them hung vibrating in the air, taking up too much space for both of us to fit in a single room. I showered in Mother's room, made breakfast early, and ate it with her. Then I began to get her ready to go out.

"You've got a fairly early doctor's appointment this morning. So we need to get you moving."

"Oh. Of course, dear. I don't feel like a bath this morning. If you'll help me into the bathroom, I can wash my face and do my hair. I'd like to wear . . . let's see. I'd like to wear trousers today. Would that be okay? The raspberry trousers and the flowered blouse? They'd be comfortable anywhere, wouldn't they?"

"Sounds good." I gathered up her clothes while she washed up and then combed and arranged her hair. Then I helped her struggle into her clothes.

My mother's nakedness is oddly comforting. At first, when she needed help getting dressed, she was embarrassed and reluctant, doing as much for herself as possible, hiding her breasts, her pubis. Now, the closeness of death has changed her relationship to her body, to her sexuality, which is simply the remnant of an existence elsewhere—in her eyes and hands and smile and mind. The lesson she needs to teach her daughter is no longer modesty and concealment but a kind of Zen, indifference and openness at the same time. We talk while we do this, but the words don't meant anything—things like "Next." Or "Easy. That's good." It's the music rather than the meaning that matters.

Once she was tidied and dressed, I found Rob in his study and asked him to help me get Mother in the car. He was too hearty about being cooperative, but I ignored that. Once we were loaded and he had waved and turned toward the house, Mother gave me a puzzled look.

"So where are we going? We never go to the doctor's on Saturday."

I threw back my head and laughed. A mad, out-of-control laugh. "You let me bully you and hurry you, all the time knowing I'd made up a story?"

"You sat by my bed last night sighing, sobbing, laughing, groaning in anger. I wouldn't have questioned anything you did this morning, my dear. So what are we really going to do? I'm in pants, so I'm ready for anything."

"How does a drive to the Eastern Townships for lunch sound?"

"Lovely! It's a perfect day for it. Early August—all those village gardens should be in full bloom."

"I wish we could take Lindsay with us, but she'll have plans with Paul."

"I'm not so sure. Something she said to Kevin when you were in the kitchen suggested that Paul had moved out. Gone somewhere for a better job?"

"And she didn't say anything?"

"Maybe she needed to decide how she felt about it before she talked to you."

"I can understand that."

"I'll bet you can. Do you have your cellphone with you?"

"It's in my purse, at your feet."

"Let me call," she said, dialling Lindsay's number. "Hello there, dear. It's your grandmother. I'm out on bail and wanted to invite you for a drive and lunch." Lindsay said something in return; I could almost hear laughter on the other end. "Your mother has decided I need a day's parole and wants to drive to the Eastern Townships. It's a perfect day. Have you been out yet?" Lindsay's response was more sedate. "We were hoping you might be free to go with us." I could hear a quiet surge of excitement. "Your mother's making an illegal U-turn this very minute. We're on our way."

Lindsay was standing on her curb when we arrived. I got out of the car and gave her a hug. It hurt in an unexpected way to hold my daughter. She kissed her gran through the open window and settled herself in the back seat. "I thought it was a perfect day to take your grandmother for a drive, and when I said it was too bad you couldn't join us, she suggested we call anyway. Just on the off chance." My voice was unnaturally bright.

"Awesome. I needed an excuse to avoid studying for my LSATs. It's too perfect to sit inside—or even on the balcony—and read over silly problem questions."

"How's that going?" Mother asked, perhaps to keep me from putting my foot in my mouth.

"It's pretty boring. A couple of the lawyers who are in and out of our offices say once I get through my first year of law school, I'll get hooked. You've got to pay your dues and do the memory work."

"That takes a lot of discipline." There's implicit praise in my mother's voice.

"I'm ready for that. This job is driving me nuts. I'm trapped. There's nowhere to go with it. It's time to move on."

Variation Three: Guilt (of course).

I hadn't heard my daughter sound like this for a long time. If she thought I was doing the wrong thing, would I give adventure a bad name? Guilt over Rob: it comes and it goes.

"You two will have to keep each other company. The drivers are crazy—even for Montreal. I've got to concentrate. Besides, I'm not entirely sure where I'm going."

There were two kinds of music in the car, Mother and Lindsay creating a fugue. There was affectionate grandmother and granddaughter talk, the music of life on the edge of something unknown, each in its different way. A light music, a springlike music on pan pipes, played by the Syrinx, even on this late July day with its full, deep greens, even with death patiently waiting in the shadows. Death quilting or playing Solitaire. Anything to pass the time quietly.

Variation Four: The status quo.

Then there was the darker counterpoint in my own mind. I was *thinking* about the traffic, about the roads, about making the right turn, about getting in the right lane, and making the best time. I didn't want to keep Mother out too long. Under that thought, my feelings jabbered incoherently. I would let thought and feeling argue and cajole, and see what emerged. I knew thought was leaning toward accepting Rob's version, which I was sure I couldn't disprove. He wasn't that careless in his lies, I suspected. Thought argued for continuity, for loyalty, for tradition and ritual.

"Look at those hills. They look like sleeping dinosaurs." We had arrived at Brome Lake. "What does that blue make you want to do?" she asked Lindsay.

"Sleep. Paint. Sing travellin' songs," Lindsay suggested, sounding slightly manic.

"That's a good start. Singing." Mother studied the intense blue for a moment, and I pulled over so she could think about it as long as she'd like. "I think I'd like to . . . to ride an elephant all the way around it, carrying an immense sun umbrella. A turquoise and gold sun umbrella." She looked at me with a whimsical smile on her face. "Thank you for this inspired outing. It's just what I needed." She patted my arm, patted Lindsay's hand, which was on the back of her seat.

It took us a while to get down to the lake and to find someplace wheelchair accessible. We rode on in companionable silence, each of us studying the landscape from her own perspective, twining it with her own thoughts. Each of us, I suspected, would have her own sense of loss and gain, of loneliness and self-respect.

Variation Five: This is all my doing.

I thought, for the thirtieth time that morning, of that slap, and of all that had gone before it in the last weeks. A purposeful disengagement, a distancing, from a man I had once loved made it possible to slap him. I had betrayed love, family, much of my past. I had been forced to do this—I thought—there was the little niggle—*I thought*—in order not to betray myself. Why did I want to believe he'd been unfaithful? Had I fallen out of love with a man who'd become *unpleasant*? Was I willing to break promises over it? Was there any justice in this? I didn't believe he was happy. Justice argued for helping him get back on track.

We finally found a little café where we could easily sit outside under the trees and eat our French Canadian fare: some lovely soup with the vegetables still tiny and crisp, good brie and bread, a raspberry crumble for dessert. We all stayed firmly in the present, each of us suspecting that to push one another outside this moment was to threaten chaos, confessions, wrong choices. When the strong coffee came, Lindsay intently watched the cream swirl in the dark liquid, settled back in her chair, and took the leap.

"It's so sweet of you two to do this. I'm sure you've both got oodles of questions about why I'm alone on a Saturday, but you haven't asked them. I've appreciated that. It's given me some time away from Montreal to think. I'd like to talk now."

"Talk away," my mother said, taking one of Lindsay's hands in two of her own and massaging it comfortingly.

"There's not that much to say. Paul's gone. We'd been having regular rows, these shouting matches about the dumbest things. Whether a racist joke was funny or not. Which movies to see. It was like we wanted to fight. Anything would do. I did it too. But the kicker was that my 'moods' were always the problem."

"It always is, my dear. 'Men don't have moods.'" My mother has resorted to ironic quotes.

Lindsay nodded ruefully. "Every time I said he just expected things to go his way, he called me a bitch. Or a whiner. I couldn't take a joke. I couldn't compromise."

"My granddaughter is not a bitch." Lindsay smiled gratefully at her grandmother.

"Music. That was the big one. He would play this inane stuff at deafening volume. The same words, over and over and over again. Many of them sexist. Most of them pointless and stupid . . ."

"Cock rock," I interjected. Lindsay looked startled.

"Yeah. Cock rock." She winced. "Sorry, Gran. When I asked him to turn it down or listened to my iPod, he'd begin his rant. The words didn't matter, he'd yell at me. There wasn't any *music* to matter, I'd say. Then I was a snob. Snobs don't listen to White Stripes. I was trying to figure out why we were together." Lindsay stared into her coffee cup, taking a moment not to cry. The waitress approached us tentatively, and Lindsay held out her cup for a refill.

"But he's the one who leaves without warning. I don't know if he was testing me or trying to find something he could blame me for. Anyway, he called me the day after he left for a business trip to Quebec City and said he was trying out a new job. If it worked out, he'd be staying there. He couldn't even tell me to my face. His voice was really matter-of-fact, like this was about *a job*. He's driving to Montreal next weekend to load up his stuff. I packed it up over a week ago and moved into the storage area downstairs. I don't intend to be there. I'll leave the key with the super."

"Well done. That's what counts: how you protect yourself." My daughter was taking care of herself. I could wish that she was never hurt, but that seems pointless. So I'll wish she continues to take care of herself.

"So what are you going to do, Mom?" She completely took me by surprise; I thought for a few moments.

"I don't know. I change my mind every two minutes. I tell myself I don't know what your father's done, if anything. I get philosophical and grown-up and simply say we've grown apart. I blame him. Then I blame myself."

"What do you blame yourself for?" I studied my questioning daughter carefully. She gave nothing away.

"For not being woman enough. Sexy enough. Young enough. Beautiful enough. Gifted enough."

"But you're all those things, Mom. Okay, except young. So why we do we do this to ourselves? Paul's behaved like a selfish bastard who avoids any kind of emotional tie or commitment when he can't have his way. So why do we blame ourselves?"

"We're told it's our job as women to keep the selfish bastard in every man under control? It's what women are for."

"Does it explain why we blame ourselves?"

"I think it does. In part. Why do you blame yourself? What have you possibly done wrong except be yourself?"

She pointed at me mockingly. "Oops. You've slipped. You've admitted it. It's our selves that are wrong in some subtle, unspeakable way. Some way we can't see or fix because we can't name it. The bastard's true gift is to make us believe there's something wrong with us we can't see."

"Oh, honey. *s.* Do you need me to say it again? *There's nothing wrong with you.* And your father's never done that to me." Or had he? Why did he make sure I knew he'd gone AWOL in Vancouver a few years ago?

"I know that."

"Your father wants us to stay together."

"I know that too. What do you want?"

"I don't know." The waitress approached and I bought time by paying the bill, searching out exact change, calculating the tip more carefully than I usually do, counting out toonies and loonies. "I don't think it will do either of us any good if we try to our situations the same way. I know that you'd like an explanation for what's happening in your life, and your father makes it tempting to blame men. That does no good. Men are a fact of our lives. If we're attracted to the opposite sex, if we want to be loved, as well as to have all those other things that make a full life—dignity, self-respect, independence, a free mind and a strong ego—we're going to have to deal with men."

"Perfect. I didn't choose Paul 'cause he's like my dad."

"No you didn't." I have to show Lindsay the best side of her father. "He supported my performing, my career, what he saw as my gifts, in so many ways. At some point, Lindsay, the decisions you make are just that: your decisions. Not a reaction to your parents. If you don't make them your own, you don't grow up."

My mother had taken Lindsay's hand between her own to get her granddaughter's attention. "My dear. Let me ask this. If Paul hadn't left, do you think you would have called it quits?"

"I think I was on my way to deciding that. I guess I'd have liked to make the decision, rather than having it made for me. I'd have liked a conversation. Though with Paul that wasn't possible."

"Why don't you pretend you did? You talked back, Lindsay: that's taking charge. Maybe neither of you could have said what wasn't right. If he hadn't buggered off, you'd have asked him to go."

"Grandma, that's making up a story!"

"So? We do it all the time. We misremember events. The 'saving fiction,' some writer called it. Your grandfather did it. It saved him from feeling poor and helpless. That allowed him to be kinder to others—a little, anyway. Why don't you be kind to yourself? If time didn't exist—and some days I think time doesn't—if Paul hadn't beaten you to the punch, you'd be the one starting a new life instead of mourning an old one. Give that to yourself as a gift. You've made a start at it by packing up his things. What else are you going to do for yourself?"

"My LSATs. He thought law school was ridiculous. That I'd never get in."

"Study your little tush off and prove him wrong, then, my dear. I'm going to have your mother transfer some of my savings into your account on Monday. Enough for you to live on for a while. Take it to buy yourself some leisure. Go for a trip—somewhere you know Paul would never like to go. Paris? That doesn't sound like his kind of place. Take time off from that appalling job. Get into law school next fall."

I could hear the tiredness in my mother's voice and started to get organized to leave. As we slowly made our way back to the car, Lindsay stopped our caravan (without elephants and turquoise sun umbrellas, unfortunately) to hug her grandmother and bury her face in her grandmother's hair. Once we were in the car, we all quieted down. My mother was exuberant and exhausted, elated at having done just the right thing for her granddaughter, and tired from a day much more active than she was used to.

We settled into that companionable quiet that's part of a lovely afternoon's drive and that gives everyone a warm space to think in. The changing light, the curving road, the dappled shadows that would suddenly open into a clearing cradled all our moods. Mother slept, so Lindsay and I were quiet. In the rear-view mirror, I could see Lindsay studying the roadside, the expression on her face sometimes numb, as if she too were exhausted from living with the vertigo you feel when you stand on the edge of a relationship's abyss. Then a tiny smile would flicker.

I had no sense of what I felt. I tried to quiet my own mind by thinking of all the songs I could remember that referred to roller coasters or merry-go-rounds or mulberry trees—occupying my mind with images of orbits. But other kinds of sound would come bursting in. Unlike Lindsay and Paul, Rob and I haven't fought. Forget infidelity. I can't prove anything.

As we entered the magnetic field of Montreal, I envied Lindsay with her pared-down apartment, with the decision—the best decision for her, I felt—already made.

I was off the expressway and onto Sherbrooke, and as the traffic became more muddled—honking, querulous, defiant, breaking as many rules as possible—I felt a sudden clarity. I still didn't have any proof. But this was not about evidence. Nor was it about infidelity. It was about wanting a different kind of partnership: a conversation. Kevin and Stuart and I could talk without words, but Rob and I couldn't talk at all. There were too many lies, too many different keys.

This was also about wanting to be alone. I thought of the naked woman in the locker room, striding off somewhere with nothing but a towel over her shoulder, maybe a gym bag with a swimsuit, T-shirt, and pair of jeans in her locker. This was not about evidence or infidelity; it was about what I wanted. To be alone in the room while I took off my clothes and took the time to study myself. It would be frightening. I would look for the flaws that he'd obviously found. But perhaps I could also see myself striding away from the mirror.

Saturday, August 3, 2002

Lila

Eighteen

"Where have you been?" When I came in Rob was slumped in a living room chair, but he leapt out of it like a bolt. "Are you all right? Is Clarice all right?" He slammed a glass with chips of ice and a thimbleful of Scotch down on the coffee table.

"Sorry. I should have called. Mom and Lindsay and I drove out to the Eastern Townships for lunch."

"You did *what*? I thought this was a half-hour doctor appointment, and I've been worried sick."

"I thought you'd figure out it was Saturday, and that going to the doctor had been a smoke screen. Look, let's talk about this later. Can you help me get Mother in? Are you okay to do that?" After the first few steps, he was steady enough, though his shoulder caught on the side of the screen door.

"I hear you've had an adventure. You must be half dead with tiredness," he said with fake heartiness. He opened the door, scooped her up, tipped his head to indicate I should get the door to the house, and then carried her on upstairs.

"I'm heating some soup," I called from the kitchen. By the time I got upstairs, Rob had Mother on the edge of the bed, her shoes and socks off. He had given her a warm washcloth to wipe her face and hands.

Mother was explaining our trip to him. "Lindsay's been a bit sad lately. Paul's buggered off for a job in Hull. No discussion, no reasons. We thought she needed a treat."

Rob smirked at Mother's frank language. Then with the suddenness of someone slightly drunk, he shifted his focus. "How is she?"

“A bit mournful. Naturally.” Mother looked at me slyly.

“I’ll go call her. You two will be all right now?”

I settled Mother into a chair where she ate her bread and soup, then undressed her for bed, washing her face and neck and hands where she sat. In the distance we could hear Rob talking to Lindsay in a paternal voice while I turned back her covers and organized her pills. I couldn’t remember the last time they had such a long conversation. There was silence, and then he appeared in the doorway.

“I’ll get us some dinner, shall I?” He looked enquiringly at me while I helped Mother into bed.

“Sure. I’ll be down in a minute to help.” The last thing I wanted was to work with Rob in the kitchen, so when I went downstairs I checked to see what he had pulled out to cook, saw it was chicken, and poured myself a glass of white wine from a bottle in the fridge. I held up the kitchen doorway.

“How was Lindsay?”

“Unexpectedly chipper. She tells me Clarice is going to give her some money so she can travel and study. That’s wonderful.”

“Do you feel vindicated?”

“Vindicated?” Rice was summering on the stove. Rob was chopping vegetables and fresh ginger for a stir fry.

“You never liked Paul.”

“I suppose I didn’t. Have I ever liked any of Lindsay’s boyfriends? Does any father?”

“Some aren’t quite so obvious about their dislike.”

Rob sneered. “Like yours, I suppose.”

“No. I was smart and never gave Dad a chance until I found you. I knew he’d like you. I never knew how I felt about that. Whether or not it was in your favour.” We might as well start at the beginning.

Again, there was that sudden shift in mood. Rob wiped his hands deliberately on the kitchen towel and came toward me, his head on one side, a flirtatious smile on his face. He put his hand high against the door frame and leaned toward me. I backed off and sat down.

“I don’t think I’m in that kind of mood tonight.” Thwarted, he turned on his heel and went back to chopping vegetables.

"Dinner will be ready in about ten minutes."

"Thanks. I think I'll go have a look at the newspaper. Would you like me to set the table first?"

"Sure. We'll just need sticks and bowls."

By the time dinner was ready, I had skimmed the news desperately for dinner-table conversation, though I was pretty sure I'd fail a pop quiz for accuracy. Verne Troyer, who played Mini-Me in *Austin Powers in Goldmember* (I don't think Rob cares about little people) was popular with the ladies. Hormone therapy was falling out of favour. (Oh dear.) Pond turtles in Santa Monica were under threat, but residents of the area could save them by animal-proofing their garbage to keep away predators and by not dumping exotic turtles in the same habitat when the family got bored with them. Five hundred Hutu rebel soldiers had been killed and a bus in Israel had been bombed by Palestinian terrorists. Only this last would really grab his interest. Turtles and terrorists: we live in both those worlds.

Dinner over, Rob put his elbows on the table, propped his chin on his woven fingers, and looked at me directly for the first time during the meal.

"So what's up?"

"I think I'd like a divorce. But we can call it a trial separation if you prefer."

"Jesus, Lila. I've just been cleared."

"Exactly. I don't need to protect you any longer."

"Protect me? Is that what you've been doing? I thought you were being my wife. You've been *protecting* me? I've been cleared. Which suggests I didn't do anything wrong."

"'Suggests.' It's funny, Rob. You can't quite lie. I think I've known for years that there were—what should we call them? Lapses? Lapses in your fidelity. In any event, it no longer matters. But the calculating—weighing every word we said to one another—made me see something. We haven't talked—not really—in quite a long time."

"In my shoes, you wouldn't have been careful about what you said and did?"

"But Rob, you could turn on the charm and concern with such ease when I figured out something was up. What does that say about the months and months when we were simply roommates? You knew perfectly well what was missing, and you conjured it up when I got suspicious."

"As if you haven't sometimes measured out your affection in eight-bar phrases. When *you* were preoccupied. *I've* been preoccupied. Look, we've been married twenty-five years. Aren't there going to be times when there isn't much romance?"

"This isn't about romance. Or at least not ours. It's about unfaithfulness that was public enough to humiliate me. You can't have been unaware of the gossip. You think too much about how the world sees you to be that naive. What would they say about you? 'He's sixty and can't get enough of it.' Did you ever think what was being said about me? 'Ah yes, menopause. She's gone frigid so he's getting it elsewhere.' You've humiliated me for the last time." Why was everything I said only half true?

"When have I ever humiliated you?"

"When you sent me out in public to do the grocery shopping with a baby and a bruise on my face."

"That was years ago! I never thought you'd hold a grudge that long."

"Fear does a good job of keeping grudges alive and well."

"Fear! What on earth have you had to fear?" He slammed his hand on the table.

"That. The fact that you hate the world so much. That you're so angry. When was I going to be the target again? When would you be unfaithful again because that anger and hatred demanded beautiful young flesh to . . . to. I don't know what." Then there was a flash of insight. "You've become like Bluebeard. An existential Bluebeard. Your bitterness has given you an enormous appetite. You chew up colleagues and undergraduates and they taste bitter. Bitter. Then you need to go fuck the nearest beautiful graduate student to get the taste out of your mouth. How many have there been?"

The look on his face said I was going to get what I deserved. "Half a dozen, give or take. Do you know when it began?" He got up out of his chair and started to come around the table. "Do you want to know when it began?" he shouted, pounding the table as he walked around it, as if to say, You've started this. You are going to see it through. "After Lindsay was born. That sick, stupid, gaping look on your face as you nursed. We couldn't make love. And then you didn't want to. 'My breasts hurt. What if she wakes up? I'm so tired.'" He mimicked an ugly whine.

"You're lying. We fucked our brains out after Lindsay was born. You loved the taste of breast milk. How many other lies are there?"

Rob smiled superciliously. "You'll never know. On the other hand, I'd like to know whether this is about a failure of communication or garden-variety jealousy. Or the fact that I haven't been romantic enough for you lately. You've given rather a lot of excuses."

"Fuck excuses. It's all true. Every one of them is true. There's nothing you can fix."

"No. That's not good enough. If you're going to end this marriage, I want to know why. You owe me that much."

"I owe *you*?"

That was a mistake. He was around the table in an instant. He grabbed my wrists and pulled me to my feet. "Yes, you owe me. You owe me for the hours of listening to scales and exercises. For listening to students playing Beethoven *Bagatelles*. Literally and figuratively. You owe me for being frigid when you were rehearsing for an important recital. God, you owe me for so much," he snarled in my face.

There was a crashing on the stairway, the sound of breaking glass and wood, and then an ominous thump-thump. Rob let go of me and we ran toward the staircase to see a picture frame at the bottom, broken glass all the way downstairs, and Mother sitting on the third stair from the top looking dazed.

"Are you all right?" I spoke first.

She shook her head. "You're not going to hurt my daughter again," she said, shaking her finger at Rob.

"No. You're right. I'm not." Rob was up the stairs in an instant. "Did you fall? Have you hit your head? Does anything hurt?"

"Slow down, please, Rob. Are you all right, Mother?"

"Yes, I think so. I think I slid a step or two, but I didn't hit my head. My fanny hurts though." She tried to move and cried out.

"Don't move. Lila, you come up here and sit next to her. Hold her steady. I'll call 911 for an ambulance and pick up the glass so they can get to her. I don't think we should mess around with this. Do you?"

I shook my head and obediently mounted the stairs. I heard Rob in a shaken but authoritative voice talking to the emergency dispatcher while I sat with my arm around Mother, her head on my shoulder, her breathing near sleep while Rob paced back and forth outside the front door. The ambulance arrived quickly. They swarmed into the stairway, gently checking for broken bones. At first glance, there didn't seem to be any, but we all thought she should have X-rays. So they eased her on to a stretcher and into an ambulance, allowing me to come with her. Rob growled that he'd follow us shortly. He needed to feed the cat.

I was waiting in X-ray when he arrived with a sweater for me and a small bag packed for mother. He handed me the sweater.

"They always keep hospitals too cold. I've brought your mother's heavy dressing gown and some of her toiletries." He took my hand and squeezed it. I was too lifeless to squeeze back. Then one of the dozens of white-gowned specialists—who knew whether he was a doctor or an X-ray technician—came towards us.

"Are you Clarice Jameson's daughter?"

I nodded mutely, and he stood in front of the two of us, making eye contact with Rob, but facing in my direction. Clearly, he thought he should be talking to me but that Rob would be the one to take in the information. Or he was a sexist asshole.

"We think she'll be fine. There's no hip fracture, which is what we would have worried about. I'd like to keep her for observation in case she hit her head and doesn't remember." I nodded. "We've done some blood tests. We always do, to see if we can figure out why someone has fallen. Hers don't look good."

"Stage IV cancer. We're not sure what kind."

"I'd assumed you knew. But needed to ask anyway, just in case. She has an oncologist?"

"Dr. Patel."

"Okay. I should probably let him know she's here."

"Wait until morning. This isn't the cancer. We were . . . Rob and I were . . ." I glanced at the grim but handsome man sitting next to me.

"Yes. She's worried about you. Would you like to go see her? Keep it short. They've taken her up to the geriatric ward. 6C."

As I stood up, Rob took the sweater from over my arm and draped it over my shoulder.

"You're shivering."

"They keep hospitals too cold."

"And you're frightened."

Driving home was awkwardly silent. To break the silence, I started talking logistics.

"I would leave—I know the house is really yours—except for Mother. I simply can't move her into an apartment now. When she's gone, I'll move out then and you can have the house."

"You can't practise in an apartment. And now is not the time to talk about this."

"When is it going to be the right time? I'll practise at the music school."

"Where will you keep your instrument? You can't practise *well* on a practice-room piano. Lila, give this a day or two. I'll sleep in my study and give you some space. You'll spend most of your time at the hospital for the next couple of days anyway. Then let's sort this out rationally. No crashing and banging. Of any kind."

"It's *your* instrument." Like everything else in my life. "Unlike you, I'm not going to pretend there's anything at all rational about what I'm feeling."

By this time we were in the house, and Rob was pouring us both a drink. Oddly, the rituals held, though instead of sitting together on the sofa we sat at either end of the marshmallow, across from the empty fireplace. Rob's hands were shaking; I could tell by the jingle of ice in his glass of Scotch. The nearly empty bottle was on the table beside his chair. We were in for a long night, I suspected.

"Look, I didn't mean to hurt you when I talked about other women. And there's only been the one affair, quite some time ago and very brief. I suppose every man says an affair doesn't mean anything, that it's just sex. But it's true."

"Oddly enough, I believe that. God, I must be mad. But tonight for example. You with Mother. Thinking to bring me a sweater. I know you care. But that doesn't erase your infidelity. Or excuse it. 'He meant well' is not a rousing endorsement."

"But there's only been the one. I haven't seen her for years."

"What about the time you disappeared after the conference at UBC?"

"Okay. Twice."

"Shit, Rob. How can I believe . . . And *that* time you *wanted* me to know, or you'd have been more subtle."

"Damn it, I will not take all the responsibility for this. Why didn't you call me on it? Why didn't you care enough to read me the riot act then? Or the other times when I'd croon on and on about a graduate student I might or might not have been screwing?"

"Because I was frightened. Because my father taught me not to ask questions."

"You didn't ask because you bloody well didn't care. You live in this ecstatic world of music, and a lot of the time what goes on around you doesn't matter."

"You envy me, don't you? You chose political history—how long ago? And it's gone sour. What has made you so bitter? Don't tell me it's knowledge. That 'knowledge naturally makes us all cynics' is a cynic's excuse for bitterness. I know people who experienced the brutality of the world first-hand, and their mouths aren't filled with ashes."

"The world is fucked. You can't pretend it isn't."

"I can pretend that a fucked world can't control the way I live. You're a bully, Rob. Nice one minute, lovely and thoughtful. Bringing warm wash cloths and warm robes. The next minute your angry fist is raised in the air. We all think if we do just the right things we can please you, because you can be so kind. But I can't do it any longer. I can't figure out how to placate you. How to keep your voice down. How to keep you from going downstairs and pounding out mortise and tenon joints. Tomorrow when I'm visiting Mother, I'd like you to take whatever you need for the next couple of weeks and find someplace. Maybe Elise will take you in while you look for a flat."

"Maybe she will. Can we call it a trial separation?" I couldn't read the look on his face, whether it was pleasure in having permission to give in to desire or to lust, or whether there was pain there as well. I wondered what Elise would think when he called and invited himself for a sleepover.

"Jesus! You're going to move in with your sweet young ass and call it a trial separation? Whatever. Just don't be here when I get back from the hospital." I lifted myself out of the chair with both arms. "I'm exhausted. I'm going to bed." I took my glass to the kitchen, and when I came back around to the stairway, he was standing there.

"Can I hold you for a while? A tribute to the past?"

"Sure. If you're willing to listen to me cry."

"I am. I am."

Sunday, August 4, 2002

Nineteen

We've come to that part of August where some of the early perennials start to give up. The bleeding hearts have turned yellow at the base and drooped down onto the Jacob's ladder in front of them. Perennials have a life cycle of their own, and even attentive watering won't stave it off. But I'm trying to keep the boxes looking as if it were early summer—deadheading, watering, weeding. The pansies and petunias, nicotiana and licorice plant don't seem to care what time of year it is. Filling the watering can is my last act of discipline and delight for today. It has been a day of discipline.

Before I left Mother last night, she asked if I was going to be okay.

"I suspect you've accomplished exactly what you set out to do. Your fall was a kind of circuit breaker. Rob's himself again. He packed your bag, and even remembered your heavy dressing gown because hospitals are so cold."

"He has his virtues. Don't come in tomorrow morning. There'll be hospital business to attend to and probably more tests. Stay home and practise. Get your Brahms ready. When you do come in, bring a book. I'm so tired these days."

"The doctor says you've been faking it. How on earth did you manage today?"

"You didn't really notice how much I've been sleeping because I lied about trying to avoid Rob. Riding in a car isn't hard work. Nor is time with you and Lindsay. It was magic. I didn't know it, but it was the one thing I wanted to do before I died: spend time with my girls."

"Sheer willpower, eh?"

"Sheer delight."

I rose before Rob, and showered in Mother's bathroom, then went to the music room. As soon as I heard Rob up and about, I started to practise. He merely put his head in the door as he was about to leave. I'm not sure we even said words—I think we merely exchanged sounds of acknowledgment. I warmed up with Brahms's "Rain Sonata", which Kevin and I know backward and forward. Then I worked hard on the trio. The very opening bars filled me with calm hope. The first movement, the Adagio, is almost twice as long as any of the other movements, so I decided to work only on it this morning. It would give me focus. In order to practise effectively, I had to hear the other voices in my head, which turned out to be a good exercise in getting out of my own. At about eleven, I packed myself a lunch of fruit and cottage cheese and set off for the hospital.

Hospitals have parallel moods, like layers of water in a stream-fed lake. There's the warm, purposeful calm of convalescence, the routines of bathing, checking vitals, dispensing medication, and being discharged. There's the colder current of panic and emergency you can hear in the ominous beep of equipment. There's also the resignation and despair of death—in the tiny chapel with its tea lights, in stoic families huddled near doors, in quiet weeping. And then there are the patients who lie dormant under their flannel blankets and wait, patients who are so absent they don't exude a mood. Their rooms are tidy—no plants or teddy bears—as if they are trying to take up as little space as possible.

Mother was asleep when I arrived at eleven-thirty, so I settled down by the window in her room to read my book—a Peter Robinson mystery, *Aftermath*. The beginning was horrific: a madman murdering a policeman with a machete, two beautiful young women sexually assaulted and then murdered, their bodies decaying in a dark basement, children kept naked in the dark. This was probably not a smart choice. I looked around for magazines but found none. Mother was startled awake when her meal came at about twelve-thirty, but smiled when she saw me.

"Did you sleep okay?"

"Off and on. Okay for a hospital. I don't know what I'd have done in the middle of the night without the male nurse who simply popped his head in and asked if I was okay. He must have been telepathic. He brought me something to help me sleep. But of course then this morning's been a bit slow. It doesn't matter. I'm here until I go, so I might as well relax. How are *you*?"

"I'm fine. I've made some important decisions. Rob is moving some things out while I'm here, and he'll be looking for an apartment. We're going to try separation. See if we can't figure out what we each want. And need." While I said this, I looked at my hands in my lap.

"I'm sure you know best, my dear." She lifted herself a bit off the bed so she could pat my hands. That seems her solution to everything these days: pat, pat.

"What were you thinking, trying to come downstairs last night? You could have killed yourself."

"If I had, it would have stopped him, wouldn't it? My life is ending soon, so keeping my daughter from being beaten doesn't seem such a bad thing to do with it."

"He wouldn't have beaten me."

"Wouldn't he? I'd heard the two of you, and I heard him get up and move toward you, striking the table. Your father was such a sly fox: he was upon you before you knew what hit you. But Rob is a bit more premeditated. He enjoys the warm-up."

"Mother, I think your illness is making you exaggerate."

"Don't lie to me. Don't lie to yourself." She turned her head away from me. "I'm tired. You read for a while," she said, pointing to the book in my lap.

I did as I was told. Or at least I seemed to be reading, straining words through my mind one at a time and turning pages. It was a relief to be unable to concentrate. Mother was clearly not sleeping, so I suddenly burst out, "What do you think you're doing, judging me? You have no idea what I've had to work with in this marriage or what I've tried to do with it. I wouldn't have let him . . ."

"Yes, you would. You love him. Sometimes you still find yourself attracted to him. So you'd have pretended something—a different kind of saving fiction." She sat up quickly to stretch forward and take my hands. "What I'm trying to do, really, is wish you well on your way.

Look, let's make this a Jameson women project. All three of us need to reinvent ourselves. And I should be the leader because, you see, if I don't, I'm going to feel it's been a tremendous waste." I had never seen her so angry.

"Yes, yes," I murmured, getting up and trying to get her to lie back down in bed. I stroked her forehead. "I think you've already done what you need to do. You're teaching Lindsay and me when saving fictions are useful and when they're destructive. I think you'll find us quick studies. You'll have done something quite important."

"For *me*. I want to do something for *me*," she cried, clutching my wrist.

"Like what? What did you have in mind?" I asked, trying to keep my voice light.

"I want to say no."

"To . . . ?"

"To death. To your father. To Rob. To having my last days stolen with this exhaustion." I looked at her face, which was grey with tiredness and with the strangeness of her feelings.

"Hush. Hush. None of us gets to say no to death. But you've already said it to my father by becoming someone remarkable after he died. You said it to Rob last night. We'll see what we can do about the exhaustion. Perhaps it's time for some vitamin B shots. Did you get a bath this morning?"

"What do you think? This is a hospital. They have sick people to take care of."

"Why don't I give you a bath? Massage your back and legs and feet. You don't even need to stay awake—drift wherever you'd like."

She had drawn herself up and buried her head in my stomach and was crying. She was never like this, even after the beatings. Now I had to love her and stay calm. I would take care of my own feelings of anger and helplessness and grief later.

Suddenly it seemed as if she was laughing. She pulled herself away slightly and said, "The nurse told me the naughtiest joke this morning. 'You can only change men if they're in diapers!'" She snorted. I hooted. Through the tears, she snuffled and hiccoughed with laughter.

"I'll get a basin with some warm water, and we'll give you a bath. The one good thing about hospitals is the great body lotion. I'll goop you up afterward and swaddle you in flannel blankets." As I found the rhythm of soaping her, then rinsing her off, I had the sense that what I was doing was both mundane and profound, and that, more wonderfully yet, it had nothing to do with self-pity and confusion and elation. It is just what people have always done for one another. I thought of the calm opening of Brahms; it's also what art tries to do sometimes, bathe the soul with its hard-earned wisdom the way a daughter tries to bathe her dying mother. What was there to mourn? I was bathing my mother, who smiled as I rubbed in the lotion, working tired but unstretched muscles, giving special attention to her feet and the small of her back. By the time I was finished, she seemed to have drifted down into the pleasures of sleep. I put my feet up on the lower frame of her bed and drifted off myself until dinner came. I prodded her to eat a little more than she would have, and then she ordered me to leave.

The house was eerily quiet. Rob's missing suitcases and clothes and toiletries, the newspaper and books he had taken with him, created a silent vacuum. I'd been alone in the house when he made trips to see his parents or do research. But this was different. It was my silence, and I moved in it purposefully, making a salad to go with the tail end of a baguette that Rob would have pronounced inedible but was quite nice toasted with goat's cheese and red pepper. Then I came out here to water.

The silence tonight is also different. The cloudy, humid weather—though I don't think any rain is in the offing—mutes the street noise. But it's also quiet simply because it's Sunday night. People who have come back from the cottage have unloaded the cars and their cranky kids, planted those kids in front of the TV while they rush and struggle to bring post-cottage, Monday-morning order to their lives. Those who stayed home this weekend are luxuriously snuggled into their couches reading or watching TV. They've painted the trim on the house, mowed the lawn, moved a new piece of furniture into the family room and put the old one out on the curb. Now women somewhere are making tomorrow's lunches and finishing up the laundry. Even the birds are quiet; they're celebrating neither sunshine nor rain. The air is almost still, though occasionally leaves fold against one another like butterfly's wings. It too is waiting for something.

For the first time in months, I am not waiting. In spite of the almost oppressive stillness and the dusk, I feel as if something is freshening: as if the air contains some dryness or tang or light that is threading its way around me like the stylized clouds in a Japanese landscape. At the simplest level, I am not waiting for Mother to call me for help or company. But more importantly, I am not waiting for proof that will allow me to make a decision, having decided that proof justifies nothing, excuses nothing. I will be glad to have Mother home, but this hiatus is not unwelcome. It will allow me to get used to being naked in the world again, without the clothing of a wedding ring, a married name, or a handsome husband.

Wednesday, August 21, 2002

Rob

Twenty

I hate assembling pre-fab furniture. Particularly bookshelves, though these are IKEA, so the hardware is clever. Still, once I've got the outer shell together, I've got to nail on bloody particle board with tiny little nails and try not to split the crappy wood. There's no alternative to pre-fab, I keep telling myself. Lila has given me quite a lot of stuff: the dishes I liked, my favourite pans and knives, towels and sheets that are suitably masculine. She also insisted I take the new leather furniture, though it's a bit out of scale in my apartment. But bookshelves were a problem. Most of the ones we had were assembled in situ, so moving them out isn't an option.

We've been civilized about the whole process. As far as I can tell, she hasn't told Lindsay that she suspects me of serial unfaithfulness; in any event, I don't notice any coolness. Instead, my daughter and I seem to be making a bond out of the fact that we've both been deserted—though neither of us says that, of course. I don't say it about her because it would be too hurtful. She's sticking to Clarice's fiction of starting life on her own terms. Of course I don't present myself as someone who's been deserted, because that brings up the issue of fault. I don't want to go there. It's still too puzzling. I know the infidelity came home to roost, and that's fair enough. But I guess I expected a last chance, not summary dismissal. Suddenly, though, I'm transformed into this ogre who's impossible to live with. Who was I the week before?

My last night at home, I told her about Claire, and about how Claire's death had made me distrust so much of the world. It was a vintage Lila moment. The new Lila, that is. She was all sympathy. First, with Claire. Then with me for not being able to stop her death.

She couldn't imagine how much grief I must feel; she could imagine how it would make one distrust every law of the universe. But then this was more proof of "our problem." Why hadn't I talked about this twenty-seven years ago? How could she possibly know when mistrust and grief would overwhelm me, when she should have simply taken me in her arms and recited everything that's beautiful about our lives? We all need someone to do this for us, she argued. But I'd cheated us by not letting her know it was needed. I pled for sympathy and got criticism.

The two weeks with Elise before I moved into this apartment were an education. Why is it so easy to love something beautiful? To wake up and see her face across the pillows was enthralling. (To be permitted to do so—forced into it, as a matter of fact—it was Elise or a hotel—added a layer of mixed feelings I tried valiantly to ignore.) I could have spent the day looking at her sleepy face and mussed-up golden hair. I could have spent hours stroking the hollows I loved. I might even have been able, with a little help from Viagra (love the sex, hate the side-effects), to make love most of the day. But that's not what Elise wanted. The activity was relentless. We breakfasted out on cold croissants and ersatz cappuccino because she thought it romantic to eat breakfast with her lover in a sidewalk café. Then we'd drive out of town someplace "romantic," like the Eastern Townships where Lila took Clarice the day she kicked me out. Elise doesn't know the history behind that, so she doesn't realize how much salt she's rubbing in my wounds. We'd go in her racy little yellow sports car; she finds my Volvo too staid. But being driven around by a careless young driver, no matter how beautiful she is, has its limits. It's hard on the heart, to be brutally frank. Then we often dined out—I could have cooked better food—but again, I felt she wanted to be "seen" with a handsome older man. This public airing of our fling began to wear. I felt like an appendage, a department of her ego. It seemed as if she noticed other people looking at her more than she noticed me. And then I'd look across the sauce-spotted tablecloth and the crumpled paper napkins (Lila preferred cloth) and I'd see this beautiful young woman with sharp and cunning eyes looking at me with desire, and nothing would matter—not her daring driving, not the indifferent food, not the constant activity. I couldn't help admire her self-interest, her self-absorption, the way one admires the adaptive behaviour of an animal perfectly suited to its environment: the tiger's smiling teeth, its pouncing spring, its confident pride. Evenings were candle-lit indulgences—long baths together, passionate and languid and self-absorbed sex. I didn't do any work. I didn't think about my research or my classes or my colleagues. In essence, I vacationed for a couple of weeks. I'd become frustrated by my latest project on Hausmann because I could only get so far given my theoretical framework. I knew I had to read Foucault but didn't have the energy or the curiosity.

And then department politics had heated up. Academic departments are relentlessly self-reflective these days, mostly because administrators compel them to be and then ignore the results. So their self-examination has this curiously ambivalent quality. It's like being too fat but wanting to gaze at your navel anyway. They resist and resist, but once inertia has been overcome, they go at it with gusto. So we're re-evaluating our curriculum, trying to bring it into the twenty-first century, and that of course brings out the tensions between the old fogies and the young farts. Naturally, I don't fall into either camp, which puts me at odds with everybody. So my little vacation with Elise was nicely timed. I dropped out of everything; I didn't go into my office to work on my article or simply read. I stopped going to department meetings.

What an enormous relief it was. It was like being lifted from among the skyscrapers of downtown Montreal and set down in the middle of the Saskatchewan prairies, seeing the land fall away beneath you for miles and miles, golden in the haze. I felt as if I was getting a clear view of my life for the first time in a long while. I'd been plucked from loathing and obedient boredom into adventure and disobedience. For the first week and a half, I was extraordinarily grateful to Elise for precipitating this break with the painful and the mundane frustrations of academic life. And then I'd be in the middle of mad, passionate lovemaking, revelling in Elise's beautiful body, entering her from behind (something Lila's never enjoyed) and studying the rise of her ass and the hollow at the base of her spine and I'd think of something I really needed to do or say. A comment to a colleague over curriculum reform. A book I needed to read that held the secret to my struggles with Hausmann. An archive I really should consult. Or I'd want to know how Lila and her mother were doing, but knew I really couldn't call. I was almost proud of my staying power, in spite of digressions.

The last half-week, I realized how grateful I was that circumstances were going to take over. I had known this affair had natural limits: Elise would be leaving for Toronto, so I had found myself a rather nice apartment—too nice for students to afford—across from Parc Mont-Royal, close to my office and libraries. At first, it felt as if I was stupidly making my world smaller. But I began to realize I *missed* the world of ideas, its continual change, and that this relationship, completely physical as it was, was doomed by her age and by mine. I found the continual activity mindless; she's starting a PHD in a matter of weeks, she's smart, but there's absolutely nothing profound about her. I was reminded of a beautiful woman in one of P.D. James's Cordelia Gray mysteries. The male character smitten with Isabella, who's left him, says he could sit at her feet for days, expecting her beauty to give rise to profound insights about life. But all she could talk about was clothes.

So I'm back to that earlier question: why is it so easy to love something beautiful? And what kind of beauty is it I love? She and I created a bubble world that other people gazed into enviously. We looked the perfect romantic couple: we held hands, we kissed publicly, we stared silently at each other. Viewers, especially men no longer young, would have felt an additional frisson, insofar as we mimed their desires. What they could not have realized was that, toward the end, that romantic staring meant we had nothing to say to each other. Elise didn't mind, as long as the sex and the meals and the handholding and the PDA's, as she called it, continued. I don't think conversation was part of her seductive repertoire. I minded, but with that smile you use to politely bite off a yawn.

So that last half-week was painful and boring and grief-stricken for me. But I was silent with it. If I had gained any understanding from Lila, it was that there was no point berating Elise for not being something she'd never promised to be. One night at the end of the first week, we had the closest thing to a contretemps we've had. We were in her huge bathroom—a chapel to the body perfect if ever there was one. But it's not the pristine chapel of hotel rooms. Bottles and jars and tubes were everywhere, many of them half open and dripping their contents on the marble countertop so it looked like a child was getting ready to fingerpaint. She was brushing her teeth, something she does with gusto, as if allowing toothpaste suds to drip down her chin proved she was thorough, and some expression of disgust must have crossed my face. "What?" she asked through the bubbles of toothpaste. "Sorry?" I queried in return, as if I was unaware of what she'd seen. But I'd fantasized sweeping everything from the counter into the wastepaper basket and then had been overwhelmed with memories of cleaning out Claire's apartment in the aftermath of her suicide.

After my sister killed herself, my family conspired to deny the relentlessness of events. We sorted through her apartment, packed up mementoes, and called the Salvation Army to take the rest; we made funeral arrangements, wrote a matter-of-fact obituary; we rifled through her personal phone book and made sure everyone was invited to the funeral; we ordered flowers. Ridiculous, massive amounts of flowers. My mother kept saying she didn't think the funeral was going to be beautiful enough for Claire. She and the organist nearly came to blows because Mother kept changing her mind about the music. She worried about beauty. We never spoke of the ugliness of Claire's need to kill herself. If my parents ever asked themselves what they did wrong when they brought up a young woman who chose to end her life rather than face the reality of pregnancy and cruel human nature, they never let me hear about it. I'm not even sure they knew she was pregnant. I didn't tell them.

We grieved, but we asked no questions. One of the ways my parents accomplished this was to leave me to deal with the more personal cleanup. Mother could sort through Claire's mail and bills. Father could organize people to take away the furniture and the clothes in Claire's closet. But I was given the task of cleaning out her bathroom. Mostly, I didn't hesitate, but simply swept everything off the counter, tipped everything out of the medicine cabinet into her wastebasket. I didn't stop to consider usefulness or economy. Half a bottle of

Aspirin, half a tube of toothpaste weren't going to make a difference to anybody. I was, as behooves a grieving younger brother, sternly unemotional.

Two things broke my resolve. Among the ointments and bandages in her vanity drawer, there was a clear plastic compact of blush. By Elise's standards, even by the standards of my twenty-first-century wife who is austere if particular about makeup, this was stone-age blush: the worn, stained, cracked plastic case, the bright pink powder with a cheap flaring brush designed to make apples out of cheeks. But how many times had I seen her heading out for life—for a class or a date—and watched her last gesture: checking her blush and her lipstick? I sniffled after this encounter, but added it to the trash in the basket.

What did me in was her laundry basket. I opened it up and smelled Claire. Her perfume, first of all. Then far underneath that, but still familiar enough that I could recognize it, the smell of a woman's body. I don't think young men are aware of their mothers' smell, maybe because it envelopes them from their first moments. So their first scent of womanhood probably belongs to their sisters. My father found me leaning into the bathroom mirror, weeping. "Stop that!" he hissed. "It's pure self-indulgence. You'll break your mother's heart." What was I to do with my dead sister's laundry? Wash it to give away to someone who needed clothing? I added it to the trash.

That brief temptation to sweep aside everything on Elise's bathroom counter was suddenly layered over with this memory, and I was overwhelmed with something I couldn't name. "Really," I said, nodding at the messy counter. "This is a beautiful room. You ought to clean it up." But Elise is quick to smell any emotion besides love, adoration, happiness.

"Missing your neat-freak wife? You've got to move in a few days. Why not get started? The movers my dad hired will take care of everything."

Christ! You'd think a man who could handle wood might be able to use a hammer without smashing his fingers. It's these tiny nails they've given me. There. God, this shelf feels flimsy as I ease it upright. It'll hold my books, but it'll probably warp within days in the Montreal humidity. The particle board will take on moisture and begin to expand, splitting the fake wood veneer. Meanwhile, the wood I bought for Lila's music cabinet is gathering dust in the basement. Lila says it's temporary. Once her mother has died, I can move back into the house. I don't want my fucking house. Every corner, every shadow, every artwork is a memory. How can I describe a fun-filled, sex-filled week and a half and be frightened of the memories enshrined in our house? I could offer you two narratives of those two weeks. There's the one I've just recounted, the narrative of a romantic facade that filled my days with pleasurable and annealing activity. Our days were full to overflowing with eating and drinking and driving and holding hands and kissing and fucking and showering and stroking and laughing. Then there's the emptiness. The pretense. The black hole of grief. The whole of grief. On many nights I laid, spent, next to Elise's unselfconscious body, unable to sleep for heartache and memories. For the truth of the matter is that while I was admiring Elise's beauty and enjoying the unrestrained sex, I missed my wife.

Every time I put on my clothes, my proper and inoffensive Dockers, the Oxford-cloth shirt, the moccasins that look worn but expensive, I thought about how people can actually allow their costumes to stand for who they are. I was so aware, during those weeks, of being divided between what I desire and who I am. Elise may be something I want: beauty, youth, lust, admiration. But Lila is who I am, who I want to be: a philosophical beauty, the wisdom of age, the vulnerability of a soul worn thin in places by her mother's dying and her music, lost in the only world I believe has any integrity. My days belonged to Elise, and I was almost—but not quite—captivated by them. I was sometimes surly, sometimes distant, but it didn't matter because Elise's egotism erased it the minute I kissed her in public or took off her clothes. My nights were Lila's.

The bathroom. Why do I keep thinking about that bloody bathroom? Because this one is so small? And the towels on the rods remind me of home? One morning, Elise was putting on her makeup while

I was shaving, and I spent ten minutes or so watching her and meditating on how we prepare our faces for our public lives. After I finished shaving, I sat on the toilet seat and studied her craft of blotting out this and emphasizing that: the special attention given to the slightly red areas where the occasional zit has recently healed. The widening of her eyes with blue or purple eye shadow and black pencil. This art was new to me: Lila—whose skin is still translucent, like her soul—uses powder, blush, a blue liquid eyeliner that she swipes across her eyelid with a casual accuracy, a touch of mascara, a subtle lipstick. Elise goes in for the full armour: some kind of undercoating, foundation, powder, blush, eye shadow, eyeliner entirely around her eye, almost daily brow tweezing and shaping. She lines her mouth in pencil and fills it in with a tiny brush. I probably make her sound a bit like a clown or a whore, but when she was done the effect was quite stunning, if a little redolent of a fashion runway, not the classroom. Do women study their faces when they put on their makeup the same way men do when they shave? We do the opposite things. My routine is pretty basic. Soap. Water. Shave. I try to expose what's underneath the night's sleep: the dreams of Mr. Hyde show up daily in the bristle on my face, and I look for the more benign Dr. Jekyll beneath. Do women create something that's not there or reveal something that's otherwise hidden? Is it a mask or a self they create? Maybe it comes to the same thing.

I moved out of Elise's apartment the day before the movers were due to come. She tried to shame me into staying with any number of narratives of my weakness. I was trying to avoid the long goodbye, which she deserved, having given me succour after my wife kicked me out. It would do me good, the last twist of the knife as she started on her new life with—who knows?—new lovers, and left me behind with my heartache. I needed a bit of moral education. This time we were in her kitchen, which, unlike the bathroom, was pristine. She never cooked, kept almost no food except rice cakes and eggs in the house. Then she wasn't tempted by things she shouldn't eat. The dishwasher was working on the dozen glasses and three plates we'd dirtied in the last two weeks, its rhythmic *swish-swish* conducting the conversation.

"Do you think your wife will take you back when she gets horny?"

"I'm not sure that's what either of us wants."

"Oh, you want it. You've been wanting it for about a week—maybe a little less. It's so clear what you want. Sex. A bit of pretend romance around the edges so it doesn't seem so crass. But you don't really like me. Maybe you should simply have a mistress and live on your own. Keep your attitude to yourself."

I had to turn away. Find something to do. This would have been the perfect moment to rearrange the fruit in the bowl on the island, except there was no bowl and no fruit. "If it was so clear, why didn't you send me packing?"

"Oh, I can use people, just like you. The boyfriend I told you about? Jean Claude? The one who's so great in bed? Well, he was more or less stalking me. You were my insurance."

"So you're not . . ."

"In love with you? No. Why do you think I'm not torn up about leaving for Toronto? You're an attractive man. Great in bed. That's about it. Not even particularly good company."

"So that's why we spent so much time in public."

"Bingo. You get the prize for the great detective."

"And all those public displays of affection."

"Boy, you're batting."

"Are you safe for the next couple of days?"

"The movers will be here. He phoned to say he's going on a business trip. That could be a lie, but I don't think so. He's not that clever. He had no idea this wasn't more or less permanent. I led him on a little. He was easily convinced you were retired and were coming with me."

Ouch. "Guess I ought to pack up."

"It's an idea." It took great control, but I didn't fling my clothes angrily into my suitcase and wipe my stuff summarily off the bathroom counter. No. That's false. It didn't take any control at all. I was a dog with my tail between my legs.

When Lindsay was ten or so, I began reading her Anne McCaffrey's books about heroines and heroes and dragons. We both liked them, and this was a cuddly time for us. We'd head for my study when Lila turned to the piano, Lindsay would snuggle in next to me on the sofa, and we'd read. Most of the time I'd read to her, but occasionally, she wanted to read to me. I concentrated on her fluty little voice with delight—though she'd look at me out of the corner of her eye from time to time to make sure I was still attentive. My memory's hazy on this, but when the dragons needed to move from place to place very quickly, they went somewhere called "between." It was essentially a portal to anywhere in their world they needed to go, a kind of physics trick. It was very cold and very dark; one couldn't stay too long. It was both nowhere and the doorway to everywhere. When dragons died, they went "between" and never returned. Lindsay thought this patently inconsistent and said so. "Between" couldn't be a means of getting somewhere and nowhere at the same time.

Between is where I am now.

Wednesday, August 21, 2002

Kevin

Twenty-One

Lila's gone to ground. And Lila's blooming.

Against Lila's wishes, Clarice has gone into the hospice. Rob's departure made it impossible for Lila to care for her mother because she couldn't get her up and down the stairs. A week after she kicked Rob out, when her mother could leave the hospital, she called me, frantic.

"Come over. Come over. We can't sort this out on the phone," I told her. So she showed up at our door looking positively schizophrenic. I swear that some of the lines on her face—the queries on her forehead and the parenthesis between her nose and mouth—have relaxed almost away. She glows with an intensity and heat that is terrifying and beautiful. If someone told you she was the passionate and consumptive heroine of a nineteenth-century novel who'd escaped both time and the space to join you in our world, you'd believe them. All she needs is a corset, a frilly white blouse, and a cameo at her throat.

"Well, I've done it this time. Kicking Rob out means that Mother can't come home."

"How does she feel about that?"

"You know Mother. Matter-of-fact all the way."

"So what's the problem? You think she's lying to you?" She seemed determined to stand in the hallway, but I had resolutely taken her arm and was leading her into the living room, seating her on the sofa, plumping pillows and wedging them behind her stiff back.

"No. Not consciously. I think she doesn't want to be a bother. I don't think she sees that she's *not* a bother."

"The truth is, you need her at home."

"Kevin. Dear Kevin. This is why I come to you. You know these things even before I tell you."

"But you can't always have what you need, Lila. Let's look at your options here. You've been thorough about finding out what kinds of home help you can get, and you always bump up against legal issues about getting her down the stairs." She nodded. "Is there any other man, besides Rob, who could get her down the stairs for you? Either Francis or I would, but neither of us is burly enough to get her down safely. Could you ask Rob to come from time to time to be pressed into service?"

"I'm sure I could. I'm sure he'd like nothing better. But I have this 'give him an inch and he'll take a mile' feeling about him. Seriously, I need him out of my life."

"Even if that's not really what he wants?"

"Fuck what he wants." This was said without heat or emphasis.

"Lila. Your heart's broken."

"No. I have two hearts right now. One of them—the one that looks backward—. You're right. It's broken. I'm sabotaged by memories. Not the big things—Lindsay's birth, the night he proposed, or our wedding. Those are almost shadowy, faded photographs, gone all sepia. But I'm constantly caught off guard by short-short films showing him with his sleeves rolled up, cooking. Or carrying my mother downstairs, making comforting small talk while he does it. Even though much of the time he was stoically quiet. Moving the sprinkler in his bare feet and rolled-up trousers to take care of his lovely lawn. Reading to Lindsay when she was young. I loved those things about him. I don't know any more whether I loved *him*. Can I have some water?"

"Wouldn't you rather have tea? Francis baked last night."

"Tea would be lovely."

"But first finish with your backward-looking heart."

"It's that these films are suddenly interrupted by—oh, let's keep to the photography metaphor and say it's stills projected onto a huge screen somewhere. They're Rob angry. Rob cynical. Rob in his own world. Sometimes even a flash of Rob fucking another woman. The conflict is nearly unbearable."

I nodded my head and started to move toward the kitchen. "And your other heart?" I asked as I filled the kettle. She had followed obediently.

"It's looking forward."

"And what does it see?" I spooned the loose tea into our kitschy tea ball that rests in a teddy bear's fat tummy after the tea's brewed and heated the tea pot.

She sat at the counter looking out into the back yard. I watched her perfectly straight back for signs. Nothing.

"Your other heart . . ." I prompted.

"Did I say I had another heart?"

"You did."

"It seems almost heretical—wicked—to have another heart."

"Not at all. Who should live—who *could* live inside those warring memories? So tell me what the other heart says." I had nuked the muffins, put them on the tray, and brought them over.

"That there's hope. Have you ever heard anything sillier? Such a slender thing, hope. Like a spider's web. Or the silk a yellow butterfly uses to spin a cocoon." She turned toward me, her eyes bright with tears. "Sometimes I am so happy. My mother is dying and my husband has moved in with his paramour, and I'm happy?" She had begun to cry, and I put my arm around her shoulders.

"Well, not this very minute. But you have moments. When you look toward the future. You haven't told me about your forward-looking heart. What does it see?"

She sighed and then looked off into the back garden. "A sunny day that's peaceful. A warm autumn day. This summer's been horrific, and I stupidly want it over. It's never a good idea to wish time would flee, but that's what I want anyway. I'm taking a long walk exactly where I want to go, taking the detours I choose, taking as much time as I need. At my own pace, stopping to look at whatever I want to see, so it's my own adventure."

Lila leans her head to one side and welcomes the reverie. "There are—let's see—this doesn't have to be real, so I can put in anything I like. The trees have just turned golden, but there are children in a swimming pool, and I can hear their shouts and see the sun sparkling off the water they're splashing high into the air. The last August roses are in full bloom, and the air is fragrant. I've just had a call from Lindsay, and she's gotten into law school. There's a street musician and he's playing Bach on his marimba. His hat's full of coins. His audience hears the magic. He smiles at me, and I'm amazed that a man wants to smile at me. This is silly. It's like bad poetry."

"Oh, Lila. Don't cut yourself off just when things are getting good."

"Okay. The blooming roses and the golden leaves and the smiling man and Lindsay getting into law school would do it. The past—the roses and the leaves—are sad but beautiful. The end of something that was once growing and blooming. The almost natural end. The present contains a small, accidental pleasure. And a future actually seems to exist. That's all I want. All I need."

"Lila. No one lives on that. What about hunger? Desire?"

Lila looked at me, bewildered. "That's not safe."

"Your mother's taught you that. 'Don't wish for anything, and you won't be disappointed.'"

"You know, I told Lindsay—earlier on the day I told Rob I wanted a divorce—not to assume that her parents' characters or habits were behind her choices. I think it's a saner way to live. But I'm not sure I've managed it."

"Your childhood was a bit more traumatic than Lindsay's."

"Traumatic? Shit. My mother's worst beating? The day of a World Series game in 1968. A couple of weeks before, the radical feminists from New York City had protested at the Miss America Pageant in Atlantic City. Boy, that sparked the dinner-table conversation. Jack started it, of course, by talking about how women ripped off their bras in public and burned them. You could tell he wanted to meet some of those radical women at university. My mother quietly told him that he might be disappointed, but that no bras were burned, much less taken off in public. Then she became slightly cheerful when she said they'd crowned a sheep Miss America because they thought beauty pageant contestants were treated like livestock. My father was eerily silent. But Jack was taken by this image. He thought it rather creative, though said that none of his friends treated their girlfriends that way. 'Yeah?' I said. 'What about Davey? Didn't he dump a girl just last week because she decided not to wear makeup?' We went on like this—Mother giving us the facts, Jack and I trading insults about how our friends treated one another. Suddenly my father stood up and announced, in his sternest, patriarchal voice, 'I will not have conversations like this at my dinner table. The subject is closed.' He got up and took his plate, which still had food on it, into the kitchen counter. If he wasn't finishing a meal, this was serious.

"Two weeks later, he was watching a World Series game. I don't usually pay attention to these things, but I can tell you who was playing that year: the St. Louis Cardinals and the Detroit Tigers. The game was being broadcast from Detroit, and Dad was on their side. Mother, probably not knowing the game had begun, started vacuuming upstairs, and Dad went storming up to tell her to stop making so much noise. He couldn't hear anything. If you can see what's going on, shouldn't you know what the score is and how well a team is playing? Do sports announcers really say anything important?"

"I think it's the air of authority that straight men love. All the while thinking they could do it as well or better."

"Well, of course, she humoured him and changed what she was doing. But laundry was also too loud. So she decided to bake his favourite muffins. He raced in, ripped the Mixmaster from her hands, and began hitting her about the head with it. 'Don't you understand anything?' he kept yelling. 'Dammit, I work hard enough to deserve a peaceful afternoon with a baseball game.' When he was finished, there was batter everywhere. I was old enough to drive, and so took Mother to emergency for stitches. She alternated between shaking and crying and trying to be funny about picking bits of batter from her hair. The doctor asked no questions; we offered no answers. Once we were back in the car, we talked frankly for a couple of minutes about what we should do. I thought we should simply drive around until Dad was tired and worried. Mother suggested some little town fifty miles away that was supposed to have wonderful ice cream. She could stay in the car while I got a couple of cones. How on earth did she make an adventure out of a beating? When we did get home, the game was over,

Detroit had won, and Dad was worried and repentant. But I always connected those two days in my head. If we hadn't talked about the Atlantic City sheep, Dad wouldn't have beaten Mother."

I poured her another cup of tea and made the kind of comforting sounds that substitute for words when you know words are inadequate. "I was suspicious about Rob's praise of his beautiful students, the disappearances. At the time time, I also denied anything was happening. Do you know what kinds of mental gymnastics it takes to count your husband's spare time and say you know he's been faithful? What kind of dishonesty? What kind of self-loathing? But now the break-up is my fault because I didn't love him enough to hold him responsible for his actions. How do you explain that, Kevin? I keep thinking that if I can find a straight line of cause and effect, I can make some sense out of all this. If I can go from the sheep to my father beating my mother to my accepting a certain amount of meanness from my husband, I can finally . . . I don't know what. Really, there's no explanation. Ever. Perhaps I could say to Rob, 'I'm not responsible. *You're* responsible.'"

"But it doesn't work that way. Desire and need and love and cruelty don't always have reasons."

"You know what my mother asked a couple of days ago?" Lila suddenly had an impish look on her face.

"Should I?"

"She looked at me archly and asked, 'How many men does it take to paper a room?'" I shrugged my shoulders. "'Depends on how thinly you slice them.' She brought it out in the middle of the most tormented, despairing conversation."

"Some imaginative nurse brought her a *Cosmo*?"

"Or a *Ms.* When she and Lindsay and I went for our drive, the advice she gave Lindsay made me swear she'd been reading *Ms.* on the sly." By this time we were both smiling. Suddenly she looked at me in a panic. "What are we doing?"

"Exactly what people do. When a friend of mine was dying of AIDS, we'd have these periods of giddiness and almost joy. It's what ya gotta do."

The first rehearsal after Rob left was almost surreal, since it seemed that Lila had tried to plant change everywhere. Rob was a bit paranoid about society's unsavoury elements, even in the leafy sanctuary of Notre-Dame-de-Grâce, so the front door was always closed. Now it was open, and sunlight was falling on a new red rug with large exploding flowers covering the slate entryway. She'd bought a small, clean-lined sofa covered in a red and white Scandinavian print. Stuart was already there, and I could hear voices coming from the kitchen, along with the smell of cinnamon and vanilla. Lila's no baker, but there was a coffee-cake on the island counter. The rack above the island that held Rob's lovely pans was gone, the holes in the ceiling expertly filled and the ceiling re-painted. It was as if it had never been there.

When I glanced up, Lila explained, "Naturally, I gave Rob his favourite pots. The ones I kept are fairly ugly. No point feeling as if doom was hanging over me while I cooked."

Stuart and I both laughed at her hyperbole, but it was an uncomfortable laugh. Maybe we both know the pissed-off, defensive exaggeration that comes after relationships have ended. You want to say "I'm in charge of my life; I'm creating the life/home/routine I've always wanted, except I had to compromise with that jerk all the time."

"A cup of coffee?" She nodded toward Stuart, who had a half-finished mug in his hands. How early had he come?

"Not really. How 'bout at half-time? Like we usually do?"

"Sure. The coffee cake is too warm now anyway."

We walked through the living room, which now had bare hooks on the walls and spaces on the shelves, toward the music room. The French doors between the two rooms were already open, and Stuart had set up his music stand and gotten his cello out of the case. Half an hour, I'd guess, at a minimum. I wondered if he made a habit of arriving early, or if he knew. How? I hadn't told him. That was supposed to happen after today's rehearsal, when we'd left. I'd almost scripted it: we'd stand on the sidewalk and have a little man-to-man conversation and I'd tell him that Rob was gone. He sat down and raised his eyebrows for an A from the piano to tune, and it was clear from the little change his cello needed that they'd done this already. I got my violin out of its case and Lila gave me another A.

It's convention that the violinist sets the tempo, at least initially, so I gave the count and then the deep inhale we all use as the "off to the races" signal. And we were off. Not in terms of speed: this first movement is broad and calm. But it was as if the three of us were threaded—like a troika—to a single carriage, and had been working together as carthorses since time out of mind. I knew, though Lila didn't seem to realize it, that Stuart had been one of our fans for some time. Perhaps he'd simply heard us often enough to intuit our approach to this music. Maybe a Ouija board came into it somewhere, some extra-musical telepathy. I didn't really spend a lot of time thinking about why this was happening: I was having too much fun. We gave the trio a single run-through and then took a deep, happy breath.

"Cool! That was fun. I've got to work on those arpeggios, though. They aren't particularly difficult. There's nothing funny about the key. They'll come."

"Of course they'll come. I'll bet an arpeggio hasn't gotten the best of you since you were about fourteen. I can see you in knee socks, stamping your foot."

That's the kind of comment that would have come from me.

"Well, I need some coffee. And I need someone to eat that coffee cake. I have no idea what possessed me to bake."

"I'll bet your mother would love a piece. Couldn't you take some to the hospice?"

"That's an idea, Stuart. Mother's not eating enough."

"How is your mother doing otherwise?" he asked.

"For a dying woman, not badly, thank you. It's awful when your mother pretends to know what's best for you. When you're fifty-three."

"But you know what's best for her?" I had to admit: Stuart had balls.

"Touché." She turned to me. "You didn't tell me that Stuart was a smart-ass and emotionally intelligent to boot."

"Emotional intelligence is the last thing you should accuse me of," Stuart said, his voice suddenly changed—down about half an octave and several decibels.

"That's okay." She patted his hand. "I'm getting rather good at having my life a mess. I've kicked my husband out of the house, and that means my dying mother can't live with me—in case you hadn't figured out the scenario. After a while you get . . . blasé? Nope. Um. You shrug your shoulders to loosen up the muscles and put your backpack on. Oddly enough, you find it steadies you."

"What should we do after our break? Do you think we should play through the whole or focus on one movement?" I asked, not changing the subject.

"Focus, focus, focus!" Lila gleefully chanted.

"Which movement?" Stuart asked.

"I need cheer—well, not cheer exactly, but energy. Let's start with the Scherzo. I think—if you'll let me be a little academic for a moment—there are two centres of gravity in this trio. The first is in the long, broad first movement. We can't possibly ignore its weight, musically speaking. But the scherzo is its counterpart. Its philosophical counterpart. When he revised the work forty years later, he left this movement almost untouched. 'Yes,' he seems to say, 'calm reflectiveness is a good thing. But there are demons you can't chase away."

"But Lila, that's only half the work. There are two more movements. They're just add-ons?" I didn't usually challenge Lila's interpretations, but that was when there were just two of us, and I could merrily ignore her and pull her in my direction. Stuart changed the dynamic.

"And that doesn't take in that lovely middle section of the scherzo," Stuart added.

"Quite right. So much for being academic. Let's go be musicians." She took our cups and plates to load in the dishwasher, threaded her arms through our elbows, and led us back to the music room.

Monday, August 26, 2002

Lila

Twenty-Two

Last night the phone rang at about ten. It's an ominous time for a phone call, so I knew it was bad news about Mother. But Stuart's voice was on the other end, asking polite questions about how I was doing. You could tell from his voice that he meant well but that this wasn't the point of the phone call, so as soon as I could I asked, "What's up?"

"I need to talk to somebody. Do you think we could go for a coffee tomorrow? Better yet, could you come to my place for a coffee?"

"Are you okay? You sound down."

"Not down. Light. So lightweight I might float away."

"Well, I'll come tie weights to your feet. If we're going to perform the Brahms trio, we can't have you floating away. What time tomorrow?"

"Ten-thirty? I can't bake, but I'll get some good scones from my local patisserie."

"You have a patisserie that makes decent scones? "

"It's right round the corner. I live on St. Denis—upstairs at 4087, almost above a shop called Au Festin de Babette. It sells marvellous food. On the west side of the street. You'll go up a set of wooden stairs on the outside. Parking is impossible."

"I'll take a taxi."

"I can take you home afterward."

"See you at ten-thirty. Or thereabouts. Taxis aren't all that reliable."

St. Denis has street life. It's not like St. Catherine's, which is where I'd have found my imaginary chap playing Bach on the marimba. More chi-chi. And a bit aloof. Everyone is searching for something—exactly the *right* thing. It's a mission devoted to *style*, whether that's medieval clothing or French Provencal fabric. I watched a slim young woman with an impeccable chignon, an only slightly rumpled linen shirt, and a chic straw shopping bag, stepping into Au Festin de Babette.

One of the ties that bound Rob and me was taste, though of course mine was educated by his. Rob's taste is understated, expensive. The Shaker furniture fits right in with the slate and wood floors, the Moroccan rugs, the good abstract art, the art glass, and antique maps. Where that ungodly white leather came from is beyond me. What I didn't realize early in our dating was that his sophisticated decorating was limited to the rooms guests would see. The bedroom was dark, masculine, and practical, so he assigned it to me. I read nesting magazines for a couple of months, worrying about doing the wrong thing, proving my feminine ineptitude. Then I walked into a little shop on St. Denis that carried lovely toiles from Provénce. I started with a cream and dusty blue toile quilt, adding pillows covered in polished cotton in varying shades of blue. I painted the room cream and painted his student desk a soft grey blue. It was a lovely room for its time, though of course it's changed over the years, often one piece at a time in the way that interiors slowly morph, building up layers of our history. Maybe that should be Rob's next academic project: an historical analysis of the politics of home decorating. Power, history, knowledge clash over the choice of an ottoman.

I thought about this as the taxi drove me slowly down St. Laurent. The driver was trying to avoid pedestrians as he searched for the address, while I imagined ways of tethering someone suffering from "the unbearable lightness of being." Tires. The complete works of Dickens. Anvils. A suit of armour. Answering my knock, Stuart greeted me in the francophone style: hands on my shoulders, kisses on each cheek.

"Are Scots allowed to do that?" I asked, stepping inside.

"I don't see why not. Providing their French is up to it."

"And is yours?"

"I teach occasionally at U de M; it had better be. My mother was francophone."

"And from her you got your sense of style?" I'd been able to take in the large room that was probably the greater part of his floor space. Three walls were white; the fourth was made of exposed brickwork embracing a fireplace. A couple of IKEA chairs stood on an emerald green rug that marked out a living room. There was no coffee table, no knick-knacks, no art on the walls. Track lighting illuminated the bookshelves at one end of the room. Another shelving unit held what was probably a top-of-the-line stereo system and rows upon rows of CDs. The oddly shaped speakers were clearly not meant to be used as extra tables. In front of the windows that looked down on St. Denis, a long workspace held a computer and all its accoutrements, along with a keyboard whose cord snaked toward the tower. Even what was clearly a busy workspace looked minimalist. Finally, one exquisitely simple wooden chair and a beautifully carved wooden music stand stood beside his cello. I wanted that space, with its promise that it's possible to create a simple life. The lack of walls: a life so unified you could hold it in a single room. What was I thinking? No life is like that.

"That's one of the things I wanted to talk to you about."

"Your interior decoration?"

"Well, yeah. It says a lot about me, don't you think?"

"That you aspire to be a monk?"

"You've got it. Come on through to the kitchen."

I didn't think the kitchen could be any more pared down, but it was a tiny galley with glass-fronted cupboards. His batterie de cuisine was perfect but minimal. It looked like he had two of everything: two cups, two saucers, two wineglasses. He certainly didn't give wild parties unless he used paper plates and plastic glasses, and somehow I didn't think so. The kettle had just come to a boil and the French press was waiting on the wooden countertop along with some scones and tiny white dishes of butter, jam, and clotted cream.

"How long have you lived here?"

"About fifteen years."

"It looks like you moved in ten minutes ago."

"I like to travel light. I don't see much point in things. Except books and music."

"Yet everything you have is beautiful."

"Or useful. I read William Morris when I was in my early twenties and was still feeling idealistic about socialism. 'Have nothing in your house which you do not know to be useful or believe to be beautiful.' For someone who sold household furnishings, his motto was the perfect antidote to consumerism. Most of the stuff they want to sell us is neither. Doing without things has given me the freedom to compose—which means living right around the poverty line. You think twice about anything you buy." He picked up the tray and I followed him back into the spacious room. It turned out that the tray had legs that allowed it to double as a portable coffee table. He poured me a cup of excellent dark roast coffee.

"I need to talk. To someone."

"That's usually how it works—'to someone.'"

"I've been as Spartan about my friendships as I have about my decor, so when things fall apart, I have no one to help me sort it out."

"Surely there's someone who's known you longer than I have?"

"Most of my friends are musicians, most of them guys. Emotionally astute—or even open—they're not."

"Okay. As long as you know the risks you're taking. What's up?"

"A custody battle of sorts."

"You want to keep a child *here*? You *have* a child?" Monks aren't supposed to have children, I think to myself.

"I've been in and out of a relationship—the same relationship—for about fifteen years. I loved Amy. I would probably still love her if we hadn't fought so much. I'm not good at domesticity. I mean, look around you."

"There's domesticity and there's domesticity. Some guys forget to pick up their socks for weeks. You, on the other hand . . ."

"Like order. I like to be able to compose at three in the morning and sleep until noon. Sometimes I perform several nights in a row. I'm an adjunct at both McGill and U de M, so I teach a lot and give lots of private lessons in order to support my composing habit. You know how it is: I teach through the dinner hour because that's when my students are free. I don't want—and I certainly don't have time for—the leave-your-socks-on-the-floor type of domesticity where my wife and I spend Saturday morning cleaning and tidying together. I usually teach on Saturday morning because—"

"That's when your students are free," I interrupted, to let him know I was listening.

"I have a life that is full of things I love—music and teaching and composing—but that doesn't mean I can't love a woman too. Yet when I didn't want to move in, when I was away for a couple of days at a time, when I'd turn down an invitation to sleep over because I had an idea I wanted to work out in the middle of the night when Montreal is asleep, Amy didn't understand."

"How do you compose in the middle of the night?"

"This is largely a commercial neighbourhood, though some people have studios on the second storey. Just in case there's a light sleeper somewhere nearby, I use earphones. Come see." We walked over to the techno part of the apartment, and he flipped some switches and put a pair of earphones on my head. "Here. Play something," he said as he seated me at the keyboard. It actually sounded like a piano. Then, as he pushed another button, a harpsichord. I tried the Bach sonatas I'd been having such trouble with and they sounded right.

"That sounds wonderful."

"I know. So do you. I also had the speakers on: I wondered what you'd play."

"Kevin and I were working on the Bach sonatas earlier in the summer, before you came into our lives with the Brahms trio. I couldn't get them to sound right . . ."

"Well, it's not your playing. They sound just fine on my keyboard."

"I'm sorry. We've gotten way off track." I untangled myself from the chords and the earphone and walked back to the seating area. "Amy? Composing at 3:00 AM?"

"She felt she was less important than my work. But because we loved one another, I guess, we'd go back at it and try again. Early on in this process, she had our baby. A daughter named Elsabeth. I did as much fathering as I could, which was quite a lot at the beginning because musicians don't work the same hours as ordinary people. I was Elsabeth's 'day care' until she went to first grade. I loved it. But I also loved it when she went home with her mother and I played my cello or taught or wrote music. Is that wrong? To have other loves in your life?"

This was a puzzle to me. How are such other loves wrong? They're an infidelity that's not unfaithfulness. "Of course it's not *wrong*. Maybe the problem is expecting—or just hoping—other people who don't have similar passions to understand ours. What does Amy do?"

"She's a teacher. A music teacher. That's how we met. And that's how we worked things out until Elsabeth went to school. Amy worked part-time, and I did the part-time day care. We really were partners. And I got to hear some of my daughter's first words, to be there when she figured out how to do a complicated puzzle. I put her to sleep and held her. There's something primal about that."

"So how does this turn into a custody battle?"

"Amy moved to Vancouver last month. They needed a French immersion music teacher, and she got the job. I can't help feeling that she choose someplace as far away from me as possible."

"Well, she could have gone to Victoria. Theoretically." No smile, just assent. "And your relationship?"

"It hasn't worked for several years. No matter how much you love each other, no matter how attracted you are to each other, or how committed you are to a child's well-being, I don't think any relationship can survive the kinds of fights we had. When I'd want to leave after dinner, she'd shout that she wasn't important. I'd shout back that I was working on a requiem commissioned by the choir at the Cathedral and had a deadline."

This was a "teachable moment" for me, not Stuart. "You can be unfaithful in many ways, Stuart. You know the cliché—'we just grew apart'? That's a kind of infidelity, needing to grow in some way that the relationship won't accommodate. Is that what happened, maybe?"

"No. Well, maybe. I finally broke it off. It seemed the only decent thing to do. I wanted her to feel free to find someone who suited her needs. I felt if I didn't call it quits, Amy's life would be . . ." He seemed unable to find a word.

"Distorted?"

"Yes. She'd wait for me to be someone I'd never become. And in the meantime, we'd fight. Even though I promised to babysit so she could have a social life, she almost seemed to try *not* to find anyone. She got an aggressive, spiky haircut and lost weight so that she looked like some kind of angry waif. Her reluctance—her failure—was an enormous guilt trip. I think she believed—and she's right—that I'd have been relieved if she found someone. She could only hurt me by taking my daughter halfway across the continent."

He was right about his lightness, its enchantments and its griefs. How could anyone be so detached? How many of us push someone away so they—both of them—can thrive? Still, as I looked around his apartment, I could see beauty in the purity and focus. I heard it in the voice of his cello.

"I'm not a bad person, Lila. I wasn't indifferent to her needs or unable to compromise. I'd keep careful score with myself. Half the time she asked me to stay overnight, even if I had plans to practise or compose, I'd stay. That only seemed fair to me. But half wasn't good enough. I'm not meant for the two-by-two march onto the Ark, trapped till the rain stops."

Funny. He didn't look like an alien. There were no obvious antennae; no beetle-green carapace looked like it would fit underneath his slim blue jeans and T-shirt. Yet as I considered his problem—clearly the source of grief I'd noticed when we met for coffee—that's how he seemed to me. Can you say to a partner, 'I'll meet your needs half the time'? How do you divide "need" in half? It's not a loaf of bread or a stick of gum.

"Sometimes I think our lives are profoundly distorted by our sense of what's 'normal.' Marriage. Two point two children, one boy and one girl; if possible, the boy first. You're not the first creative person who found conventional relationships a challenge. Doris Lessing. D.H. Lawrence. Though Frieda was more mother than lover, I sometimes think. Or the worst of both. Leonard and Virginia Woolf. Is there some reason you deserve the integrity many of us compromise when we make commitments? What is integrity? At some point, it has to involve something beyond *you*. Otherwise, it's just selfishness."

I wasn't helping. "For me it wasn't a matter of deserving something other people couldn't have. It was simply what I was. I think I was willing to go halfway between what I would ideally have liked my life to be without encumbrances and what Amy and Elsabeth needed. Because Amy became pregnant and Elsabeth was my daughter." He face reddened slightly, as if he was trying to struggle with tears. "And because I *want* love in my life. But halfway wasn't far enough. You have no idea how it hurt . . ."

"Maybe I do."

"Maybe you do. Being told you're lazy, selfish, self-absorbed, well, you take only so much of it. So yeah, I broke off the relationship in part because I wanted her to find someone else. But I also broke it off because I couldn't take the attack on me any longer."

"And you feel guilty about that?"

"Of course."

"Why? Guilt's overrated. We use the word *guilt* when we know we've done something wrong that we have no intention of doing any differently. It changes nothing and makes us feel bad. Rob's feeling guilty, I'm sure, but it's pointless."

"How are you doing? Not to change . . ."

". . . the subject." I looked at my watch. "We haven't talked about the custody thing yet. But I promised my mother I'd visit around noon. She likes company for her lunch."

"What will you eat?"

"Oh, I'll pick something up on my way."

"Except you don't have your car."

I made some noise of frustration. How did I manage to plan so badly?

"Look, I'll take you. I'll make you a sandwich, and I've got some fruit. Shall I make you a Thermos of tea before we leave?"

"That would be kind. I'll take a taxi from the hospice to the house this afternoon."

"How long do you stay?" He spoke from the doorway of the kitchen, where he'd put the kettle on. Then he turned to go back to the kitchen, and I heard the rattle of a cutting board on the counter.

"Two or three hours. Depends on how tired she is. I've got my book, as I always do. Sometimes she naps and I just sit there and read."

"What are you reading?" It sounded like he had his head in the refrigerator. I walked to the doorway to answer.

"An appalling book by Peter Robinson. *Aftermath*. It's well written. His always are. But it's about some sex crimes that make your hair stand up."

"That's not what you need right now." He put his arm around my shoulders as he walked me toward his bookshelves. "You need something slow. But profound." He searched his shelves. "Have you read *Austerlitz* by Sebald?"

I looked at the startling photograph on the front, the sticker announcing it was a National Book Critics Circle award winner. I shook my head.

"Take this with you. It's a much better book for sitting *shiva*. Which is what I suspect you're doing, though she hasn't died. Look, call me when you want to go home, and I'll come pick you up."

"I don't want to interrupt your day like that." The kettle had begun to boil, and he'd returned to the kitchen to make the tea and finish the sandwich.

"I've got some really tedious work to do. The composer's equivalent of stretching canvas. It would be a relief to know I've got a break to look forward to."

So I visited my mother with a lunch packed by Stuart McTaggart. There was brie on a baguette with watercress; a just-ripe pear, and a few squares of dark chocolate, as well as a Thermos of excellent tea. Mother ate a bit of her lunch and then slid down into a long nap. I must call Margaret tomorrow morning and suggest she come soon if she wants to spend time with Mother before she dies.

Finally, at around four-thirty, I felt I couldn't hold Stuart's plans hostage any longer, and when Mother seemed as if she would sleep for the rest of the day, I called him. He asked if I could wait until about five, and I said I'd read another endless paragraph of the Sebald. I could wait in Mother's room and he'd come get me there. He arrived slightly late, but Mother had woken and I was able to feed her some of her broth for dinner with the promise that once she'd finished it, she could eat her chocolate pudding.

"No need to rush," he said when he could see that I didn't know whether I should stop feeding Mother and leave with him. "Do you suppose they'd mind some music in here, since it's dinnertime and everyone should be awake?" Mother shook her head between sips. He pulled a harmonica from his pocket and turned to look out the south window at the early evening light: it still has the sharpness of August, but the shadows of the trees angle nostalgically across the fronts of the old three-storey houses opposite. He began meditatively to play something that sounded like an old Appalachian or Maritime tune—Copland meets a nineteenth-century musician with modest resources. A nurse stopped in the doorway and beyond her a patient in a wheelchair had paused. But he was not performing; he was entirely unassuming about what he was doing, and seemed unaware that he was gathering an audience. He was simply a musician passing the time with music. He'd come to the end of a tune, doodle a little segue, and then move on to another. They were plangent and simple: a people's response to the beauty and tragedy of a harsh landscape.

When we had finished her broth and the pudding, Mother turned to him. "I'm afraid I'm too tired to enjoy any more. Will you come again and play for me?"

"Would you like me to bring my cello?"

"For right now, I like the harmonica. I like something about the fact that you carry it in your pocket. How does a cellist learn to play the harmonica?"

"It's a lot easier for busking than a cello. I'll be back Thursday. I'm sure Lila will let me?"

"Of course."

"Someday, we'll bring a little portable keyboard of mine, and Lila can play for you again."

"Would you?" There was a smidgeon of energy and delight in Mother's voice that I hadn't heard for about a week. "I'd so love that."

When we got out to his car, a Cooper Mini, I could see that there was a basket in the back.

"I've been presumptuous," he confessed, once he had eased his way out of the parking spot. "I suspect I've messed up your day by keeping you so long this morning and not driving you home on time when you called. So I've brought your dinner. Enough for both of us, actually. I'd hoped we could share it in your back garden. I'm not much of a cook, so I picked it up on St. Denis. Eggplant Parmesan, a baguette, fruit salad, a decadent chocolate mousse. And a bottle of excellent Merlot, of course."

Did he have no idea how tired I was? "Well, it will save me from one of the ad hoc meals Rob would have such contempt for. And we need to finish the conversation. We hadn't even gotten to Elsabeth and how you're going to keep her part of your life. We should do that."

Once out on the back deck with our trays of reheated eggplant and large glasses of Merlot, the compliments about the flowers gone through, I reopened the earlier conversation.

"So tell me what Elsabeth thought about the move."

"She was mostly curious about the change in her life. But before she left, she visited, and talked about what Vancouver was like—the Internet version anyway. Maybe she's inherited my sense of detachment. She walked around and around the apartment, talking about Vancouver and touching everything: the speakers, my keyboard, the backs of the chairs. She ran her hand along the books, and stared at the titles, picking them out to look at the covers. Like many twelve-year-olds, she's a slim little colt of a girl, prone to trot everywhere. But this was a serious walkabout. Finally, she picked up the only work of art in the room, a folk carving of a trio of musicians, about a foot high, and asked if she could take it with her. Of course I said yes."

"Can you ask for visitation rights? Four weeks in the summer, for example? Is there a room for her in your flat?"

"Yes, there's a tiny bedroom. I've got a bunk bed in there with a desk and dresser underneath. She likes sleeping there. It's a kind of adventure. But I'm not on record as her father. I don't have a legal leg to stand on. If I could have that—well, it would be something. But I don't want to be a kind of vacation in her life. I don't know how she'd react to coming for a month and being without her mother."

"Could you ask her? After talking to Amy, of course."

"Yes." He shook his head at his own obtuseness. "That's always a good idea: ask. Do you want any more eggplant?

"I'm fine. But I'll get you some more." I stood up to go in, but he took my arm and gently tugged me back down into my chair.

"Where'd you learn that?" he asked.

"Probably from my mother."

"Why don't you try to unlearn it?" He got up and went inside. When he came back out, he started right where we left off.

"I said that I didn't want to be a *vacation*. That's not quite the right word. Maybe it's easier to say what I *do* want. I want to be an integral part of her life. With the emphasis on *integral*. I want there to be some integrity to what I do. I want to be there when the unexpected happens—when she gets chosen for the basketball team, when her new girlfriend mocks her hair, when she gets an A on a science test or struggles to write an English essay."

"How portable are you?" I was thinking of that spare apartment. There wasn't much to move. "Could you move to Vancouver?"

"I have absolutely no musical connections in Vancouver. No connections means no teaching, no playing, no eating, no heating."

"Do you need heat in Vancouver?" I was trying to leaven the conversation, which was now saturated with anguish.

"Fuck. She's done it. Amy's done it. I have to choose between my daughter and myself. I've got a stable of wonderful students and fairly regular teaching. I've got enough of a reputation in Quebec that I get regular commissions. I've got the promise of this wonderful partnership with you and Kevin. I'd have to be ready to give all that up."

There was no response to that, except to put my hand on his forearm. He moved and took my hand in his and began reading it over with his fingers the way a blind man reads Braille. "I could put out some feelers in Vancouver," I told him while he read. "I know someone at UBC. That might get you started. If you were a vacation for a couple of years, and then rearranged your life to be part of hers, your presence might be even more valuable."

"I don't want to be valuable. That's not what parents are. I want to be *there*."

I felt an attack of wise righteousness coming on, in spite of the intimate, subtle conversation our fingers were having. Polar opposites: righteousness and intimacy.

"We can't always have what we want."

"I know that."

"Do you? I don't say that as a challenge. I honestly don't know."

He came as close to a guffaw as was in his nature. "My dad. He did, basically, manual labour, and after his mid-fifties was in a lot of pain, on and off Worker's Comp. My mom was nearly illiterate, but boy was she a miracle worker with starch and soap and bleach. Not having what I wanted was part of my childhood. Except for music lessons. How they managed those, I have no idea."

"My mother got beaten for wanting me to have more than five years of lessons."

His hand continued its study of mine.

"Do you remember a time I drove you home about twenty years ago after a summer party? There's no reason you should."

"You drove back after you took the babysitter home and sat on guard outside the house. What were you waiting for?"

"You *do* remember. I was afraid you weren't quite safe."

"You were probably right. Except he was too drunk."

We sat in the secret light of late August that makes me so happy and so sad. Its duskiness creates the impression of paths to everywhere that might be found between the flowers or through the trees in the distance. But it also means fall is upon us. And then winter.

Monday, September 9, 2002

Lila

Twenty-Three

Last Friday, the frosty morning had cleared the air. I could see my breath as I walked to the garage, dressed, for the first time this fall, in the social carapace of a suit. I was off to teach a class at McGill, where one of the music history professors has suddenly become ill. Callously I didn't ask what was wrong: it's not someone I know, so my sympathy would have been artificial anyway. The suit felt good, not only the well-shaped warmth of greeny-gold wool greeting the exhilarating air, miming the colour-to-come of the leaves, but the social shape of it. I felt the thrill of the informal new year that comes every fall as we resume our lives, our learning, our responsibilities, shucking off the languor and laziness of summer spent with coolers and detective fiction. I felt, I think for the first time really, that something new might replace what I had broken.

"A summer spent." I like the contradiction in that word, *spent*. The depletion, the exhaustion. A spent marriage. A spent desire. The cum on the bedsheets. Mary Pratt's wonderful orange bed with the universe of light behind it, sheets rumpled suggestively.

But also the sense of wealth carefully, deliberately allocated here and there. The abstract traded for the concrete. Pieces of paper and bits of metal traded for a hand-made bowl, a wooden spoon, a bottle of perfume. The abstraction of loneliness traded for the concrete of a lover's scent, for the precise weight of a palm on your shoulder.

Margaret came last weekend, arriving late in the day after I taught my first class in years. It was too late to go see Mother, so we had a pyjama party, complete with adolescent munchies and the magazines

Margaret had bought in Winnipeg to amuse herself during the layover. As Margaret handed the popcorn bowl across my bed, she held up a picture in *Oprah.*

"What about some new colour for your hair?"

"Nope."

"You didn't even look."

"Was it blond or red?"

"Neither. White streaks. Like Susan Sontag or Lucrezia Borgia."

"How do you know what Borgia looked like?"

"Isn't there a portrait somewhere?"

"Dunno," I said as I poured myself another martini and handed the cold, dewy shaker to her. We were being really adolescent and drinking chocolate martinis with the popcorn. Foofy drinks. Because they go down so easily, we were getting quite drunk.

"How much did you know and when did you know it?" I asked her. I must have been in a masochistic mood.

"Okay. Do you really want an answer?"

"I don't know. Do I?"

"Well, Mother said on the phone she thinks you're blaming yourself. This might change your mind."

"Top up my drink. Then give it to me." I reached across the bed with my glass in hand.

"It's already full," she said impatiently. "I don't know that much. Jack checked up on Rob before you were married. He thought it was something your father would have wanted him to do. I frankly thought it was a bit of a male pissing contest. As if Jack had assumed some kind of ownership. I wasn't impressed and didn't listen all that carefully. But Jack found something and let Rob know he was watching. Which he couldn't exactly do effectively once we moved to Calgary. I think Rob's depressed."

"Oh, great. Rob says he's intellectually engaged. I think he's become an emotionally lazy cynic, and you think he's depressed."

"Comes to the same thing."

"Does it?"

"Yeah. He was hard to live with."

"That's it? I kicked him out because he was hard to live with?"

"There has to be more? He was ornery, bossy, and superior with it. Life's too short." She made it sound so simple.

"What about Jack?"

"Ah, yes. What about Jack?"

"He was no bed of tulips."

"Roses."

"What?"

"'Bed of roses,' my dear. Goodness, we've both had too much. Here. Have some more." She emptied the last of the martini shaker into the swirly red glasses I'd bought because they weren't tasteful. I hoped it was mostly melted ice.

"Oh. Right. Well, Jack wasn't. A bed of roses." Contradictory memories of my brother raise up from the quilt. Jack threatening to quit hockey to make sure I could still have music lessons. Jack verbally abusing his son.

"No. And Jack's dead because of it. And I miss him terribly. God, he could fuck." We giggled uncontrollably, like a pair of teenage girls apologizing for their dirty minds by mocking themselves. "He had staying power, your brother."

"Rob didn't. Rob easily became bored. ADDF."

"ADDF?"

"Attention deficit disorder fucking. He just wanted to do it. The faster the better. Maybe that was his problem. With ADD, he simply couldn't concentrate. He couldn't remember who he was supposed to do it with." Now I was crying the maudlin tears of the drunk rejected woman.

Margaret did her "There, there," imitation and changed the subject. "So what about this new guy?"

"New guy? It's a little early for a new guy. And where do middle-aged women meet new guys anyway?"

"Look, you mention somebody once on the phone, and it's just in the course of telling me about your life. Stuart? The cellist." I nodded while she took a sip of her martini, made a little face, and put the nearly empty glass down on the bedside table. "You mention him twice, and

I think to myself here's this little wish swirling around in your life. But three times in a single conversation means that something's up. You're preoccupied. So? What's up?"

"Like I said, it's a little early . . ."

"No, it's not. Not for a healthy little fling. Let me turn your question around. How much did you know and when did you know it?"

"I know I saw signs. Did I ignore what I suspected? Or was I being charitable and looking for clear evidence?" How does one watch one's mind at work, catch it in its inconsistencies? "It's like the particle in Heisenberg's uncertainty principle. You can see how fast it's going or where it is, but not both at the same time."

"Heisenberg is a little much for a drunk woman who's spent the better part of the day on airplanes and in airports. Except the Heisenberg joke. Do you know the Heisenberg joke?" I shake my head. "This cop pulls Heisenberg over on the LA expressway and says, 'Do you know how fast you're going?' 'No,' Heisenberg responds. 'But I know exactly where I am.'" We laugh with mock hysteria.

"Let's get back to the new guy."

"Well, I think Heisenberg comes up here as well. I feel like I can either observe or just go with the flow. Not both."

"Hooray! Lila, you think too much. Go with the flow. But tell me about it first." She snuggles down into the bed and hugs one of the extra pillows to her chest.

"There's nothing to tell." I told her about Stuart standing guard twenty years ago after the party, about his custody troubles, about the advice I gave him to move to Vancouver.

"Are you crazy?"

"There's nothing going on. We've held hands. Twice. He's given me the tenderest, most . . ." Here I searched for words. "Inquisitive. Yes, inquisitive kisses. He was asking a question and not insisting on an answer."

"Why on earth tell him to move to Vancouver?"

"He has commitment problems. No, that's not accurate. He stayed with Amy for fifteen years, trying to work things out. He needs a lot of solitude. I'm not sure he wants . . . What would we have at this point?

I'm not ready. I've got too many issues, and I'm not going to take some poor, unsuspecting man with a good heart and make him the boxing bag where I work those out."

"Punching bag."

"Yeah. Anyway, I'm not."

"How can you decide in advance what's good for the two of you? Why not talk it over the next time he gives you one of those tentative kisses? Oh, my dear, you should see the look on your face when I bring those little kisses up.

"After Jack died—about six weeks after the funeral, I started a randy affair with an older friend of Jack's, a sort of mentor at work whose wife had died of cancer three months earlier. Viagra. Hotel rooms. The whole thing. We both knew exactly what we were doing. It lasted about three months and did us both a world of good. I know it's a cliché, but it was oddly life-affirming. We both knew when it had run its course and ended it amiably. Lila, living in your head makes you a wonderful musician. It's helped you raise a daughter who's not too damaged by her father's negative whatever. You've been an angel about taking care of Mother. But sometimes we all need to be a little animal." Here she growled like a lioness, and I burst out laughing while Brahms, who'd joined us on the bed, looked at her haughtily. "Put a little tiger in your tank. Remember pleasure and fun."

"Stuart doesn't seem much like a tiger. The pace is relentlessly, beautifully adagio. When I'm not telling myself that it's too soon, I'm simply resigning myself to moving forward at that persistently curious pace, the way a child falls backward slowly into a deep swimming pool."

"Well, given Rob's attention deficit disorder fucking . . ." We both giggled and scowled at the same time. "Maybe that's exactly what you need. God, am I tired. It's only nine in Calgary, but I'm heading to bed. I'll leave you to think whatever thoughts you like."

We gave each other a sisterly kiss, and Margaret padded off to Mother's room, where she was staying for the long weekend she was spending in Montreal. Brahms seemed relieved to see her go, and claimed the space where Rob's chest would normally have lain. I lay on my back and put my hand on his soft, grey fur. The room wobbled slightly.

Margaret and I were much more sober the next morning—literally and figuratively. On Saturday, we were no longer concerned with my love life but with Mother's life. I gave Margaret the short version of Mother's medical status.

"She has maybe a month to live. You'll be shocked at how thin and frail and worn she is. Through most of this, I've been able to see my mother in the shape of her face, the turn of her head, the cadence of her voice. But now all that's left of her is her eyes and her smile. She's on a lot of pain medication, so sometimes she's not very sociable.

"I should come clean about something else. You'll find out sooner or later anyway. Sometimes Stuart comes to play for her. Sometimes he brings his cello and plays works for solo cello, particularly the Bach suites. Sometimes he simply has his harmonica in his pocket and gives us folk tunes. He usually comes at meal times."

"And you tell me nothing's going on?"

"Watch. Tell me what you see."

"Margaret. Thank you for coming. How are you?" whispered my mother in a voice coming from somewhere else with its own ghostly music.

I think of the Prokofiev violin sonata, with the passages Oistrach played at Prokofiev's funeral that sound like ghosts in a graveyard. The portentousness, the sweetness and melancholy of that movement all melded by the alchemy of art. It's what art does: talks to us, reassures us about the contradictions and complexities of our lives, tells us that this is its normal richness, not some joke with a punchline we don't get. Maybe that's false comfort, but we seem to need it.

"I'm fine, Clarice."

"So am I." Margaret smiled knowingly at Mother. "You think I am ironic or lying."

Margaret smiled, kissed mother's wasted cheek, and took her hand. "I think you are lying. And telling me the truth."

"I have little pain. The doctor and the nurses are good about that. I sleep a great deal. I am ready to sleep even more. Except for Lila." She looked at me meaningfully. "Can you teach her to let me go and get on with her life? She can make it up as she goes along. That'll work just fine. That's all any of us do."

"That's not what you've been doing since Gregory died. You've been making yourself up with a vengeance."

"But there's a difference. Don't you think? Between creating oneself and creating one's life? The most interesting people are slightly out of focus. Only the unimaginative or the greedy seem whole. No contradictions." The ghost laughed hoarsely.

"I don't know, Clarice," said Margaret. "You're too philosophical for me."

"We don't need you philosophical. You're our reality check and our shit detector," Mother says, laughing hoarsely. "That's all for now, girls. If you want to stay, be quiet."

"What are you all still doing here?" Mother growled just as Stuart walked in with his cello. "I'm busy. Go away and let me get on with it."

Stuart gave the impression of not having heard her as he opened his cello case, though a quick look to me indicated he heard perfectly well what she'd said. I ignored her crankiness for a few moments by making quiet, polite introductions. Margaret barely managed not to be too delighted to meet him.

The Stuart turned back to Mother. "I've brought you some Bach today. And some other solo suites by Ernest Bloch. He wrote them for his muse, Zara Nelsova."

"Goodness. I remember her. I saw her perform in some smallish concert hall. A large, statuesque blond women with big hair and a flowing scarf and a full taffeta skirt. She looked weirdly out of style. Entirely herself. As if she had a persona, and she knew it was a persona. But it was completely comfortable for her. Supportive. Like a well-fitting bra."

What he plays is abstract, urgent, and mournful, its moods changing as quickly as hers.

"Now I want some Bach. For balance. Maybe next week you'll bring your keyboard so I can hear Lila play?"

"I'd love to." He plucked his strings lightly to make sure they were still in tune. "I've been working on the D minor. Would that be okay?"

"Whatever," she said airily, as if she were a teenager.

At the end of the meditative prelude, which Stuart played so questioningly that it seemed he was unwinding something unknown as he went, Mother stopped him. "Too beautiful. Too sad. Please go away now. All of you. I'm done for today. You'll have to watch somebody else die if that's what you want to do."

"Mother. Stuart simply came . . ."

"I know why Stuart's here. I know *all* the reasons Stuart is here." She looked meaningfully at me with an unexpected glint in her eye—or was it a tear? "And there are many, not the least of which is pity. He's making a conversation between the eternity of music and the eternity I'm facing. I don't want to hear any more of it. I want to sleep."

As we walked down the hallway, Stuart told me not to worry. He didn't elaborate on what I should or shouldn't worry about, as if I knew perfectly well what he meant. At the door of the hospital, he kissed me on the cheek the way old couples do: affectionately but without passion or unintended meanings.

That night, Margaret and I did not repeat the experiment with chocolate martinis but each drank a single glass of wine on the back deck with our toasted brie sandwiches and bowls of fruit. It had been almost hot today, but it cooled quickly, as it does in early September.

"She's been like this more and more lately; her mood changes so quickly, from wise and resigned to funny and angry. I don't know what to do."

"Why do you need to do anything? All you need to do is be a witness. It's *her* experience, not yours."

"Maybe that's why we had that weird conversation about coherence tonight."

"Dunno. But I can well imagine that dying is a little incoherent. Maybe it's a relief. As well as a terrifying unknown. I can imagine those at the same time."

“And a grieving for herself.”

“Which is why she seems just a shade envious of you and Stuart.”

“Margaret. You’re reading into . . .”

“Don’t BS me. Why on earth would a man *voluntarily* drag his cello into a hospice where *everyone* is dying, except to court his lady-love?”

“Because he’s kind?”

“Well, he’s obviously that. I like the way he almost turns his back to the door and everyone else in the room. An audience is the last thing he’s thinking about. It echoes that quality in Mother’s voice.”

“The absence?”

“No, that’s not quite it. It’s a quality of self-possession so profound that . . .” She furrowed her brows.

“It’s self-sufficient? It doesn’t depend on anyone’s blame or praise?

“Yes. That’s it exactly. It’s not humility. It’s got more integrity than humility,” she says with obvious satisfaction.

“It’s one of the things about him that frightens me,” I admit, thinking that Margaret’s the perfect person, really, to help me work this through. Her response is to hand me her empty wineglass.

“Okay, fillerup.” She kicks off her shoes under the table. “Let’s get down to it.”

“Well, that I’m attracted to him goes without saying. I went to his flat about ten days ago because he wanted advice and thought I’d understand his dilemma if I saw where he lived. You can’t imagine any place more bare bones—beautifully so. That in itself was seductive, though I can’t say why.”

“The archetype of the wanderer?”

“Brando in *The Wild One*?” I snorted. “Can you think of anyone less like Stuart?” Margaret, sipping her wine, shook her head. “That’s never done it for me. Men like that have always seemed a bit juvenile.”

“Ya think?”

“What would it be like to have a relationship with someone so self-sufficient? Would it be easier to be yourself? If they seem to have no need of others, can they love you? Would you matter less to them? Or more—because you’d be seen as you are, not as a projection?”

"Does it make sense to do all this guessing? Lila. What does your gut—or your intuition because I'm not sure you've got a gut—tell you? Things can only get better for you." She rubbed my calf affectionately with her bare foot. The sun had set and the garden was getting the secretive look it takes on in the autumnal dusk, as if there's a whole world just out of the reach of light.

"Oh, no. That's not true. If I let myself hope, things could get a *lot* worse."

"So that's what you're doing? Waiting for permission to hope?"

"Oh, what I'm doing is much sillier than that. I'm trying to understand *need*."

"God, Lila. You might as well understand the universe. 'Need' is right up there with gravity and subatomic particles."

"Maybe 'need' *is* gravity and subatomic particles. Maybe it's that essential to our emotional universe. I've thought a lot about Rob's needs, about how much I didn't understand about them, and how much I ignored."

"Put Rob out of your mind. He was hard to live with. That's all there is to it."

"No, it isn't. Maybe I should let your little sentence settle the guilt . . ."

"There you go."

"But that isn't all there is to it. Rob had a responsibility to tell me what he needed, not to play games. If he needed me to dress up in a thong and pull-up stockings, like his little sluts undoubtedly did, he should have told me. Then we could at least have negotiated."

"Lila, you shock me. You're actually mad at him."

"Indeed, I am. But I also know that for me not to admit these needs sloshing around in our relationship was culpable. I suddenly found, after Lindsay was born, that I didn't know who I'd married."

"He beat you, didn't he? Like your father?"

"No. He hit me. And it only happened once. No, it's not the threat of violence. Something quite essential about him changed. Maybe it had always been there, like a seed. He came back from France edgy and arrogant and pushy. Always pushing against something. It was puzzling and frightening at the same time. But he was also cooking and being a lovely father, and we were redecorating the kitchen and eating the most exquisite food, and I simply pretended I didn't see the other things. Maybe I didn't really see them. Maybe I saw only shadows. What is it about memory? How can we possibly run our lives, depending on something so unreliable?"

Margaret had no answers to these questions, of course. She stayed several more days, going with me to the hospice, chiding Clarice playfully for her sleepiness but holding her hand while she slept. Stuart came several more times, once bringing his harmonica (thinking perhaps, that folk tunes were safer emotional territory), once bringing his keyboard. He called to tell me he'd be doing that, and I said I'd see if Kevin might come and the two of us play for her. "Surely you have some solo repertoire," Stuart chided. I brought Bach and Debussy and Brahms, playing for hours while Mother seemed to sleep, then occasionally surface.

How will I remember this summer ten years from now? Will those faulty memories be dominated by the death of my mother or the end of a twenty-seven-year marriage? Or will I think of the beginning of a musical partnership that has sustained me after my divorce? Or the brief love affair of my life? Perhaps the memories will come back to me the way my mother's do, as postcards. The message on the back will read, undoubtedly, "Ha, ha!" with twenty-first-century scare quotes. What will be on the front? A group of people playing volleyball on a nude beach? An illuminated manuscript ?

Thursday, September 19, 2002

Lila

Twenty-Four

For the next two weeks, Stuart came almost every evening to play for Mother between six and seven. He never promised to come, and sometimes didn't, but he was there most nights. At the beginning, he played while she ate, but soon she wasn't interested in eating or even in being conscious. He would play anyway, settling himself in the corner of her room next to the door, invisible to anyone who wasn't with us, and play as if he were having a quiet conversation with his cello.

While they talked about eternity, I watched change. At first I noticed the sharpening of shadow and the lengthening of light as the sun moves south. Then the colours began to change every day, deepening, becoming more golden, more olive, more umber, more bronze. The street became secretive. The shadows dropped by trees, and houses suggested hidden whispering behind the rustle of leaves and the husky songs of crickets. The pale gold light in the houses opposite was a penumbra around all those hidden lives you know are taking place but don't think about.

Every night, I watched a novel unfold in a house across the street. It was a brick house that had been converted to open modernity, probably sometime during the eighties, inhabited by a woman with long salt-and-pepper hair that she wore differently arranged every day. Somewhere in the house, I thought, there is a drawer full of combs and barrettes and clips in tortoise and silver and ebony. During the two weeks I studied the street, she had several dinner guests. There was a little boy who set the table and then sat down to colour while she cooked. He climbed into her lap after dinner and she read to him, occasionally burying her face in his neck and making him laugh. There was a blond teenage girl whose tight pullover didn't reach her low-rise jeans. My grey-haired heroine kept tickling the girl, who would scrunch up defensively. There was a young man in a brown suit who carried a leather briefcase and drank amber liquid before dinner while he talked to the empty room. A white-haired woman joined my imaginary heroine for dinner: the two of them sat at the dinner table bobbling their heads from side to side in time to music I couldn't hear.

But there were also nights when she ate alone. She set the table and disappeared for a while, returning with her plate of food and a half-empty glass of wine. She read a hardcover book (hardcovers stay open more cooperatively, I've learned during the last month) and looked up at the window from time to time—which, since it was dusk, probably meant studying herself in the imperfect mirror of the windows.

I continued to teach and to ignore the illness of the person I was replacing. Kevin and Stuart and I continued to practise, but we were at the more pedestrian stage, where we just got things clean and nicely in sync. The making of music had come before, and would come afterward: now we were making order. We were reining in our personalities, trying to finger the net of meaning that connected each voice to the other. Every day, I put on clothing as a knight puts on armour, as a kind of protection, an attempt at invulnerability that only the truly wounded need. It was possible, though not likely, that I'd run into Rob on campus, and each time I wanted to look self-sufficient and unbroken.

Then the hospice called me yesterday morning and said Mother's breathing was more laboured and perhaps I'd better come. I could not do this alone, so I called Stuart and Lindsay. He was the first to join me. He'd brought his cello, but it remained in its case.

It didn't take long. Each breath sounded like a struggle—the sound came, the nurses explained, from her inability to clear her throat. I chose—with determined struggle, I made the choice—to believe that she was straining to enter another world, not to leave this one. I held her hand while I willed her to leave me and find herself elsewhere—all the while knowing that I was losing my guide to aloneness, my guide to growing inside aloneness. She was so particular to me in those moments in a way she'd not been during the last week of unconsciousness: I had not little postcards but tiny film strips playing in my memory: my mother laughing as we trained the dog, my mother rapt as she listened to me play while I was a child, my mother baking cookies or shopping for new clothes in Montreal, looking youthful after my father's death. Stuart held my other hand while my heart filled with nothing—with my mother's last breaths, which had a cosmos of deep blue silence between them. Just before Clarice died, Lindsay, who had farther to drive, arrived to kiss her grandmother and then stand half-looking out the window, listening to the long pauses in Clarice's breathing. Briefly, in one of those irrational eruptions of thought that nestles up to powerful feeling, I wondered if Lindsay was watching my heroine's breakfast routine, and I wanted to ask her whether the woman's hair was wound up yet for the day, whether she was drinking tea or coffee, eating a croissant or a bagel.

Not long after Mother died, the hospice workers kicked into gear. A doctor was brought in, the body was arranged. The bustle was unseemly and necessary, apologetic around the edges. It was all right: I could have told them that this flesh was not my mother's. Stuart squeezed my hand before saying that he had to rush: he had a rehearsal he couldn't miss.

"Mom? Do you need to be here?"

"No. What should I do?"

"Could you eat some breakfast? Have a coffee?"

She took my hand and led me down the hall. "After the call this morning, all I did was get dressed. Did I do it right? Am I presentable?"

"You look fine, Mom." She studied my face, brushed one of my eyebrows with her finger, and massaged the creases on my forehead.

"Where should we go?" At that moment, I couldn't think of any place in all of Montreal to eat breakfast.

"How about that decadent little place on St. Laurent? You know the one—with the to-die-for almond croissants?"

"How do I get there?"

"Look. You're parked right behind me. Just follow me. If we get separated, meet me at the corner of St. Laurent and Milton."

Lindsay drove in her little red beater with what seemed supernatural competence through the crisp blue day. She was the needle threading through the formal grey streets of Montreal; I the thread that simply followed her. She drove at the stately pace required by Sherbrooke, past the McGill campus, where the leaves had just begun to turn, past the McCord Museum, a place I'd always intended to visit when I had some spare time (the museum was all about time, I'd been led to believe), past Pollock Hall where Kevin and Stuart and I would give our recital in about ten days. She turned up St. Laurent and pulled up in front of a patisserie with a black and white awning whose sharp stripes hurt my eyes. The thick green glass made the pastries in the window look as if they were otherworldly sea creatures, deep under water.

Inside, Lindsay made suggestions: "How about a cappuccino? They don't skimp on the espresso here the way they do at Starbucks. You could use a shot of espresso."

"And a chocolate croissant. I want chocolate."

"You sit down. Over there." She pointed to a table near the window. "I'll bring everything."

Everything around me seemed faded, fogged in, dusted over with icing sugar. I stared at the glassed-in counter full of glazed and frosted pastries, tarts adorned with glassy fruits, cookies thick with gothic decorations, and felt hunger and satiety at the same moment.

"What's your favourite story about your grandmother? Or your favourite memory?"

Lindsay barely paused to think. "Do you remember the year I was twelve, and you and Dad decided to take a couple of weeks and go to France?" I nodded. Unfortunately, it was not a particularly happy memory for me—two weeks following Rob around while he ranted about his passions. Perhaps it was the first time I heard the little motif, that tune I began hearing again half a year ago.

"Well, Grandma was afraid I'd be bored. She didn't know any kids in her neighbourhood, and though we spent time at the park near the end of her street, we didn't really find any friends my age. But she'd begun to collect things when you and Dad began talking of leaving me there."

"What kinds of . . . ?"

"Well, from what I remember, she started with a couple of costumes sold by the local opera company as a fundraiser. Weird, heavy velvet gowns in colours like wine and apricot. Up close they were rather tacky, but from a distance they were spectacular. They came with fancy turbans with enormous feathers. Then she'd wandered the antique shops and found straw hats with flowers on the brim and lacy dresses and this crocheted thingy that I wore everywhere. Kind of like a shrug. Also, boys' trousers and old-fashioned shirts without collars. A sailor suit that fitted me. Because she didn't know any kids, we played together for those two weeks. After breakfast and our morning errands, we'd survey this wardrobe, which she'd put in the closet in my room—your old room—and decide who we were to be for that day. I loved the velvety gowns, though they made it hard to move, so I never wore them for very long. I remember we put her favourite opera on the record-player and stood dramatically in the middle of the living room, making grand gestures and singing along. She warbled, Grandmother did. Rather spectacularly. During the evenings, we'd start a fire in the fireplace and roast hot dogs and marshmallows for s'mores, and make popcorn. We pretended we were in a cabin deep in the woods, surrounded by bears and wolves. She gave me respect for playfulness. What's your favourite memory?"

"I like yours. It *does* capture her playfulness. I saw so much of that these last few months." Frantically, I search for a favourite story, or piece of a story. Nothing. It's as if her days have been erased with her breath. "My memory seems to have shut down. She talked about 'postcards' that popped into her head over the last month or two. That's about all I've got. Gestures, a word, a pose. That's not enough."

"You're in shock." She took my hand.

"In shock? This day has been coming for how long? I have no right to be unable to remember my favourite story of her. Why haven't I been spending the last months going over them all and choosing the half-dozen best ones?"

"You've been busy making more stories?"

I'm silenced by something quite different. My mother was a paradox in so many ways. She was vulnerable to my father's brutality, but she also transcended it. Maybe she tolerated his beatings because she knew she was stronger than any beating he could give, that his need to beat her was his weakness. A false or a true knowledge? Ethical or culpable? Only she could have told me that, but now I can't ask. Now I feel the need to come up with the *one* story that encapsulates her.

"It's as if the stories are frozen in layers. I can see through to them, but they're vague and unreal because the ice is so thick. My happiest memories come from the time before I realized my father beat her. Then there's this big, restless blank—all the stories I don't want to remember. They started coming back to me, bursting in where they weren't wanted when I suspected your father . . ."

"Don't go there now." Is there a shade of defensiveness in her voice? Or a note of comfort? I know that she and Rob have been talking and spending time together—a good thing, I thought.

"How can memory be so unreliable? So stubborn?" I was near tears.

"I should have taken you back to my place and made you coffee."

"No. I'm okay." I wrapped my hands defensively around my thick white cup, as if trying to kindle something. And then, there it is. At the bottom of the ice, there are toys: my Barbara Ann Scott doll, Jack's hockey skates, a Monopoly game and Jack's View Master, which he had to share with me. I liked the ones with the Grand Canyon; he liked the stories about Hopalong Cassidy and the Cisco Kid. My memories were like those tiny transparent images in the round cards. We'd fight about the View-Master: Jack wanted to push the lever and show me each view; that way, I wouldn't break his toy. I wanted the continuity of seeing them in a stream. Mother patiently mediated, trying to get Jack to see his little sister with less jealous contempt. And I'm laughing. Because my mother loved life, I'm laughing.

I tried to explain the View-Master to Lindsay, but she couldn't quite imagine anything not electronic. "They were fast and slow at the same time. You would put the card in the View-Master, which was kind of like a boxy pair of plastic binoculars, and push the lever to change the picture as quickly as you could. Quicker made the story easier to construct. You drew the lines in between—the story lines in between. But you could only do that if you'd already looked at the pictures slowly."

"And this is relevant how?" Lindsay is gently herding me toward my task.

I gaze through that thick green glass in the shop front. "The only thing I can come up with is a series of snapshots. No stories. There's my mother playing badminton with her best friend in some kind of tournament. She'd told me about the fancy bloomers Gussy Moran wore at Wimbledon, so I see her in a short skirt with fancy underwear (with her own cotton briefs underneath, of course), though she probably wore a modest pair of Bermuda shorts. Riding a bicycle in a long skirt, her hem weighted with . . . what? Something. Something to keep it from ballooning in the breeze. Endlessly playing double solitaire with me the one time we rented a cottage and it rained most of the week. Teaching me to make snow angels in the back yard. Once, just once when I was a kid, she had a part in a local theatre production. Linda, in *Death of a Salesman*. My father went on opening night and was horrified. Willy Loman was too much like him. He almost forbade her to do the last two performances, but she convinced him she couldn't let the rest of the actors down. I think she did some acting after his death, but I never went to see her. Why? Didn't I take her seriously? How many times has she watched me perform?"

"We went once, you and I. Don't you remember?" Since my face and memories were blank, Lindsay prompted me. "It was over Easter break. They were putting on a play for the kids, to keep them out of their parents' hair for an afternoon. *Little Women*. She was Marmee. A wonderful Marmee. When she told Jo to be more patient, to hold her tongue, I thought she was talking right to me."

"How is it I don't remember this?" My memory is a sieve that will never hold my mother. It's not a cradle or a grave, a pantry filled with food or an attic where you've stored the photograph albums and boxes of letters. It's a basket; memories keep draining through the gaps in the weaving.

"Do you remember every performance you've ever given? Every book you've ever read? Surely there are some limits to how much sticks in our memories?"

"But she had a whole self I knew nothing . . ."

"So do you. So do I." Lindsay held both my hands in her own, then let go of one to find a tissue in my purse and handed it to me. "Which is probably the way it should be. It's hard enough to live with ourselves. Other people shouldn't have to live with us."

I closed my eyes, snuffled for half a minute, and then opened them to concentrate in Lindsay's presence. Then the taste of the lukewarm but sweet cappuccino.

"'That'll put hair on my chest,' as Mother used to say. How do they manage to keep all the espresso in the bottom of the cup?" We both grimaced at my silliness and then smiled. "You're a gift, you are." I started to collect myself.

"Would you like me to call Dad? He'll want to know."

"Yes. I'd appreciate it. He was good to her while she lived with us."

"You gonna be okay?"

"Yup. You and espresso and chocolate have helped me get over the shock. Really. Each day that she's stayed mostly unconscious has gotten me ready for this. The moment of her dying just took me by surprise. You don't really expect life to change in a single moment. Though it does all the time." How long did it take a husband to decide to be unfaithful? "An automobile accident or a plane crash takes a second. Love takes longer. Unless it's your daughter." We hugged; she pulled my arm through hers and walked me to the car.

"Call if you need anything. Call anyway. Call before you go to bed so I won't worry."

"Okay. Sure." We hugged and kissed one another's cheeks. I got into the car and found I was starving again. Well, it would be time for lunch in an hour or so.

I wasn't home ten minutes before Stuart called. He had two rehearsals that day, he told me, but he'd be by after the second if I wanted. I said I'd like to be alone, and he understood. I sat and worked out new fingerings for Bach's *Goldberg Variations*. My copy dated from my student days, and had fingerings (in pencil of course) that I wouldn't use now. So first, I erased everything.

There's a story about the work—apocryphal, we're sure, but it won't die—that Bach wrote it for Count Hermann Karl von Keyserling, a Russian ambassador to the court of Saxony, who had insomnia. He asked Bach to write a piece of music for his harpsichordist, Johann Gottlieb Goldberg, of a "smooth and somewhat lively character to cheer him on his sleepless nights." The result was Bach's only foray into the theme and variation form; although no cure for insomnia, it was one of the most mathematical and analytical of works in its way of devising variations not on some trite tune but on the bass line. It is also the most unearthly combination of rigour and humanity I know. Its one minor variation is a study in grief: it has the most halting, unpredictable rhythms. It will be a good guide for this time in my life.

Unable to concentrate any longer, I looked through the new music I hadn't yet filed. Then I spent the late afternoon looking for something I couldn't name. I opened my mother's closet and sat staring at it. I had taken the few things she needed to the hospice weeks ago. Clearing out her closet seemed taboo. But I sat in the chair where I'd held her hand so many nights and studied what was left. There were the insistently cheerful clothes of an older woman in shades of fuchsia and coral and scarlet. Limp on their hangers, they looked surreal, like the alternate realities of one of Dali's paintings. There was a row of pretty boxes along the top shelves that I ought to get down. Some were the boxes you find in photographers' or frame shops, meant to hold photographs or videotapes. But there were also a couple of old hatboxes covered in toile and chintz. Suddenly hungry, I went downstairs and searched through the fridge and cupboards for something I might possibly want to eat. Surely, I'd know it when I saw it. But I didn't. I put some crackers and cheese and a glass of wine on the living room coffee table and went back upstairs and began pulling down all the boxes and piling them up on the little desk in her room.

They were all labelled, but the labels had been, perversely, turned to the wall. I piled four boxes up, braced the top one under my chin, and took them downstairs where I could sit more comfortably. Predictably, there was a box labelled "Lila," containing my programs, press clippings, and publicity photographs. Holding the pile of papers down was a sugar bowl that read "Meito China, Hand Painted, Made in Japan" on the bottom. There was no lid for it. I set this aside. Of course there was a box marked "Jack," holding his cowl, newspaper clippings about his teams, his wedding photograph. Nestled protectively in the cowl was a cluster of dried oak leaves with two acorns attached, a Matchbox racing car, and a lock of blond hair I didn't think belonged to anyone in the family. I took out the car, hair, and oak leaves to join the sugar bowl and set the rest aside to give Margaret. There was a box with "Gregory" written on it, containing my father's letters to her during the war. These I remember reading aloud to her shortly after she moved in; they were warm and romantic, sometimes out of control with love. Jingling in the bottom were coins from the various islands in the Pacific where his ship had docked, and some patches from his uniform, various certificates, a newspaper article about his retirement. But here again, some things seemed out of context. There was a tacky little replica of the Eiffel Tower. Mother had gone to Paris on a tour about five years ago, but it seemed more than five years old and didn't look like the kind of thing she'd buy. There was also a baggie of miscellaneous baby teeth. At the very bottom of the box there was a packet of letters in a rubber band. Turning it over, I recognized her handwriting and stationary at the bottom of the pile, but the letter on top, which had no envelope, was in handwriting I didn't know. I unfolded it and read

> Dear Clarice,
> I'm doing what you asked against my better judgment. I don't really think it's right to say to a friend 'I'm dying of cancer. Go away.' I know you think you're doing this for me, trying to protect me from another loss. Honey, I've lost so much I don't know what found looks like. That's not true. It looks like you. It's got curly white hair and red toes. Found has got joy and laughter and warmth in her voice. And life. Unlike some people, you'll live till you die. I'd like that life to hold me in some way.

So here are your letters. I don't know why you want to take them from me too.

I've cheated though. I made copies.

Wildly yours,

Glen

What other surprises could there be? I opened up the last box, the largest, to find old books—a copy of *Evangeline*, *Idylls of the King*, du Maurier's *Rebecca*, *Daddy Long Legs* by Jean Webster, a forty-five recording of "Something's Gotta Give." There were other forty-fives: Tommy Dorsey, Glen Miller. Suddenly a memory cracks through that ice I was trying to describe to Lindsay. My mother is trying to teach my father the two-step because the two of them are going to a dance—something to do with the Veterans—and the only thing he can do is a waltz. They are both laughing at his confusion. It is quick-quick-slow or slow-quick-quick? It depends on the music, my mother tries to explain as she extricates herself from his arms to rifle through the forty-fives and choose another one to put on.

I put my head back in the wing chair and hope my father's box is simply sentimental, not some kind of archive I can't read. This is such a puzzle—*she* was such a puzzle—and it feels good to simply lean my head back and close my eyes and think about that. Revel in it and be frightened by it.

I had just closed my eyes when I heard Stuart softly calling my name. It was dark in the room. I had left the front door open to catch the late afternoon light.

"Lila?" he queried, standing at the entryway to the living room. "Do you really want to be alone? I wanted to check in person. I knew I couldn't tell from your voice on the phone." He stood stock still there, clearly not wanting to invade.

"Come in, come in. I'd fallen asleep. I'm still half asleep." He came over to the chair and leaned down to kiss my forehead. "I've learned this afternoon that my mother probably had a lover before she was diagnosed—or at least a boyfriend. Their whole correspondence is here. She was a puzzle. A complete puzzle. Look what I've found in her carefully organized boxes of memorabilia. It makes no sense to me to store oak leaves and acorns in Jack's box of academic and sports relics. And this sugar bowl without a lid. I found it in my box. I've never seen it before."

He pulled up a chair to sit across from me. "What would we find if we went through your jewellery box right this minute?"

I began to laugh. "Well, you'd mostly find jewellery. But there are also Lindsay's baby teeth and a handful of stones I've picked up various places. I know where they've come from and when, but they wouldn't mean anything to anyone else. Also a red button that reads 'Somewhere in Texas a village is missing its idiot.' A handful of blown glass marbles from Old Montreal. Also a Hello Kitty Pez dispenser. I couldn't resist it. *Jack* was the one who got Pez dispensers, not me."

He began laughing with me. "I rest my case."

"But I haven't organized that. Its compartments aren't labelled to organize my connections with other people. This was deliberate. A purposeful attempt to confuse."

"Well, she's entitled."

"I think I should write the lover. Don't you think so? Or call him. I haven't read the whole package of letters, and maybe I won't. But I should let him know she's died and that she kept his letters, don't you think?"

"I think she'd love that. He would too. Do you have an address?"

"The only letter I've read probably came in a large envelope, because he writes about agreeing to return her letters. Another gesture I can't figure out. This isn't the nineteenth century and she wasn't still married: he couldn't blackmail her with their letters. So why ask for them back?"

"So you could find them?"

"And so I'd know. But I don't know. They make her more of a puzzle, not less."

"Maybe that's the reason, then. We tend to simplify the dead, don't we?"

I sorted through the pile and found one with a return address. "Should I do it now?"

"Tomorrow, I think. Is there anything you need to do about arrangements?"

"Oh, god. The obituary. There's no service; she didn't want a service; she knew very few people here outside her bridge cronies. But I have to do an obituary."

"Have you had dinner?"

"No. Apparently I slept through dinner."

"Only on North American time. I brought some food; it's in the car. I suspected you wouldn't have eaten. Let me heat it for us while you write the obituary." He went to the music room where he knew he could find a pen and paper, brought it to me, brought me a glass of wine, and left me to my task. I heard him leave the house, return, and move around in the kitchen.

I felt rebellious. I wanted to create a community of mourners to protect her. After much scratching, this is what I had:

> Peacefully, after a long conversation with cancer and mortality. She is survived by her loving daughter, Lila Jameson; her dependable son-in-law, Robert Dowling; her humorous daughter-in-law, Margaret Jameson, who creates such funny family sanity; gifted, loving, and admiring grandchildren Lindsay Dowling, and Devon and Jackie Jameson. Predeceased by her husband, Gregory, and her son, Jack. In lieu of flowers, contributions can be made to agencies opposing violence against women, or to the Clarice Jameson Memorial Scholarship for young actors at McGill.

Then, on the back of the draft for my mother's obituary, I started a list of hopes that would morph over the next couple of months. A list was rational, linear. I'd let it contain seven things, and whenever I wanted to add something new, I'd have to take something else off. That way, I'd be forced to see what I really wanted.

1. Run away and join the circus. The absurdity reminded me of rebellion's pitfalls. This would never change.

2. Take up ballroom dancing. Something that celebrated my body. But I had no partner. Maybe Francis? A few days later, I thought of yoga. Brahms would like that.

3. Learn the *Goldbergs*.

4. Fewer bar lines. These two were contradictory, and I thought that was just fine.

5. Become a vegetarian. I had a long way to go on this one. The next—contradictory—step was "eat a hot dog on a street corner." Then "eat frozen dinners when you feel like it." The primal rebellion: food. Too much or too little.

6. Clean the basement. Clean your closet. Empty your head. Silence the noise. Love the silence. Somehow I've always believe paring down starts in the basement. Or that it's easier to deal with the basement, since the things you've moved there have already been exiled from your daily life. But I learned that "clean the basement" was a metaphor for all kinds of other housecleaning and mindcleaning.

7. Red. This puzzled even me. I wasn't sure what it meant.

Not my obituary. My hungers. My private birth announcement.

Sunday, October 6, 2002

Twenty-Five

Being discreet is overrated, don't you think? If I didn't suspect that Lila and Stuart had been extraordinarily discreet for some time, I'd tell you that right after Friday's rehearsal for the Brahms recital they raced back to his studio—or hers—and shagged like mad. His desk. Her comfy chair. Maybe Stuart is really inventive and brought in a big black garbage bag full of animal furs to spread on the floor. There were sexual fireworks going off everywhere by the end of the very successful dress rehearsal. If we all weren't fairly reliable musicians, I'd have worried: often a bad dress teaches you to concentrate during the performance. But concentration wasn't what we needed. Nor was restraint. Audiences often don't realize how much pleasure they get out of a quiet sexual frisson as they watch performers. The fireworks weren't going to hurt us.

I shouldn't have been surprised to see Rob in the audience. At least he had the tact to find a seat in the back shadows of the auditorium, on the keyboard side so he could see Lila's hands but so he'd be in her blind spot. I wish I could say he looked sheepish or the worse for wear, but his hair was tidy and well-cut, as always, and he wore his usual ensemble of button-down shirt and tweed jacket. The place was packed. Unlike me, Lila doesn't face the audience as she plays, and while she does her program notes, she can't see anyone for the lights, so it was unlikely she'd know he was there unless he showed up at the reception afterward.

It wouldn't be too much to say that Lila's exquisitely prepared program notes are one of the reasons our concerts are so successful. They're always delivered as if she made them up on the spot, though she has small note cards for quotations and dates, and more often than not they're rehearsed so we're ready to provide the examples she needs to get them to make sense. Tonight she was dressed in red: not the restrained, winy red she usually wears but a pure vibrant silky red dress with bands of black at the hem and on the rather décolleté neckline, black repeated at the wrists, front edge, and hem of its jacket. Normally, when she delivers her program notes, she stands primly, holding her hands before her in a stance that is almost pleading. Not tonight. Her left hand rested almost languidly on the corner of the piano where it could pick up her notes if need be, her right accompanied her thoughts. She looked open and unafraid, strong, and frankly seductive.

> Both pieces on tonight's concert are linked to Brahms's love for Clara Schumann and to his involvement in her life after the suicide attempt and death of Robert Schumann.
>
> Toward the end of February 1854, Robert Schumann was plunged into his final conversation with the underworld of mental illness. He had been hearing voices for quite some time when he began to write a series of variations on a theme he told Clara had been dictated to him by an angel who, in the succeeding days, became hideous . . . Schumann attempted suicide by leaping into the Rhine, only to be fetched out by a fisherman and returned home dripping wet. He was taken to Endenich, a rather progressive private asylum . . . At the time, Clara was pregnant with her youngest son, Felix, who would become her last link to Schumann.
>
> Hearing the news of Schumann's suicide attempt, the twenty-one-year-old Brahms (he was fourteen years younger than Clara) rushed to Düsseldorf and moved into the Schumann home . . .
>
> Both Robert and Clara had a pervasive effect on Brahms's life. Robert had predicted Brahms's greatness with a double-edged pronouncement that he was the next Beethoven . . . Clara would arguably remain his lifelong

muse. We have letters giving us evidence of Brahms's passion for Clara; we do not have evidence that this passion was ever consummated.

Brahms wrote his first violin sonata, the Opus 78, the summer after the death of Felix Schumann, the child Clara was carrying when her husband attempted suicide. Brahms based the final movement on one of Clara's favourite songs of his, his Opus 59 "Rain Song" or "Regenlied." When he sent her the score, Clara responded, "How deeply excited I am over your sonata . . . you can imagine my rapture when in the third [movement] I once more found my passionate loved melody . . . I say 'my,' because I do not believe that anyone feels the rapture and sadness of it as I do."

Here are some of the words of the "Regenlied" written by Klaus Groth:

Plash down, rain, plash down,
Awaken in me those dreams,
That I dreamt in childhood,
When the wetness foamed in the sand!

When the wet summer sultriness
Fought lazily against the fresh coolness
And the pale leaves dripped dew,
And the fruitful fields took on a deeper blue.

What joy to stand in the downpour
At such times with bare feet,
To dance in the grass,
And to grab with one's hands the foam.

Plash down, rain plash down,
Awaken my old songs
That we sang in the doorway
When the drops tapped outside!

I would gladly hear them again,
So their sweet moist rustling,
My soul, tenderly bedewed
With that holy, childlike awe.

> Perhaps Brahms's use of this poem meant to offer Clara comfort by implying that the wonder of childhood can never be recaptured, and that Felix, having lived to the age of twenty-four, had already experienced the best years of his life. But Brahms plays another game with the "Regenlied" which suggests that this sonata is saturated with another nostalgia. As you will hear, one of the characteristics of the song is its rhythm.

Lila and I played the song, Lila in her role as accompanist, I the singer for whom it was written. Then Lila explained that the dotted motif that begins the song is used throughout, playing snippets from each movement.

> The way these dotted motifs saturate each movement gives the sonata an unusual aesthetic unity. But it achieves something else: the first and second movements' rhythmic references to a song that has not yet come set up a kind of nostalgic longing for something that Brahms will never experience.

During the first half, Stuart was sitting in the front row right in Lila's line of sight; I saw him leap clapping to his feet before he raced to the Green Room at the interval. Francis and I walked up and down the hallway outside the Green Room; when I'm nervous, I need to move. Francis is oddly turned on when I perform—something, he says, about the white tie and tails, the way the stage lights turn my cheeks red, and my absolute unavailability—so while I'm worrying about the second half, thinking my way through some of the difficult bits, he's keeping up a slippery, quiet patter of flirtation with frank sexual innuendo as we walk the halls. He doesn't need any response from me. Perhaps he doesn't want it. Thank heaven that my tails cover his hand on my ass.

About the third time we walked past the Green Room, there was Lila, leaning against the wall, Stuart with his hands either side of her shoulders. He'd taken off his tails, so the scene was a little composition in red, black, and white. He'd splurged and bought a new shirt with French cuffs for the occasion and had unearthed some old onyx and gold cufflinks. They looked somehow like an erotic Sargent painting, his crisp white shirt and the drape of her silk seeming to belong more to the nineteenth century than to the twenty-first. The next time we walked past, she'd taken his curly head in her hand, and they were kissing without any restraint. On the next fly-by, she was fixing her hair and makeup, and it was almost time to get ready for the second half.

> In the days following Schumann's suicide attempt, Brahms remained at Shadowplatz, comforting Clara and making music in the evening. There he played the draft of his *B Major Trio*, the first of his chamber works he'd allowed to survive. Clara found it puzzling: "I cannot quite get used to the constant change of tempo in his works, and he plays them so entirely according to his own fancy that today . . . I could not follow him, and it was very difficult for his fellow-players to keep their places." Malcolm MacDonald suggests that in this version his Romantic expressiveness surpassed his Classical control of structure.
>
> In the summer of 1889, he wrote to Clara about his latest project: revision of the first Piano Trio, telling her, "It will not be as wild as it was, but whether or not it will be better—? . . . I did not provide it with a wig, but just combed and arranged its hair a little." This is an unusual work, then, containing both the young, adventurous Brahms (the second movement scherzo is almost unchanged) layered over or even reformed by the mature craftsman. Enjoy the interplay between his youthful enthusiasm and his mature world view and wise aesthetic control.

There was so much to get through before I could finally cuddle with Francis and talk about what I needed to talk about. There was the reception. Rob managed to speak to me but kept clear of Lila. He couldn't help seeing the chemistry with Stuart: they didn't come unglued from each other for the entire time, sometimes simply standing holding hands, sometimes with Stuart's arm around Lila's shoulder. Rob made a quick exit after asking me to tell her he thought she was wonderful and was glad she had something to look forward to after her mother's death. I decided to leave that last detail alone.

Our rituals were entirely changed: there was no pyjama party, merely drinks at Lila's while we ran through the performance. It's been a while since we performed in Montreal, so I should have expected some changes: there was no reason for the tin of nuts, for example. Stuart seems to be preternaturally astute about where you can buy prepared food and had delivered a large plate of delicious nibblies before the concert. Garlic-stuffed olives, prosciutto-wrapped melon, Quebec goat's cheese. I'd have preferred something a little more basic, a little more hedonistic, a little less swanky. Some weird new flavour of potato chips and chipotle squirt cheese on Triscuits. This tradition was becoming all too healthy and mainstream. At least he didn't question why Francis was there when the two of us arrived together. Lila had probably prepared him.

Stuart insisted on gushing about Lila's performance. Stuart's a composer, a twenty-first-century composer, so if anyone has all the skills to be abstract and analytical, he does. But they weren't on display tonight. What I saw was a man deeply, helplessly in love. I thought to myself, Look, guys, I arranged this, in case you wanna know. But this isn't what I'd planned. You owe something to the planner to ask what he was about.

The conversation quickly crumbled into predictions about how the reviews would be and what it would do for our careers. Because in my humble opinion, we cooked tonight. We made something temporary but exquisite, and people will want us to do it again. So what happens to us? Do we keep to tonight's formula and combine sonatas and trios? Get an all-Beethoven program up and running? Maybe the restraint of two voices seems too moderate for the twenty-first century. Maybe everyone thinks of their lives in terms of a ménage a trois, and the trios give them a little hint of that scene.

Francis and I didn't stay long. We knew that *discussion* wasn't quite what was wanted. They seriously wanted to find a way to end the words. I, on the other hand, wanted *more* words with Francis, and then I wanted to fuck and then to sleep until noon the next day in my lover's arms.

So when we got home, I began the therapeutic whine: "A couple of weeks ago, when I went to her studio, she was working on one of the *Goldberg Variations*. Pianists don't fiddle with these just to keep their hands in; it's a serious undertaking. She's gonna leave me. She's going solo. Which means I'll have to learn a whole new repertoire or get used to a new accompanist. I'm too old for a whole new repertoire. Way too old for a new accompanist."

"Dear boy, you're not too old for anything. Except to be up this late. Get ready for bed, and we'll talk under the covers."

And talk we did. Francis believes in her, and I don't think Francis is a dolt. "She would never desert you. It's not really how she's made, now is it? Look how long it took her to get rid of *him*. For *cause*. She loves working with you. You know that. With good reason." Francis was getting amorous; I love that, not knowing when the words are going to stop and the real action will begin. Maybe I'm a bit of a masochist that way. "She's got time on her hands, with her mother gone and her husband hung out to dry. She's doing what any sane person does after a break-up: first, hunker down. Then try to grow."

How could I not believe everything he said?

Monday, October 28, 2002

Rob

Twenty-Six

My god, that man can lie. Can you imagine being so comfortable and authoritative about your own fictions? Weapons of mass destruction, my ass. You can be sure if Bush had any real evidence, he'd let us know, security risk or no. He'd be so *proud* he wouldn't know any better. I stake my life, little as that's worth, that there are no significant chemical, biological, or nuclear weapons in Iraq—never mind that Bush is threatening us with a mushroom cloud in the next terrorist attack. Ronald Cleminson, a former RCAF pilot now specializing in intelligence, put it this way: how do you verify absence? And the minute that goes through my head, I'm thinking of Lila for about the twentieth time today. Since it's 2:30 AM, the day is only a couple of hours old. How do you verify absence? Didn't she say something like that last August? In September, once the exciting, painful thing with Elise was over, once I'd moved into my apartment, once I had my classes rolling along, I have to admit that unverifiable absence was about all I consisted of.

They've got the TV on overhead, in case I can't sleep, I guess—which I can't—but there's no sound. Watching the silenced TV makes you think it's quiet in here; then you begin to hear the beeping, dripping, whishing-whooshing sound of heart monitors and drugs being dispensed. When that silence becomes a bit too ominous, you go back to the voiceless TV. The only thing that seems to be on this hour of the morning is footage of the last couple of days' demonstrations. I'd seen it Saturday night, when I was making my decision to take part in yesterday's march in Montreal. It's this absence thing, this cynicism that Lila accused me off—I've begun to take her seriously. There's nothing like the silence of an empty apartment—I'm not even allowed a cat—to convince you of your own existential crisis. That and the whining sound of your own disaffected mind like a vacuum cleaner with a belt that's slipping and squealing and can't quite take anything in. September being a "new year" in academia, I thought I'd try a bit of a change in the classroom. Couldn't I feign a little more warmth, a little more interest in my students, a little more tolerance of their jejune views? After all, it was my job, I reasoned, to make them less immature, less credulous. If I didn't need to do that, I wasn't necessary. I worked hardest in my first-year course. There were a couple of helpful students: a young woman named Lucy, slightly plain, with straight blond hair and a miraculous voice; a young black man named Joe with Rastafarian hair who was more politically astute than his classmates, probably from necessity; and a mature student named Ken who was better informed than your average eighteen-year-old. These three helped me create an environment where it seemed safe to ask questions.

Then one day we were talking about the historical relationship between politics and security. A young noodle named Rick asked whether it wasn't important to put a significant amount of money into Canada's own kind of Homeland Security to ensure that Al-Qaeda didn't open up shop here. Really, shouldn't we protect ourselves? I tried to suggest that perhaps the *real* Canadian way to ensure our security might be to address some of the problems that create terrorists, like poverty and injustice. We couldn't do anything like that, he argued. Not on a world scale. We'd better protect ourselves and buy more intelligence-gathering stuff and more guns. No. I tried again: we'd better see to our relations with the Muslim community in Canada. The little bulldog felt that I just wasn't getting it and tried again. So I lost it. This was isolationist, militarist, right-wing thinking and it hadn't worked in the past and wouldn't work in the future. It gave us the fiction of control and safety, where no such things existed. History had certainly demonstrated that. After my little rant, the world got quiet all over again. Yeah, I did my job and taught them something about critical thought and history, but it was the end of trust, though Lucy tried from time to time to ask questions I'm sure she knew were safe.

With that sweet voice of hers, she'd try to carve out confidence in the academy as a place of free inquiry. Most students haven't bought it so far, though I'm not giving up yet.

So if something wasn't going to happen in the classroom, I decided it would have to happen on the street. Seeing Saturday's demonstrations, I was suddenly moved by the feeling of solidarity among the protestors. Surely a cure for my cynicism about public process was taking part in something with a purpose. Montreal's own march was supposed to start near the Place des Arts and march west down St. Catherine Street then turn south past the US consulate on St. Alexandre Street. I dug out a backpack I haven't used for years and packed a large Thermos of coffee against the day's chill, a book to read while I bussed my way downtown and waited for things to get started, a handful of business cards, a notebook, and a pen.

It was like a carnival, and a long check-in line at the airport, and a crowded coffee house all in one. There was a certain cheerful electric energy in the air that was almost celebratory. At the same time, when we hadn't moved for fifteen minutes after the march was to have begun, there began to be some grumbling. A heavy woman behind me in a bright green coat moaned that standing was harder for her than walking. She didn't know how much longer she'd be able to take this. People began to spot friends in the crowd, but for the most part we stood around and listened to one another's conversations, hoping to get invited in. I was one of the few loners. On my left there was an idealistic beautiful blond husband and wife with a toddler in a canvas contraption on the husband's back. His wife held the baby's hand and cooed at her when she threatened to get bored. I tried to help with the entertainment, bringing out my vocabulary of animal sounds from some long-lost place they've been hiding for a couple of decades. To my right were two couples in their mid-thirties who were obviously old friends; the husbands talked to each other about politics while the wives shared their struggles with adolescents and sexist supervisors.

Once the march actually started, we were like a single animal flowing down narrow, trendy St. Catherine's, something fluid like an otter or a tiger. Being in the crowd was both terrifying and oddly empowering. It wasn't so much the placards, which were pretty standard: "Iraq isn't your ranch, Mr. Bush" and "Stop Bush! Stop War!" Rather, it was what I suppose Lech Walesa felt during the Solidarity movement: you suddenly discover the presence of a collective spirit; you find that people are eager to give up their individual wills to see if together they can achieve something larger than all of them individually. This is made visceral by the movement of people around you as they march *en masse*, cooperatively trying not to step on one another or get in one another's way.

We'd gotten about halfway down Ste. Catherine before we were to turn off on St. Alexandre toward the US Consulate when it seemed like a gorilla pounded his fist into my chest. I dropped to my knees; the person behind me stumbled over me, falling painfully over my shoulders and spilling hot coffee on my back (*Where* did he get *hot* coffee? was my immediate and irrational thought) as he exclaimed "Fuck." But the woman in the green coat quickly took in what had happened and mobilized a couple of guys to get me onto the sidewalk while she hunted up one of the ubiquitous police officers there to ensure the crowd didn't get out of control. Turns out having a heart attack in the middle of an anti-war demonstration isn't unusual. They hustled me into an ambulance that noisily rushed down one of the side streets. In Emergency, there were, of course, countless tests, and it turns out it was a mild attack, a kind of warning. The doctor tells me I've got to change some things.

"You look fit," he acknowledged, "so I can't tell you to quit smoking, lower your cholesterol, and lose twenty pounds. Some lifestyle changes, maybe? Reduce stress? Cut down your hours at work?"

How about getting my wife back? About half an hour ago, I called the nurse in. Like Claire used to be, she was warmly brisk, checking the monitors, the drip. "Can't sleep?" she observed. I shook my head, not trusting words yet. "I'll take your blood pressure since I'm here," she offered.

"I'd like you to call my wife in the morning."

"Your wife? You told us there wasn't anyone."

"Separated. Still, I need someone to know, and I don't want to alarm my daughter. She's a little vulnerable since the break-up. Someone needs to call my department head in the morning and find a substitute for my classes. How long will I be in here?"

"Couple more days. You'll need help at home and someone to check on you for a while." She studied my chart. "The doctor's giving you something to reduce the risk of a second attack." She tucked her stethoscope into the large pocket in her smock, crossed her arms, and looked at me appraisingly. "I'm sure Dr. Gates told you to change your lifestyle and avoid stress. How about giving up the loner habits? You're probably human too, like the rest of us."

I didn't trust my voice, so I grunted an assent. How lucky men are to get away with saying so little by using their vocabulary of authoritative basso noises.

The silence here is daunting. Maybe even worse than the whine of my apartment. Here's the most damning conclusion I've come to: I didn't think about it. Cynicism has a long and respected tradition. I didn't think about what it would do to either my relationship with others or my engagement with the world. I'm worse than my undergraduates.

What will I say to Lila? The nurse has said she'll bring me a phone sometime between seven and eight so I can call about having my classes covered. I think I'll be matter-of-fact. Just ask her if she'll call Ben and get him to either find a replacement or put up a notice. I'll contact him myself just as soon as I know when I'll be in action again.

What would I *like* to say to Lila? "I'm finding this really hard?" Would understatement be the right strategy? "I don't like myself very much, so it's hard living alone. I need your help?" "You moved me. I love you." Why would she believe me?

Monday, October 28, 2002

Lila

Twenty-Seven

Raw. The air is raw; my nerves are raw. I'm trying to think of ways to describe being tired, cold, lonely, and hungry that aren't self-pitying. There: crisp. The bare trees dotting the campus are a smoky intaglio against a sky that never quite darkens in downtown Montreal. It's cloudy tonight, and students haven't begun arriving for their evening classes, so my route from the hospital to the music school through campus is quiet. There's the swoosh of traffic on Sherbrooke and on Pine, and the odd horn in the distance. Occasionally, I hear a set of footsteps—usually the soft thud of sneakers, but sometimes the brittle sound of another pair of heels—or pass a quiet conversation about a puzzle so different from my own. "Why?" "How?" sometimes even "When?" these academic questioners ask one another. My own footsteps echo slightly as I walk past buildings and sound much more certain than I actually feel. I'll reach my new studio soon, and can unpack my curry and naan, and study Bach's *Goldberg Variations* while I eat. Then I'll practise for a while before I begin to get more settled. I unloaded half a dozen boxes before I went to see Rob, so I'll be staying late. One by one, the voices in the music school will go out and I'll be left with silence. It's a delicious silence, full of promise. It's a musical silence that lets me hear my own voice but promises that others will join mine soon.

Stuart's in Vancouver for six months, and I've just moved into his apartment. Rob's just out of intensive care, terrified by his heart attack, I can tell, though he's putting on a brave face, seeming to fear loneliness more than mortality. Lindsay will probably be gone by next fall. This little room in the music school is waiting for me, to be filled with students and colleagues and new music. Our triumphant all-Brahms concert opened up new possibilities for me. These are all the lines in the fugue of my life, and it refuses to settle into a major or minor key. A vulnerable but boldly naked woman is directing the lines, holding the fugue together.

At first I didn't understand why Rob called me this morning. If he could speak to me, he could also speak to his department head. But my visits made everything clear. I went to his apartment to pick up his pyjamas, robe, and slippers. It was an odd experience. There were pieces of our past everywhere, but they looked unfamiliar out of context. These were eked out by some new furniture: bookshelves and a small kitchen table and two chairs, probably from IKEA. Given Rob's taste for beautifully, laboriously made furniture, the pieces from IKEA made it look like he was camping out. Among the temporary and the out of place, the large white leather sofa and ottoman from Roche Bobois looked grotesque. I saw a man in crisis. He's always been a tidy person, and he could easily afford a cleaning woman. But there were mounds of unwashed dishes piled on top of the empty dishwasher (yes, I looked), and books and papers everywhere. While I searched for a bag to put things in, I also did a bit of reconnaissance. Why had an obsessively fit man suddenly had a heart attack?

I went into his bedroom to see if I could find a book to take him to read, and actually found he was reading fiction at bedtime. I added *Such a Long Journey* to the pile of things I was taking. He'd left letters scattered on his desk, which I read in an attempt, I told myself, to gauge his frame of mind. There was a letter from his publisher making what were probably idle but encouraging threats if he didn't get his manuscript in by the end of November. There was a chatty and decidedly unromantic letter from Elise, written in round, girlie longhand on lined paper ripped out of a notebook, reporting on the young men in her classes she was sizing up for their prospects as a lover or husband. Probably her version of class notes. As I sat to read this a second time, I stared out the window above the desk, which faced Parc Mont-Royal with its bare trees.

Part of my intelligence-gathering, as I sat studying those trees, had simply to do with me. What was I feeling about his heart attack? What was I feeling as I sat in his empty life, looking at his unmade bed, reading a kiss-off letter from the woman he probably committed adultery with? I realized these were the right questions, but I couldn't come up with any answers. Silence. But an expectant, curious, friendly silence.

Seeing him in the hospital clarified things. When I arrived, he was asleep, curled up on his side, his hospital gown open along his back, looking vulnerable. I felt pity but no love, no longing to *do* something to alleviate his situation. It would be good for him to find a way to take care of himself. I'd brought work with me and was making some notes on the bedside table, which I'd lowered to my chair, when I heard, "Well, hello!"

"Hello, yourself. How are you feeling?"

He let out an exhausted jet of air. "Given that my heart tried to murder me yesterday, not bad."

"I've brought your pyjamas and robe. Slippers." I held them up. "Your super let me in. I thought you deserved to have your backside covered."

His smile at my thoughtfulness was bitten off with sudden embarrassment. "It doesn't take Freud or rocket science to see I've been having a bad time."

"Your teaching?"

"Okay. Quite okay, actually. I'm not so prickly, and the kids seem to be a bit more engaged."

"There you are, then." I did not say that *not* to completely fall apart when your wife kicks you out and your hot young lover deserts you was commendable. "When I arrived, the nurse said you'd been brought in from some kind of demonstration?"

"I thought I needed to remember what it was like to take part in communal—and vainly hopeful—political action. The coming war in Iraq?"

"What happens next? Do they send you home soon?"

"Apparently there's home help for victims of heart attacks who don't have family to take care of them. Once I've got my health under control, would you think of some cautious . . . time spent together?"

"No."

"That was fast."

Just at that moment, a life-saving nurse came in, armed with blood pressure monitor, thermometer, a whole raft of pills, and picked up his chart to study it. I turned away, looking out the window, to give them some privacy for her businesslike conversation with him. It was dusk, and moment by moment the view out the window receded. I saw my slightly doubled reflection—one in the outer storm window, one in the room itself—more and more clearly.

The night my mother died, Stuart stayed with me. Time-lapse photographs would have found us in any number of positions on the living room sofa—sleeping, talking, curled up, at opposite ends. We did all this fully clothed; this was not the night for death-defying sex. The next morning, I made breakfast, and he proposed we walk the stiffness out of our bodies by taking his tour of musical Montreal. We began at Sacre Coeur, where one of his friends practised every Friday morning for the Sunday service. We sat in the dim, chilly silence and listened for half an hour to mistakes and fresh starts, to experiments with the organ stops: the same music played over and over again, sounding slightly different each time: sometimes crisp and clean, sometimes heavy and regal. Then Stuart thought I needed some sunshine to warm me up. So we got hot dogs and ate in a corner of the botanical gardens especially known for its birds. Every time I'd try to talk, he'd shush me playfully, reminding me to close my eyes and simply listen to the cacophony and fugues the birdsong made.

"What's that one that says, 'Reschedule, reschedule, reschedule'?"

"Shush. Just listen. No words." He held my hand and smiled.

Our final destination was a park where an artist had created a fence out of pieces of cast-off metal. There was the plumbing from a trombone and a trumpet, a whole row of dangling spoons and forks, the lids of pans, car ornaments and hubcaps, a brass teapot that had been flattened.

"Pretend you're a percussionist," he said, handing me a small Swiss Army knife he kept attached to his keychain, its longest blade extended. "Or a child. See how the world sounds." I couldn't get quite the playfulness I wanted, that of a good jazz musician; I was too interested in predictable rhythms and motifs in different timbres. "All of this—the organ, the birds, this metal—makes you so aware of how the world sounds. It's like going to a beautifully filmed movie and coming out and seeing that the world looks different."

Of course he smiled. "Can you come back to my place? I've got some ideas I need to write down before they evaporate."

So I sat in one of the simple chairs and read about the world's preoccupation with building better fortresses in *Austerlitz* while he doodled for a while. Then in the early evening, he pulled me out of the chair and took me off to bed.

It was not lightning-bolt sex. It was being in a library studying each promising book carefully so you knew which one you wanted to read. It was walking down a long portrait gallery of black and white photographs: each subject caught in a moment of extraordinary inward knowledge but unaware of the photographer. You smiled because you recognized a similar moment of conversation with yourself. It was a painter's studio, where you needed to turn the half-painted canvases from the wall and consider how they might be finished. It was Saturday-morning people-watching at the coffee bar. There was no selfish impatience, only curiosity. And desire that had been building over the weeks, weaving its way around death.

I have never known such attentive kindness as the time we spent together. Rob in our most romantic days couldn't come close. But afterward, there came a quiet, subtle disengagement: he would disappear for days at a time—never without warning and never defensive about it. This was fine with me, particularly after the Brahms concert, and a series of changes in my professional life. Shortly after Mother's death, I was asked to take on some piano students that a senior professor couldn't devote enough time to. One of these—a gifted young man named Andrew—overheard me playing some Bill Evans in my studio one afternoon while I prepped for my class. He confessed a passion for Evans's jazz, for the way his technique built a bridge—third stream, he called it—between jazz and classical. I'm his classical coach, but he, in turn, is teaching me some of the rudiments of jazz improvisation. After his lesson, we simply play—like children—for an hour.

Then I was hired for another class in the winter term. Finally, a new agent approached me after the concert and wanted to sit down and talk about solo repertoire. All this meant, of course, that Rob wouldn't need to pay alimony and could have the house back. I could move the Heintzman into the music school and find myself an apartment that would take Brahms. I could liberate Rob and in turn myself.

These changes meant reading, learning, considering, listening. Practising. At all hours, practising. It was engrossing. I didn't want a lover who strode dejectedly, needfully through the living room (as I realized Rob was often wont to do in a manoeuvre that had kept my musical life contained within my partnership with Kevin) as I prepared the *Goldberg Variations* for a concert next February. Next July and August, Kevin and I both will be playing chamber music at the Festival of the Sound in Parry Sound, sometimes together, sometimes with other musicians. We'll grow and revise ourselves for other ensembles, and then we'll come back to being the pair we've always been, a little changed, mostly the same.

Sometimes when I play Bach or Brahms or Beethoven, I think that the universe is pulsing in time to the music: expanding, contracting—breathing. Time breathes along with it, also expanding and contracting. Aren't space and time somehow connected? After my mother's death, I felt time's breath with a painful exhilarating intensity. It was the first time in years when I wasn't responsible for someone's else's daily well-being. Stuart's deep affection (it was too soon to call it love) and his need for time to himself gave me the sense that the universe—and so time—were expanding lazily around me, giving me time to think and practise and read but not in some lonely vacuum. Time changed; the nature of time changed. It became more personal, more fluid. But then a corner of the music room where the light didn't quite reach, or a false note, or a certain chill on the early morning air, or Brahms's decision to sleep at the foot of the bed rather than propped against my shoulder, and the reality of my aloneness—motherless, husbandless—would suddenly contract my heart—and with it my sense of the generosity of the cosmos. Sometimes I thought I couldn't breathe, so tight was the grip of grief in the clean void of blue space that gave me such time. So here were the two of me reflected in Rob's hospital window: one woman jubilant and liberated, one grieving and still sad. Some things hadn't been changed by Rob's departure; others were entirely different. So be it.

The nurse finally left. He broke the uncomfortable, diagnostic silence.

"So we can't stay friends?"

"Oh, let's *do* stay friends. I think it would be better for all of us. Especially Lindsay. No uncomfortable choices. You've got what you want. I've got what I want. And in fact, I've got something you want."

"Slow down a minute. What do you think it is I want?"

"Freedom to explore your desires. You've always talked about the honesty of unbridled desire. Go for it."

"She's left."

"There'll be another." There's always been another, I thought before realizing I didn't really know.

"And what do you want?" He was trying to pull himself up in bed, to sit with a little less vulnerability. I helped him raise himself.

"Do you want me to crank up the bed?"

"Yes. That would help." Once he was upright, he continued, "Now, what do you want? What surprises has my wife of nearly thirty years—"

"Twenty-seven."

"Twenty-seven years got for me?" There, in his hospital gown, he had pulled his kingly cape around him. It was in his tone of voice, his precise, professorial diction with a thin overlay of laboured patient good humour. He sat, imperious and frightened, at the height of the white bed.

"Solitude. Music. Uncomplicated emptiness. I'm exhausted. By my mother's death. And by the years of working so hard to pretend we were truly happy, the perfect couple with our congenial domestic routines. I want frozen dinners and empty rooms."

"The least you could do is be honest with me. I saw you at the concert . . ."

"He left last week for seven months in Vancouver. And it's frankly none of your business. But I've got something you want. The house. I've moved out. McGill has given me one of their nicer studios, and I moved the piano in there. I've found a small apartment for Brahms and me." I didn't tell him it was Stuart's.

"I don't *want* you out of the house," he growled. A strategic mistake. "I don't *need* you out of the house," he said with laboured calm and less panic.

"*I* needed to be out." He opened his mouth to interrupt, to correct, to chastise, but I soldiered on. "Doubtless you think it unnecessarily hurtful or childish. I don't care what you think." The ultimate liberation.

He began involuntarily weeping. He spread his arms. Look at me! the gesture said.

"I know. You're vulnerable. Why do you think I went to the trouble of bringing you proper clothes? And something to read? But you test and test and test. And push. And demand. Even your silence is demanding. I want—"

"You want?" he entreated.

"Just silence. A quiet flat."

I don't know why I thought this curry would stay warm until I got to my studio. Well, it's not cold, and there's lots of naan to dunk in it. I'm not that hungry.

When Stuart told me of Amy and Elsbeth's move to Vancouver, I'd put out feelers among my connections on the West Coast. Sure enough, just as we'd settled rather into our on-again, off-again intimate separate lives, an offer came from UBC where a cello teacher with a complicated pregnancy needed to be replaced. They offered him seven months of work—from mid-October through to the end of April. Disciplined by new selfishness, I told him to take it. This was an opportunity to test the waters, make connections, spend some time with his daughter. I reasoned, not quite truthfully, that our relationship would flounder if half his heart was somewhere else. I've never been jealous of an twelve-year-old I haven't seen.

Why is it we fight in airports? Have you ever noticed the difference between arrivals and departures? Arrivals are full of relief and jubilation and beginnings. New Year's in miniature: full of resolutions and a belief we can change. Departures are soaked in anxiety, a desire to have the whole thing over with. I've picked more fights in airports. It's a way of wanting to be relieved to be alone. How many women leave a child or husband or lover at the airport with plans for their precious solitude? Only to have the car break down on the expressway and the cat get desperately sick.

Waiting to go through security, Stuart asked the inevitable question. Again.

"Why are we doing this?"

"So when you get back in seven months, we can tell ourselves we've gone through the test that's set for every couple. Like something out of *The Magic Flute*. We'll know what to do. Maybe they'll love you and the pregnant cellist won't want to stop being a mother and we'll decide to move to Vancouver and pay an arm and a leg for a little closet somewhere on the ocean where we can walk every day in the rain."

"The Christmas holidays are only a couple of months away. Less."

I kissed him as passionately as one can in public. "I miss you already. It will be so good to have you back."

He looked puzzled. "I thought you were coming to Vancouver."

"I can't come to Vancouver. That would be leaving Lindsay at Christmas. I can't bring her because that would be leaving Rob alone. And where would we stay? Where did you say they were parking you?"

"Graduate housing."

"Right. So can you see all of us piling into your grad digs for two weeks of rain. Or paying for a hotel. Christmas in a hotel?"

"But I thought you'd come to Vancouver because you knew I'd want to spend Christmas with Elsabeth."

"But I *can't* come to Vancouver. I've explained. Why did you *assume* I'd come to Vancouver?" I was near angry tears, but he pulled me toward him.

"Hush. Tell me again why we're doing this?"

"Because you need to go. We need to think what to do. Once you've spent some time with Elsabeth, you'll be able to *reason* about what to do. It won't be so raw, that need to be a father. You can think it through. Surely we're creative enough, between the two of us, to figure something out."

"And we'll figure something out for Christmas. I'll come early. Or come on Boxing Day. Something will occur to us. We'll suddenly know how this can be solved. It's not the most complicated thing that's happened to us."

"You'd better go. They're calling your flight and you've still got to get through security."

"I'll call you early tomorrow morning. This evening is likely to be chaotic."

"In the morning, then. I love you."

Sometimes the biggest surprises in our lives aren't something momentous: winning a lottery or making all the lights when you need to pick your daughter up at dusk from her swim meet or getting in the right line at the grocery store or even finding the right partner. By the time we're thirty, most of us have figured out that life is unpredictable, a cross between a crap shoot and a blind date, and that these things happen—or not—with no respect for who we are or what we deserve. So the big surprises, sometimes, are what we allow ourselves to do. That night, I found myself a window and watched planes take off until I knew his plane had surely left. One by one, these stiff, giant birds barrelled down the runway and made it safely into the air. I had no idea which one might be his, but all the same I was wishing him—and everyone else in those planes—godspeed. And I was thinking about what it meant to do that—to fly, to say goodbye. The universe was once again contracting painfully, yet I felt as if I had something—some sense of gravity or well-spring of generosity—that would make the next seven months bearable. And then the next phase, the next challenge after that. And the next.

Because it's clear Stuart won't be back. One of my twins—the one that picked the fight—knew he wouldn't be back even before he left. But I lied to myself long enough to be gracious about this opportunity and see him on the plane and get over the worst of the sense of loss. He loves relationships on a schedule and that's exactly what he's got with

Elsabeth, who was overjoyed to see him. Amy left for Vancouver not to hurt Stuart but because she'd found someone online. So the four of them sat down shortly after he arrived and worked out a rational schedule.

Meanwhile, my to-do list has morphed. The top of the list still reads *Run away and join the circus.* Francis has found a way to help. I went to another opening at his gallery, where I found brightly painted folk-art figures of circus performers. I bought several, and Francis has constructed some nearly invisible Plexiglas boxes to display them on Stuart's white walls. We're keeping our eyes open for more. Ballroom dancing became yoga, though Brahms didn't like it as much as I thought he would. Next term, I'm going to try kick boxing. Yes, I'm learning the *Goldbergs*, as planned, but I'm also playing some jazz and have a quiet duo piano gig in a little club toward the end of November. Probably I'll be the straight guy—like Evans so often in *Kind of Blue*, where he just creates predictable moments that allowed everyone else to let loose, get lost, and find the music again. Andrew'll do most of the improvisation, but I suspect he'll find a way to encourage me to let go. That's taking care of some of the bar lines. Occasionally, I'm bumping against others and doing a little syncopated gigue around them.

I haven't solved the food thing. Some days I think vegetarian is the way to go—healthier and better for the planet. Other days, I crave meat. Perhaps the principle here is to have no principles. Cleaning my closet, my head, or the basement—moving into Stuart's apartment cornered me into that, because I want the unencumbered simplicity he's created. Mostly, it was just a matter of leaving things behind. Rob can call in the dump trucks if he likes.

Red. I'm still not sure what that means, unless it's simply instructions to let every joy into my life. So I'm letting my eye—and my budget—be highjacked by burnt orange boots and briefcase, by the red print rug and sofa I bought when Rob took his marshmallows, as Kevin calls them, to his apartment. Fire engine red; orangey red; winey red. Food, clothing, decor—whatever. Let it in, along with indigo, lime green, deep purple—which I should practise this week. Peter de Rose's old standard, not the rock group.

It's late: Brahms will wonder where I am, but he won't complain too much because he has half the bed all to himself now. One by one the voices have gone out in the music school, voices plangent and triumphant and curious. A pianist close by was practising the *Well-Tempered Clavier*. Farther away, someone was nailing the difficult horn part in Bruckner's *Third*. Another voice was trying Byrd, or some other early English composer, on a virginal. It's like Stuart's sound-world, this conversation between all the voices that have ever sung their world in music.

I've been working on the *Goldbergs*, largely for my mother. I can imagine them being written for the metaphysical insomniac, and hope they will put her wishes for me to sleep. She would have loved the paradoxical simplicity and complexity of them, the wordless portraits of moments of being we have no need to describe to others since Bach has done it for us. Some are contemplative, and move with the fluidity of lucid, personal thought. Others are extroverted and social. I could explain those differences by talking about the dance forms of Bach's time. But you would say I'm being slightly dishonest, or even disingenuous. Some of them are lived; others are merely thought or dreamed. It's hard work to get your hands to express these differences but worth the effort. And to remain, suspended, in that musical effort, is enough.

Acknowledgments

I want to thank my mother for her surprising determination to introduce me to classical music when I was seven. Even when she was far away in body or in mind, music has been a comfort, a challenge, a joy for me.

I want to thank one of the University of Regina's most versatile and helpful reference librarians, Larry McDonald.

This manuscript had a few readers whose encouragement was crucial. Ken Probert read a very early version with patience and acumen. Stephen McClatchie helped me with the musicology, and tweaked Kevin's voice. Medrie Purdham gave me encouragement at a crucial, disheartened moment.

I want to thank my daughter, Veronica, for her gifts as a photographer, and for helping create the perfect cover image. Veronica's art and vision help feed my creative hungers and encourage me to see a more intriguing world.

Thanks also to Hannah Sauchyn, who willingly modeled for Lila.

Deepest thanks to my publisher, Ruth Linka, who kept pushing because she believed in me and cares about good books. Yes, Ruth, one more revision was a great idea!

There is no way to thank my husband, Bill Ursel. His generous encouragement, which seems to know no limits, is part of the air I breathe.

Kathleen Wall is an English professor at the University of Regina, an award-winning teacher, and the author of two books of poetry. As a scholar, she is completing a study of Virginia Woolf's use of form, arguing that Woolf believed that art plays an important role in our civil lives by encouraging conversations. Kathleen's poetry collection *Time's Body* won a Major Manuscript Award for Poetry from the Saskatchewan Writers Guild. Kathleen lives in Regina, Saskatchewan, surrounded by family, music, and cats. *Blue Duets* is her first novel.